## "THEY'VE COME FOR YOU!"

"What have you done, what have you done?" cried the girl, in one of those heart-piercing whispers of fear. "They have come for you—a whole crowd of armed men—they're outside the door! What have you done? It was something done for me, I know!"

Donnegan suddenly transferred his wrath from big George to the mob.

"Outside my door?" he asked. And as he spoke he slipped on a belt at which a heavy holster tugged down on one side, and buckled it around him.

"Oh, no, no, no!" she pleaded, and caught him in her arms.

Donnegan allowed her to stop him with that soft power for a moment, until his face went white—as if with pain. Then he adroitly gathered both her wrists into one of his bony hands; and having rendered her powerless, he slipped by her and cast open the door.

# MAX BRAND

## DONNEGAN

**LEISURE BOOKS**  **NEW YORK CITY**

A LEISURE BOOK®

October 1996

Published by special arrangement with Golden West
Literary Agency.

Dorchester Publishing Co., Inc.
276 Fifth Avenue
New York, NY 10001

Printed in the United States of America.

**DONNEGAN**

# DONNEGAN

### CHAPTER I

#### TALE OF DONNEGAN

THE fifty empty freights danced and rolled and rattled on the rough road bed and filled Jericho Pass with thunder; the big engine was laboring and grunting at the grade, but five cars back the noise of the locomotive was lost. Yet there is a way to talk above the noise of a freight train just as there is a way to whistle into the teeth of a stiff wind. This freight-car talk is pitched just above the ordinary tone—it is an overtone of conversation, one might say—and it is distinctly nasal. The brakie could talk above the racket, and so, of course, could "Lefty" Joe. They sat about in the center of the train, on the forward end of one of the cars. No matter how the train lurched and staggered over that fearful road bed, these two swayed in their places as easily and as safely as birds on swinging perches. The brakie had touched Lefty Joe for two dollars; he had secured fifty cents; and since the vigor of Lefty's oaths had convinced him that this was all the money the tramp had, the two now sat elbow to elbow and killed the distance with their talk.

"It's like old times to have you here," said the brakie. "You used to play this line when you jumped from coast to coast."

"Sure," said Lefty Joe, and he scowled at the mountains on either side of the pass. The train was gathering speed, and the peaks lurched eastward in a confused, ragged procession. "And a durned hard ride it's been many a time."

"Kind of queer to see you," continued the brakie. "Heard you was rising in the world."

He caught the face of the other with a rapid side glance, but Lefty Joe was sufficiently concealed by the dark.

"Heard you were the main guy with a whole crowd behind you," went on the brakie.

"Yeh?"

"Sure. Heard you was riding the cushions, and all that."

"Yeh?"

"But I guess it was all bunk; here you are back again, anyway."

"Yep," agreed Lefty.

The brakie scratched his head, for the silence of the tramp convinced him that there had been, after all, a good deal of truth in the rumor. He ran back on another tack and slipped about Lefty.

"I never laid much on what they said," he averred. "I know you, Lefty; you can do a lot, but when it comes to leading a whole gang, like they said you was, and all that—well, I knew it was a lie. Used to tell 'em that."

"You talked foolish, then," burst out Lefty suddenly. "It was all straight."

The brakie could hear the click of his companion's teeth at the period to this statement, as though he regretted his outburst.

"Well, I'l be hanged," murmured the brakie innocently.

Ordinarily, Lefty was not easily lured, but this night he apparently was in the mood for talk.

"Kennebec Lou, The Clipper, and Suds. Them and a lot more. They was all with me; they was all under me; I was the Main Guy!"

What a ring in his voice as he said it! The beaten general speaks thus of his past triumphs. The old man remembered his youth in such a voice. The brakie was impressed; he repeated the three names.

"Even Suds?" he said. "Was even Suds with you?"

"Even Suds!"

The brakie stirred a little, wabbling from side to side as he found a more comfortable position; instead of looking straight before him, he kept a sideglance steadily upon his companion, and one could see that he intended to remember what was said on this night.

"Even Suds," echoed the brakie. "Good heavens, and ain't he a man for you?"

"He was a man," replied Lefty Joe with an indescribable emphasis.

"Huh?"

"He ain't a man any more."

"Get bumped off?"

"No. Busted."

The brakie considered this bit of news and rolled it back and forth and tried its flavor against his gossiping palate.

"Did you fix him after he left you?"

"No."

"I see. You busted him while he was still with you. Then Kennebec Lou and The Clipper get sore at the way you treat Suds. So here you are back on the road with your gang all gone bust. Hard luck, Lefty."

But Lefty whined with rage at this careless diagnosis of his downfall.

"You're all wrong," he said. "You're all wrong. You don't know nothin'."

The brakie waited, grinning securely into the night, and preparing his mind for the story. But the story consisted of one word, flung bitterly into the rushing air.

"Donnegan!"

"Him?" cried the brakie, starting in his place.

"Donnegan!" cried Lefty, and his voice made the word into a curse.

The brakie nodded.

"Them that get tangled with Donnegan don't last long. You ought to know that."

At this the grief, hate, and rage in Lefty Joe were blended and caused an explosion.

"Confound Donnegan. Who's Donnegan? I ask you, who's Donnegan?"

"A guy that makes trouble," replied the brakie, evidently hard put to it to find a definition.

"Oh, don't he make it, though? Confound him!"

"You ought to of stayed shut of him, Lefty."

"Did I hunt him up, I ask you? Am I a nut? No, I ain't. Do I go along stepping on the tail of a rattlesnake? No more do I look up Donnegan."

He groaned as he remembered.

"I was going fine. Nothing could of been better. I had the boys together. We was doing so well that I was riding the cushions and I went around planting the jobs. Nice, clean work. No cans tied to it. But one day I had to meet Suds down in the Meriton Jungle. You know?"

"I've heard—plenty," said the brakie.

"Oh, it ain't so bad—the Meriton. I've seen a lot worse. Found Suds there, and Suds was playing Black Jack with an old gink. He was trimmin' him close. Get Suds going good and he could read 'em three down and bury 'em as fast as they came under the bottom card. Takes a hand to do that sort of work. And that's the sort of work Suds was doing for the old man. Pretty soon the game was over and the old man was busted. He took up his pack and beat it, saying nothing and looking sick. I started talking to Suds.

"And while he was talking, along comes a bo and gives us a once-over. He knew me. 'Is this here a friend of yours, Lefty?' he says.

" 'Sure,' says I.

" 'Then, he's in Dutch. He trimmed that old Dad, and The Dad is one of Donnegan's pals. Wait till Donnegan hears how your friend made the cards talk while he was skinning the old boy!'

"He passes me the wink and goes on. Made me sick. I turned to Suds, and the fool hadn't batted an eye. Never even heard of Donnegan. You know how it is? Half the road never heard of it; part of the roads don't know nothin' else. He's like a jumping tornado; hits every ten miles and don't bend a blade of grass in between.

"Took me about five minutes to tell Suds about Donnegan. Then Suds let out a grunt and started down the trail for the old Dad. Missed him. Dad had got out of the Jungle and copped a rattler. Suds come back half green and half yeller.

" 'I've done it; I've spilled the beans,' he says.

" 'That ain't half sayin' it,' says I.

"Well, we lit out after that and beat it down

the line as fast as we could. We got the rest of the boys together; I had a swell job planned up. Everything staked. Then, the first news come that Donnegan was after Suds.

"News just dropped on us out of the sky. Suds, you know how he is. Strong bluff. Didn't bat an eye. Laughed at this Donnegan. Got a hold of an old pal of his, named Levine, and he is a mighty hot scrapper. From a knife to a toenail, they was nothing that Levine couldn't use in a fight. Suds sent him out to cross Donnegan's trail.

"He crossed it, well enough. Suds got a telegram a couple of days later saying that Levine had run into a wild cat and was considerable chawed and would Suds send him a stake to pay the doctor?

"Well, after that Suds got sort of nervous. Didn't take no interest in his work no more. Kept a weather eye out watching for the coming of Donnegan. And pretty soon he up and cleaned out of camp.

"Next day, sure enough, along comes Donnegan and asks for Suds. We kept still—all but Kennebec Lou. Kennebec is some fighter himself. Two hundred pounds of mule muscle with the brain of a devil to tell what to do—yes, you can lay it ten to one that Kennebec is some fighter. That day he had a good edge from a bottle of rye he was trying for a friend.

"He didn't need to go far to find trouble in Donnegan. A wink and a grin was all they needed for a password, and then they went at each other's throats. Kennebec made the first pass and hit thin air; and before he got back on his heels, Donnegan had hit him four times. Then Kennebec jumped back and took a fresh start with a knife."

Here Lefty Joe paused and sighed.

He continued, after a long interval: "Five minutes later we was all busy tyin' up what was left of Kennebec; Donnegan was down the road whistlin' like a bird. And that was the end of my gang. What with Kennebec Lou and Suds both gone, what chance did I have to hold the boys together?"

# CHAPTER II

## DONNEGAN SLEEPS

THE brakie heard this recital with the keenest interest, nodding from time to time.

"What beats me, Lefty," he said at the end of the story, "is why you didn't knife into the fight yourself and take a hand with Donnegan."

At this Lefty was silent. It was rather the silence of one who cannot tell whether or not it is worth while to speak than it was the silence of one who needs time for thought.

"I'll tell you why, bo. It's because when I take a trail like that, it only has one end. I'm going to bump off the other bird or he's going to bump off me."

The brakie cleared his throat.

"Look here," he said, "looks to me like a queer thing that you're on this train."

"Does it?" queried Lefty softly. "Why?"

"Because Donnegan is two cars back, asleep."

"The devil you say!"

The brakie broke into laughter.

"Don't kid yourself along," he warned. "Don't do it. It ain't wise—with me."

"What you mean?"

"Come on, Lefty. Come clean. You better do a fade off this train."

"Why, you fool——"

"It don't work, Joe. Why, the minute I seen you I knew why you was here. I knew you meant to croak Donnegan."

"Me croak him? Why should I croak him?"

"Because you been trailing him two thousand miles. Because you ain't got the nerve to meet him face to face and you got to sneak in and take a crack at him while he's lying asleep. That's you, Lefty Joe!"

He saw Lefty sway toward him; but, all stories aside, it is a very bold tramp that cares for argument of a serious nature with a brakie. And even Lefty Joe was deterred from violent action. In the darkness his upper lip twitched, but he carefully smoothed his voice.

"You don't know nothing, pal," he declared.

"Don't I?"

"Nothing," repeated Lefty.

He reached into his clothes and produced something which rustled in the rush of wind. He fumbled, and finally passed a scrap of the paper into the hand of the brakie.

"My heavens," drawled the latter. "D'you think you can fix me with a buck for a job like this? You can't bribe me to stand around while you bump off Donnegan. Can't be done, Lefty!"

"One buck, did you say?"

Lefty Joe expertly lighted a match in spite of the roaring wind, and by this wild light the brakie read the denomination of the bill with a gasp. He rolled up his eyes and was in time to catch the sneer on the face of Lefty before a gust snatched away the light of the match.

"Well?" queried Lefty Joe.

They had topped the highest point in Jericho Pass and now the long train dropped into the down grade with terrific speed. The wind became a hurricane. But to the brakie all this was no more than calm night. His thoughts were raging in him, and if he looked back far enough he remembered the dollar which Donnegan had given him; and how he had promised Donnegan to give the warning before anything went wrong. He thought of this, but rustling against the palm of his right hand was the bill whose denomination he had read, and that figure ate into his memory, ate into his brain.

After all what was Donnegan to him? What was Donnegan but a worthless tramp? Without any answer to that last monosyllabic query, the brakie hunched forward, and began to work his way up the train.

The tramp watched him go with laughter. It was silent laughter. In the most quiet room it would not have sounded louder than a continual, light hissing noise. Then he, in turn, moved from his place, and worked his way along the train in the opposite direction to that in which the brakie had disappeared.

He went expertly, swinging from car to car with apelike clumsiness—and surety. Two cars back. It was not so easy to reach the sliding side door of that empty car. Considering the fact that it was night, that the train was bucking furiously over the old roadbed, Lefty had a not altogether simple task before him. But he managed it with the same apelike adroitness. He could climb with his feet as well as his hands. He would trust a ledge as well as he would trust the rung of a ladder.

Under his discreet manipulations from above the door loosened and it became possible to work it back. But even this the tramp did with considerable care. He took advantage of the lurching of the train, and every time the car jerked he forced the door to roll a little, so that it might seem for all the world as though the motion of the train alone were operating it.

For suppose that Donnegan wakened out of his sound sleep and observed the motion of the door; he would be suspicious if the door opened in a single continued motion; but if it worked in these degrees he would be hypersuspicious if he dreamed of danger. So the tramp gave five whole minutes to that work.

When it was done he waited for a time, another five minutes, perhaps, to see if the door would be moved back. And when it was not disturbed, but allowed to stand open, he knew that Donnegan still slept.

It was time then for action, and Lefty Joe prepared for the descent into the home of the enemy. Let it not be thought that he approached this moment with a fallen heart, and with a cringing, snaky feeling as a man might be expected to feel when he approached to murder a sleeping foeman. For that was not Lefty's emotion at all. Rather he was overcome by a tremendous happiness. He could have sung with joy at the thought that he was about to rid himself of this pest.

True, the gang was broken up. But it might rise again. Donnegan had fallen upon it like a bight. But with Donnegan out of the way would not Suds come back to him instantly? And would not Kennebec Lou himself return in admiration of a man who had done what he, Kennebec, could not do? With those two as a nucleus, how greatly might he not build!

Justice must be done to Lefty Joe. He approached this murder as a statesman approaches the removal of a foe from the path of public prosperity. There was no more rancor in his attitude. It was rather the blissful largeness of the heart that comes to the politician when he unearths the scandal which will blight the race of his rival.

With the peaceful smile of a child, therefore, Lefty Joe lay stretched at full length along the top of the car and made his choice of weapons. On the whole, his usual preference, day or night, was for a revolver. Give him a gat and Lefty was at home in any company. But he had reasons for transferring his alliance on this occasion. In the first place, a box car which is reeling and pitching to and fro, from side to side, is not a very good shooting platform—even for a snapshot like Lefty Joe. Also, the pitch darkness in the car would be a further annoyance to good aim. And in the third and most decisive place, if he were to miss his first shot he would not be extremely apt to place his second bullet. For Donnegan had a reputation with his own revolver. Indeed, it was said that he rarely carried the weapon, because when he did he was always tempted too strongly to use it. So that the chances were large that Donnegan would not have the gun now. Yet if he did have it— if he, Lefty, did miss his first shot—then the story would be brief and bitter indeed.

On the other hand, a knife offered advantages almost too numerous to be listed. It gave one the deadly assurance which only comes with the knowledge of an edge of steel in one's hand. And when the knife reaches its mark it ends a battle at a stroke.

Of course these doubts and considerations pro and con went through the mind of the tramp in about the same space of time that it requires for a dog to waken, snap at a fly, and drowse again. Eventually, he took out his knife. It was a sheath knife which he wore from a noose of silk around his throat, and it always lay closest to his heart. The blade of the knife was of the finest Spanish steel, in the days when Spanish smiths knew how to draw out steel to a streak of light; the handle of the knife was from Milan. On the whole, it was a delicate and beautiful weapon—and it had the durable suppleness of—say—hatred itself.

Lefty Joe, like a pirate in a tale, took this weapon between his teeth; allowed his squat, heavy bulk to swing down and dangle at arm's length for an instant, and then he swung himself a little and landed softly on the floor of the car.

Who has not heard snow drop from the branch upon other snow beneath? That was the way Lefty Joe dropped to the floor of the car. He remained as he had fallen; crouched, alert, with one hand spread out on the boards to balance him and give him a leverage and a start in case he should wish to spring in any direction.

Then he began to probe the darkness in every direction; with every glance he allowed his head to dart out a little. The movement was like a chicken pecking at imaginary grains of corn. But eventually he satisfied himself that his quarry lay in the forward end of the car; that he was prone; that he, Lefty, had accomplished nine tenths of his purpose by entering the place of his enemy unobserved.

# CHAPTER III

### HE WAKES

BUT even though this major step was accomplished successfully, Lefty Joe was not the man to abandon caution in the midst of an enterprise. The roar of the train would have covered sounds ten times as loud as those of his snaky approach, yet he glided forward with as much care as though he were stepping on old stairs in a silent house. He could see a vague shadow—Donnegan; but chiefly he worked by that peculiar sense of direction which some people possess in a dim light. The blind, of course, have that sense in a high degree of sensitiveness, but even those who are not blind may learn to trust the peculiar and inverted sense of direction.

With this to aid him, Lefty Joe went steadily, slowly across the first and most dangerous stage of his journey. That is, he got away from the square of the open door, where the faint starlight might vaguely serve to silhouette his body. After this, it was easier work.

Of course, when he alighted on the floor of the car, the knife had been transferred from his teeth to his left hand; and all during his progress forward the knife was being balanced delicately, as though he were not yet quite sure of the weight of the weapon. Just as a prize fighter keeps his deadly, poised hands in play, moving them as though he fears to lose his intimate touch with them.

This stalking had occupied a matter of split seconds. Now Lefty Joe rose slowly. He was leaning very far forward, and he warded against the roll of the car by spreading out his right hand close to the floor; his left hand he poised with the knife, and he began to gather his muscles for the leap. He had already taken the last preliminary movement—he had swung himself to the right side a little and, lightening his left foot, had thrown all his weight upon the right—in fact, his body was literally suspended in the instant of springing, catlike, when the shadow which was Donnegan came to life.

The shadow convulsed as shadows are apt to swirl in a green pool when a stone is dropped into it; and a bit of board two feet long and some eight inches wide crackled against the shins of Lefty Joe.

It was about the least dramatic weapon that could have been chosen under those circumstances, but certainly no other defense could have frustrated Lefty's spring so completely. Instead of launching out in a compact mass whose point of contact was the reaching knife, Lefty crawled stupidly forward upon his knees, and had to throw out his knife hand to save his balance.

It is a singular thing to note how important balance is to men. Animals fight, as a rule, just as well on their backs as they do on their feet. They can lie on their sides and bite; they can swing their claws even while they are dropping through the air. But man needs poise and balance before he can act. What is speed in a fighter? It is not so much an affair of the muscles as it is the power of the brain to adapt itself instantly to each new move and put the body in a state of balance. In the prize ring speed does not mean the ability to strike one lightning blow, but rather that, having finished one drive, the fighter is in position to hit again, and then again, so that no matter where the impetus of his last lunge has placed him he is ready and poised to shoot all his weight behind his fist again and drive it accurately at a vulnerable spot. Individually the actions may be slow; but the series of efforts seem rapid. That is why a superior boxer seems to hypnotize his antagonist with movements which to the spectator seem perfectly easy, slow, and sure.

But if Lefty lacked much in agility, he had an animallike sense of balance. Sprawling, helpless, he saw the convulsed shadow that was Donnegan take form as a straight shooting body that plunged through the air above him. Lefty Joe dug his left elbow into the floor of the car and whirled back upon his shoulders, bunching his knees high over his stomach. Nine chances out of ten, if Donnegan had fallen flatwise upon this alert enemy, he would have received those knees in the pit of his own stomach and instantly been paralyzed. But in the jumping, rattling car even Donnegan was capable of making mistakes. His mistake in this instance saved his life, for springing too far, he came down not in reaching distance of Lefty's throat, but with his chest on the knees of the older tramp.

As a result, Donnegan was promptly kicked head over heels and tumbled the length of the car. Lefty was on his feet and plunging after the tumbling form in the twinkling of an eye, literally speaking, and he was only kept from burying his knife in the flesh of his foe by a sway of the car that staggered him in the act of striking. Donnegan, the

next instant, was beyond reach. He had struck the
end of the car and rebounded like a ball of rubber
at a tangent. He slid into the shadows, and Lefty,
putting his own shoulders to the wall, felt for his
revolver and knew that he was lost. He had failed
in his first surprise attack, and without surprise to
help him now he was gone. He weighed his revolver, decided that it would be madness to use it,
for if he missed, Donnegan would instantly be
guided by the flash to shoot him full of holes.

Something slipped by the open door—something
that glimmered faintly; and Lefty Joe knew that
it was the red head of Donnegan. Donnegan, soft-
footed as a shadow among shadows. Donnegan on
a blood trail. It lowered the heart beat of Lefty
Joe to a tremendous, slow pulse. In that moment
he gave up hope and, resigning himself to die,
determined to fight to the last gasp, as became one
of his reputation and national celebrity on "the
road."

Yet Lefty Joe was no common man and no
common fighter. No, let the shade of "Rusty" Dick,
whom Lefty met and beat in his glorious prime—
let this shade arise and speak for the prowess of
Lefty Joe. In fact it was because he was such a
good fighter himself that he recognized his helplessness in the hands of Donnegan.

The faint glimmer of color had passed the door.
It was dissolved in deeper shadows at once, and
soundlessly; Lefty knew that Donnegan was close
and closer.

Of one thing he felt more and more confident,
that Donnegan did not have his revolver with him.
Otherwise he would have used it before. For what
was darkness to this devil, Donnegan. He walked

like a cat, and most likely he could see like a cat in the dark. Instinctively the older tramp braced himself with his right hand held at a guard before his breast and the knife poised in his left, just as a man would prepare to meet the attack of a panther. He even took to probing the darkness in a strange hope to catch the glimmer of the eyes of Donnegan as he moved to the attack. If there were a hair's breadth of light, then Donnegan himself must go down. A single blow would do it.

But the devil had instructed his favorite Donnegan how to fight. He did not come lunging through the shadows to meet the point of that knife. Instead, he had worked a snaky way along the floor and now he leaped in and up at Lefty, taking him under the arms.

A dozen hands, it seemed, laid hold on Lefty. He fought like a demon and tore himself away, but the multitude of hands pursued him. They were small hands. Where they closed they tore the clothes and bit into his very flesh. Once a hand had him by the throat, and when Lefty jerked himself away it was with a feeling that his flesh had been seered by five points of red-hot iron. All this time his knife was darting; once it ripped through cloth, but never once did it find the target. And half a second later Donnegan got his hold. The flash of the knife as Lefty raised it must have guided the other. He shot his right hand up behind the left shoulder of the other and imprisoned the wrist. Not only did it make the knife hand helpless, but by bearing down with his own weight Donnegan could put his enemy in most exquisite torture.

For an instant they whirled; then they went down,

and Lefty was on top. Only for a moment. The impetus which had sent him to the floor was used by Donnegan to turn them over, and once fairly on top his left hand was instantly at the throat of Lefty.

Twice Lefty made enormous efforts, but then he was done. About his body the limbs of Donnegan were twisted, tightening with incredible force; just as hot iron bands sink resistlessly into place. The strangle hold cut away life at its source. Once he strove to bury his teeth in the arm of Donnegan. Once, as the horror caught at him, he strove to shriek for help. All he succeeded in doing was in raising an awful, sobbing whisper. Then, looking death in the face, Lefty plunged into the great darkness.

# CHAPTER IV

## HE ENDS ONE TRAIL

WHEN he wakened, he jumped at a stride into the full possession of his faculties. He had been placed near the open door, and the rush of night air had done its work in reviving him. But Lefty, drawn back to life, felt only a vague wonder that his life had not been taken. Perhaps he was being reserved by the victor for an Indian death of torment. He felt cautiously and found that not only were his hands free, but his revolver had not been taken from him. A familiar weight was on his chest—the very knife had been returned to its sheath.

Had Donnegan returned these things to show how perfectly he despised his enemy?

"He's gone!" groaned the tramp, sitting up quickly.

"He's here," said a voice that cut easily through the roar of the train. "Waiting for you, Lefty."

The tramp was staggered again. But then, who had ever been able to fathom the ways of Donnegan?

"Donnegan!" he cried with a sudden recklessness.

"Yes?"

"You're a fool!"

"Yes?"

"For not finishing the job."

Donnegan began to laugh. In the uproar of the train it was impossible really to hear the sound, but

Lefty caught the pulse of it. He fingered his bruised throat; swallowing was a painful effort. And an indescribable feeling came over him as he realized that he sat armed to the teeth within a yard of the man he wanted to kill, and yet he was as effectively rendered helpless as though iron shackles had been locked on his wrists and legs. The night light came through the doorway, and he could make out the slender outline of Donnegan and again he caught the faint luster of that red hair; and out of the shadowy form a singular power emanated and sapped his strength at the root.

Yet he went on viciously: "Sooner or later, Donnegan, I'll get you!"

The red head of Donnegan moved, and Lefty Joe knew that the younger man was laughing again.

"Why are you after me?" he asked at length.

It was another blow in the face of Lefty. He sat for a time blinking with owlish stupidity.

"Why?" he echoed. "Oh, my heavings!"

And he spoke his astonishment from the heart.

"Why am I after you?" he said again. "Why, confound you, ain't you Donnegan?"

"Yes."

"Don't the whole road know that I'm after you and you after me?"

"The whole road is crazy. I'm not after you." Lefty choked.

"Maybe I been dreaming. Maybe you didn't bust up the gang? Maybe you didn't clean up on Suds and Kennebec?"

"Suds? Kennebec? I sort of remember meeting them."

"You sort of—the devil!" Lefty Joe sputtered the words. "And after you cleaned up my crowd, ain't it natural and good sense for you to go on and try to clean up on me?"

"Sounds like it."

"But I figured to beat you to it. I cut in on your trail, Donnegan, and before I leave it you'll know a lot more about me."

"You're warning me ahead of time?"

"You've played this game square with me; I'll play square with you. Next time there'll be no slips, Donnegan. I dunno why you should of picked on me, though. Just the natural devil in you."

"I haven't picked on you," said Donnegan.

"What?"

"I'll give you my word."

A tingle ran through the blood of Lefty Joe. Somewhere he had heard, in rumor, that the word of Donnegan was as good as gold. He recalled that rumor now and something of dignity in the manner with which Donnegan made his announcement carried a heavy weight. As a rule, the tramps vowed with many oaths, here was one of the knights of the road who made his bare word sufficient. And Lefty Joe heard with great wonder.

"All I ask," he said, "is why you hounded my gang, if you wasn't after me?"

"I didn't hound them. I ran into Suds by accident. We had trouble. Then Levine. Then Kennebec Lou tried to take a fall out of me."

A note of whimsical protest crept into the voice of Donnegan.

"Somehow there's always a fight wherever I go," he said. "Fights just sort of grow up around me."

Lefty Joe snarled.

"You didn't mean nothing by just 'happening' to run into three of my boys one after another?"

"Not a thing."

Lefty rocked himself back and forth in an ecstacy of impatience.

"Why don't you stay put?" he complained. "Why don't you stake out your own ground and stay put in it. You cut in on every guy's territory. There ain't any privacy any more since you hit the road. What you got? A roving commission?"

Donnegan waited for a moment before he answered. And when he spoke his voice had altered. Indeed, he had remarkable ability to pitch his voice into the roar of the freight train, and above or beneath it, and give it a quality such as he pleased.

"I'm following a trail, but not yours," he admitted at length. "I'm following *a* trail. I've been at it these two years and nothing has come of it."

"Who you after?"

"A man with red hair."

"That tells me a lot."

Donnegan refused to explain.

"What you got against him—the color of his hair?"

And Lefty roared contentedly at his own stale jest.

"It's no good," replied Donnegan. "I'll never get on the trail."

Lefty broke in: "You mean to say you've been working two solid years and all on a trail that you ain't even found?"

The silence answered him in the affirmative.

"Ain't nobody been able to tip you off to him?" went on Lefty, intensely interested.

"Nobody. You see, he's a hard sort to describe. Red hair, that's all there was about him for a clew.

But if any one ever saw him stripped they'd remember him by a big, blotchy birthmark on his left shoulder."

"Eh?" grunted Lefty Joe.

He added: "What was his name?"

"Don't know. He changed monikers when he took to the road."

"What was he to you?"

"A man I'm going to find."

"No matter where the trail takes you?"

"No matter where."

At this Lefty was seized with unaccountable laughter. He literally strained his lungs with that Homeric outburst. When he wiped the tears from his eyes, at length, the shadow on the opposite side of the doorway had disappeared. He found his companion leaning over him, and this time he could catch the dull glint of starlight on both hair and eyes.

"What d'you know?" asked Donnegan.

"How do you stand toward this bird with the birthmark and the red hair?" queried Lefty with caution.

"What d'you know?" insisted Donnegan.

All at once passion shook him; he fastened his grip in the shoulder of the larger man, and his finger tips worked toward the bone.

"What do you know?" he repeated for the third time, and now there was no hint of laughter in the hard voice of Lefty.

"You fool, if you follow that trail you'll go to the devil. It was Rusty Dick; and he's dead!"

His triumphant laughter came again, but Donnegan cut into it.

"Rusty Dick was the one you—killed!"

"Sure. What of it? We fought fair and square."

"Then Rusty wasn't the man I want. The man I want would of eaten two like you, Lefty."

"What about the birthmark? It sure was on his shoulder, Donnegan."

"Heavens!" whispered Donnegan.

"What's the matter?"

"Rusty Dick," gasped Donnegan. "Yes, it must have been he."

"Sure it was. What did you have against him?"

"It was a matter of blood—between us," stammered Donnegan.

His voice rose in a peculiar manner, so that Lefty shrank involuntarily.

"You killed Rusty?"

"Ask any of the boys. But between you and me, it was the booze that licked Rusty Dick. I just finished up the job and surprised everybody."

The train was out of the mountains and in a country of scattering hills, but here it struck a steep grade and settled down to a grind of slow labor; the rails hummed, and suspense filled the freight car.

"Hey," cried Lefty suddenly. "You fool, you'll do a flop out the door in about a minute!"

He even reached out to steady the toppling figure, but Donnegan pitched straight out into the night. Lefty craned his neck from the door, studying the roadbed, but at that moment the locomotive topped the little rise and the whole train lurched forward.

"After all," murmured Lefty Joe, "it sounds like Donnegan. Hated a guy so bad that he hadn't any use for livin' when he heard the other guy was dead. But I'm never goin' to cross his path again, I hope."

# CHAPTER V

## HE SEES A VISION

BUT Donnegan had leaped clear of the roadbed, and he struck almost to the knees in a drift of sand. Otherwise, he might well have broken his legs with that foolhardy chance. As it was, the fall whirled him over and over, and by the time he had picked himself up the lighted caboose of the train was rocking past him. Donnegan watched it grow small in the distance, and then, when it was only a red, uncertain star far down the track, he turned to the vast country around him.

The mountains were to his right, not far away, but caught up behind the shadows so that it seemed a great distance. Like all huge, half seen things they seemed in motion toward him. For the rest, he was in a bare, rolling country. The sky line everywhere was clean; there was hardly a sign of a tree. He knew, by a little reflection, that this must be a cattle country, for the brakie had intimated as much in their talk just before dusk. Now it was early night, and a wind began to rise, blowing down the valley with a keen motion and a rapidly lessening temperature, so that Donnegan saw he must get to a shelter. He could, if necessary, endure any privation, but his tastes were for luxurious comfort. Accordingly he considered the landscape with gloomy disapproval. He was almost inclined to regret his plunge from the lumbering freight train. Two things had governed him in making that move.

First, when he discovered that the long trail he followed was definitely fruitless, he was filled with a great desire to cut himself away from his past and make a new start. Secondly, when he learned that Rusty Dick had been killed by Joe, he wanted desperately to get the throttle of the latter under his thumb. If ever a man risked his life to avoid a sin, it was Donnegan jumping from the train to keep from murder.

He stooped to sight along the ground, for this is the best way at night and often horizon lights are revealed in this manner. But now Donnegan saw nothing to serve as a guide. He therefore drew in his belt until it fitted snug about his gaunt waist, settled his cap firmly, and headed straight into the wind.

Nothing could have shown his character more distinctly. When in doubt, head into the wind.

With a jaunty, swinging step he sauntered along, and this time, at least, his tactics found an early reward. Topping the first large rise of ground, he saw in the hollow beneath him the outline of a large building. And as he approached it, the wind clearing a high blowing mist from the stars, he saw a jumble of outlying houses. Sheds, barns, corrals —it was the nucleus of a big ranch. It is a maxim that, if you wish to know a man look at his library, and if you wish to know a rancher, look at his barn. Donnegan made a small detour to the left and headed for the largest of the barns.

He entered it by the big, sliding door, which stood open; he looked up, and saw the stars shining through a gap in the roof. And then he stood quietly for a time, listening to the voices of the wind in the ruin. Oddly enough, it was pleasant to Donnegan. His own troubles and sorrow had poured upon him so thickly in the past hour or so that it was soothing to find evidence of the distress of others. But perhaps this meant that the entire establishment was deserted.

He left the barn and went toward the house. Not until he was close under its wall did he come to appreciate its size. It was one of those great, rambling, two-storied structures which the cattle kings of the past generation were fond of building. Standing close to it, he heard none of the intimate sounds of the storm blowing through cracks and broken walls; no matter into what disrepair the barns had fallen, the house was still solid; only about the edges of the building the storm kept murmuring.

Yet there was not a light, neither above nor below. He came to the front of the house. Still no sign of life. He stood at the door and knocked loudly upon it, and though, when he tried the knob, he found that the door was latched, yet no one came in response. He knocked again, and putting his ear close he heard the echoes walk through the interior of the building.

After this, the wind rose in sudden strength and deafened him with rattlings; above him, a shutter was swung open and then crashed to. So that the opening of the door was a shock of surprise to Donnegan. A dim light from a source which he could not direct suffused the interior of the hall; the door itself was worked open a matter of inches and Donnegan was aware of two keen old eyes glittering out at him. Beyond this he could distinguish nothing.

"Who are you?" asked a woman's voice. "And what do you want?"

"I'm a stranger, and I want something to eat and a place to sleep. This house looks as if it might have spare rooms."

"Where d'you come from?"

"Yonder," said Donnegan, with a sufficiently non-committal gesture.

"What's your name?"

"Donnegan."

"I don't know you. Be off with you, Mr. Donnegan!"

He inserted his foot in the closing crack of the door.

"Tell me where I'm to go?" he persisted.

At this her voice rose in pitch, with squeaky rage.

"I'll raise the house on you!"

"Raise 'em. Call down the man of the house. I can talk to him better than I can to you; but I won't walk off like this. If you can feed me, I'll pay you for what I eat."

A shrill cackling—he could not make out the words. And since patience was not the first of Donnegan's virtues, he seized on the knob of the door and deliberately pressed it wide. Standing in the hall, now, and closing the door slowly behind him, he saw a woman with old, keen eyes shrinking away toward the staircase. She was evidently in great fear, but there was something infinitely malicious in the manner in which she kept working her lips soundlessly. She was shrinking, and half turned away, yet there was a suggestion that in an instant she might whirl and fly at his face. The door now clicked, and with the windstorm shut away Donnegan had a queer feeling of being trapped.

"Now call the man of the house," he repeated. "See if I can't come to terms with him."

"He'd make short work of you if he came," she replied. She broke into a shrill laughter, and Donnegan thought he had never seen a face so ugly. "If he came," she said, "you'd rue the day."

"Well, I'll talk to you, then. I'm not asking charity. I want to pay for what I get."

"This ain't a hotel. You go on down the road. Inside eight miles you'll come to the town."

"Eight miles!"

"That's nothing for a man to ride."

"Not at all, if I had something to ride."

"You ain't got a horse?"

"No."

"Then how do you come here?"

"I walked."

If this sharpened her suspicions, it sharpened her fear also. She put one foot on the lowest step of the stairs.

"Be off with you, Mr. Donnegally, or whatever your outlandish name is. You'll get nothing here. What brings you——"

A door closed and a footstep sounded lightly on the floor above. And Donnegan, already alert in the strange atmosphere of this house, gave back a pace so as to get an honest wall behind him. He noted that the step was quick and small, and preparing himself to meet a wisp of manhood—which, for that matter, was the type he was most inclined to fear—Donnegan kept a corner glance upon the old woman at the foot of the stairs and steadily surveyed the shadows at the head of the rise.

Out of that darkness a foot slipped; not even a boy's foot—a very child's. The shock of it made Donnegan relax his caution for an instant, and in that instant she came into the reach of the light. It was a wretched light at best, for it came from a lamp with smoky chimney which the old hag carried, and at the raising and lowering of her hand the flame jumped and died in the throat of the chimney and set the hall awash with shadows. Falling away to a point of yellow, the lamp allowed the hall to assume a certain indefinite dignity of height and breadth and calm proportions; but when the flame rose Donnegan could see the broken balusters of the balustrade, the carpet, faded past any design and worn to rattiness, wall paper which had rotted or dried away and hung in crisp tatters here and there, and on the ceiling an irregular patch from which the plaster had fallen and exposed the lathwork. But at the coming of the girl the old woman had turned, and as she did the flame tossed up in the lamp and Donnegan could see the new-comer distinctly.

Once before his heart had risen as it rose now. It had been the fag end of a long party, and Donnegan, rousing from a drunken sleep, staggered to the window. Leaning there to get the freshness of the night air against his hot face, he had looked up, and saw the white face of the moon going up the sky; and a sudden sense of the blackness and loathing against the city had come upon Donnegan, and the murky color of his own life; and when he turned away from the window he was sober. And so it was that he now stared up at the girl. At her breast she held a cloak together with one hand and the other hand touched the railing of the stairs.

He saw one foot suspended for the next step, as
though the sight of him kept her back in fear. To
the miserable soul of Donnegan she seemed all that
was lovely, young, and pure; and her hair, old gold
in the shadow and pale gold where the lamp struck
it, was to Donnegan like a miraculous light about
her face.

Indeed, that little pause was a great and awful
moment. For considering that Donnegan, who
had gone through his whole life with his eyes ready
to either mock or hate, and who had rarely used
his hand except to make a fist of it; Donnegan who
had never, so far as is known, had a companion;
who had asked the world for action, not kindness;
this Donnegan now stood straight with his back
against the wall, and poured out the story of his
wayward life to a mere slip of a girl.

# CHAPTER VI

EVEN the old woman, whose eyes were sharpened by her habit of looking constantly for the weaknesses and vices of men, could not guess what was going on behind the thin, rather ugly face of Donnegan; the girl, perhaps, may have seen more. For she caught the glitter of his active eyes even at that distance. The hag began to explain with vicious gestures that set the light flaring up and down.

"He ain't come from nowhere, Lou," she said. "He ain't going nowhere; he wants to stay here for the night."

The foot which had been suspended to take the next step was now withdrawn. Donnegan, remembered at last, whipped off his cap, and at once the light flared and burned upon his hair. It was a wonderful red; it shone, and it had a terrible blood tinge so that his face seemed pale beneath it. There were three things that made up the peculiar dominance of Donnegan's countenance. The three things were the hair, the uneasy, bright eyes, and the rather thin, compressed lips. When Donnegan slept he seemed about to waken from a vigorous dream; when he sat down he seemed about to leap to his feet; and when he was standing he gave that impression of a poise which is ready for anything. It was no wonder that the girl, seeing that face and that alert, aggressive body, shrank a little on the stairs. Donnegan, that instant, knew that these two women were really alone in the house as far as fighting men were concerned.

And the fact disturbed him more than a leveled gun would have done. He went to the foot of the stairs, even past the old woman, and, raising his head, he spoke to the girl.

"My name's Donnegan. I came over from the railroad—walked. I don't want to walk that other eight miles unless there's a real need for it. I——" Why did he pause? "I'll pay for anything I get here."

His voice was not too certain; behind his teeth there was knocking a desire to cry out to her the truth: "I am Donnegan. Donnegan the tramp. Donnegan the shiftless. Donnegan the fighter. Donnegan the killer. Donnegan the penniless, worthless. But for Heaven's sake let me stay until morning and let me look at you—from a distance!"

But, after all, perhaps he did not need to say all these things. His clothes were rags; upon his face there was a stubble of unshaven red, which made the pallor about his eyes more pronounced. If the girl had been half blind she must have felt that here was a man of fire. He saw her gather the wrap a little closer about her shoulders, and that sign of fear made him sick at heart.

"Mr. Donnegan," said the girl, "I am sorry. We cannot take you into the house. Eight miles——"

Did she expect to turn a sinner from the gates of heaven with a mere phrase? He cast out his hand, and she winced as though he had shaken his fist at her.

"Are you afraid?" cried Donnegan.

"I don't control the house."

He paused, not that her reply had baffled him, but the mere pleasure of hearing her speak accounted for it. It was one of those low, light voices which are apt to have very little range or volume, and which break and tremble absurdly under any stress of emotion; and often they become shrill in a higher register; but inside conversational limits, if such a term may be used, there is no fiber so delightful, so purely musical. Suppose the word "velvet" applied to a sound. That voice came soothingly and delightfully upon the ear of Donnegan, from which the roar and rattle of the empty freight train had not quite departed. He smiled at her.

"But," he protested, "this is west of the Rockies— and I don't see any other way out."

The girl, all this time, was studying him intently, a little sadly, he thought. Now she shook her head, but there was more warmth in her voice.

"I'm sorry. I can't ask you to stay without first consulting my father."

"Go ahead. Ask him."

She raised her hand a little; the thought seemed to bring her to the verge of trembling, as though he were asking a sacrilege.

"Why not?" he urged.

She did not answer, but, instead, her eyes sought the old woman, as if to gain her interposition; she burst instantly into speech.

"Which there's no good talking any more," declared the ancient vixen. "Are you wanting to make trouble for her with the colonel? Be off, young man. It ain't the first time I've told you you'd get nowhere in this house!"

There was no possible answer left to Donnegan, and he did as usual the surprising thing. He broke into laughter of such clear and ringing tone—such infectious laughter—that the old woman blinked in the midst of her wrath as though she were seeing a new man, and he saw the lips of the girl parted in wonder.

"My father is an invalid," said the girl. "And he lives by strict rules. I could not break in on him at this time of the evening."

"If that's all"—Donnegan actually began to mount the steps—"I'll go in and talk to your father myself."

She had retired one pace as he began advancing, but as the import of what he said became clear to her she was rooted to one position by astonishment.

"Colonel Macon—my father——" she began. Then: "Do you really wish to see him?"

The hushed voice made Donnegan smile—it was such a voice as one boy uses when he asks the other if he really dares enter the pasture of the red bull. He chuckled again, and this time she smiled, and her eyes were widened, partly by fear of his purpose and partly from his nearness. They seemed to be suddenly closer together. As though they were on one side against a common enemy, and that enemy was her father. The old woman was cackling sharply from the bottom of the stairs, and then bobbling in pursuit and calling on Donnegan to come back. At length the girl raised her hand and silenced her with a gesture.

Donnegan was now hardly a pace away; and he saw that she lived up to all the promise of that first glance. Yet still she seemed unreal. There is a quality of the unearthly about a girl's beauty; it is, after all, only a gay moment between the form-lessness of childhood and the hardness of middle age. This girl was pale, Donnegan saw, and yet she had color. She had the luster, say, of a white rose, and the same bloom. Lou, the old woman had called her, and Macon was her father's name. Lou Macon—the name fitted her, Donnegan thought. For that matter, if her name had been Sally Smith, Donnegan would probably have thought it beautiful. The keener a man's mind is and the more he knows about men and women and the ways of the world, the more apt he is to be intoxicated by a touch of grace and thoughtfulness; and all these age-long seconds the perfume of girlhood had been striking up to Donnegan's brain.

She brushed her timidity away and with the same gesture accepted Donnegan as something more than a dangerous vagrant. She took the lamp from the hands of the crone and sent her about her business, disregarding the mutterings and the warnings which trailed behind the departing form. Now she faced Donnegan, screening the light from her eyes with a cupped hand and by the same device focusing it upon the face of Donnegan. He mutely noted the small maneuver and gave her credit; but for the pleasure of seeing the white of her fingers and the way they tapered to a pink transparency at the tips, he forgot the poor figure he must make with his soiled, ragged shirt, his unshaven face, his gaunt cheeks.

Indeed, he looked so straight at her that in spite of her advantage with the light she had to avoid his glance.

"I am sorry," said Lou Macon, "and ashamed because we can't take you in. The only house on the range where you wouldn't be welcome, I know.

But my father leads a very close life; he has set ways. The ways of an invalid, Mr. Donnegan."

"And you're bothered about speaking to him of me?"

"I'm almost afraid of letting you go in yourself."

"Let me take the risk."

She considered him again for a moment, and then turned with a nod and he followed her up the stairs into the upper hall. The moment they stepped into it he heard her clothes flutter and a small gale poured on them. It was criminal to allow such a building to fall into this ruinous condition. And a gloomy picture rose in Donnegan's mind of the invalid, thin-faced, sallow-eyed, white-haired, lying in his bed listening to the storm and silently gathering bitterness out of the pain of living. Lou Macon paused again in the hall, close to a door on the right.

"I'm going to send you in to speak to my father," she said gravely. "First I have to tell you that he's different."

Donnegan replied by looking straight at her, and this time she did not wince from the glance. Indeed, she seemed to be probing him, searching with a peculiar hope. What could she expect to find in him? What that was useful to her? Not once in all his life had such a sense of impotence descended upon Donnegan. Her father? Bah! Invalid or no invalid he would handle that fellow, and if the old man had an acrid temper, Donnegan at will could file his own speech to a point. But the girl! In the meager hand which held the lamp there was a power which all the muscles of Donnegan could not compass; and in his weakness he looked wistfully at her.

"I hope your talk will be pleasant. I hope so." She laid her hand on the knob of the door and withdrew it hastily; then, summoning great resolution, she opened the door and showed Donnegan in.

"Father," she said, "this is Mr. Donnegan. He wishes to speak to you."

The door closed behind Donnegan, and hearing that whishing sound which the door of a heavy safe will make, he looked down at this, and saw that it was actually inches thick! Once more the sense of being in a trap descended upon him.

# CHAPTER VII

## HE SEES THE DEVIL

HE found himself in a large room which, before he could examine a single feature of it, was effectively curtained from his sight. Straight into his face shot a current of violent white light that made him blink. There was the natural recoil, but in Donnegan recoils were generally protected by several strata of will power and seldom showed in any physical action. On the present occasion his first dismay was swiftly overwhelmed by a cold anger at the insulting trick. This was not the trick of a helpless invalid; Donnegan could not see a single thing before him, but he obeyed a very deep instinct and advanced straight into the current of light.

He was glad to see the light switched away. The comparative darkness washed across his eyes in a pleasant wave and he was now able to distinguish a few things in the room. It was, as he had first surmised, quite large. The ceiling was high; the proportions comfortably spacious; but what astounded Donnegan was the real elegance of the furnishings. There was no mistaking the deep, silken texture of the rug upon which he stepped; the glow of light barely reached the wall, and there showed faintly in streaks along yellowish hangings. Beside a table which supported a big reading lamp—gasoline, no doubt, from the intensity of its light—sat Colonel Macon with a large volume spread across his knees. Donnegan saw two high lights—fine silver hair that covered the head of the invalid and a pair of white hands fallen idly upon the surface of the big book, for if the silver hair suggested age the smoothly finished hands suggested perennial youth. They were strong, carefully tended, complacent hands. They suggested to Donnegan a man sufficient unto himself.

"Mr. Donnegan, I am sorry that I cannot rise to receive you. Now, what pleasant accident has brought me the favor of this call?"

Donnegan was taken aback again, and this time more strongly than by the flare of light against his eyes. For in the voice he recognized the quality of the girl—the same softness, the same velvety richness, though the pitch was a bass. In the voice of this man there was the same suggestion that the tone would crack if it were forced either up or down. With this great difference, one could hardly conceive of a situation which would push that man's voice beyond its monotone. It flowed with deadly, all-embracing softness. It clung about one; it fascinated and baffled the mind of the listener.

But Donnegan was not in the habit of being baffled by voices. Neither was he a lover of formality. He looked about for a place to sit down, and immediately discovered that while the invalid sat in an enormous easy-chair bordered by shelves and supplied with wheels for raising and lowering the back and for propelling the chair about the room on its rubber tires, it was the only chair in the room which could make any pretentions toward comfort. As a matter of fact, aside from this one immense chair, devoted to the pleasure of the invalid, there was nothing in the room for his visitors to sit upon except two or three miserable backless stools.

But Donnegan was not long taken aback. He tucked his cap under his arm, bowed profoundly in honor of the colonel's compliments, and brought one of the stools to a place where it was no nearer the rather ominous circle of the lamp light than was the invalid himself. With his eyes accustomed to the new light, Donnegan could now take better stock of his host. He saw a rather handsome face, with eyes exceedingly blue, young, and active; but the features of Macon as well as his body were blurred and obscured by a great fatness. He was truly a prodigious man, and one could understand the stoutness with which the invalid chair was made. His great wrist dimpled like the wrist of a healthy baby, and his face was so enlarged with superfluous flesh that the lower part of it quite dwarfed the upper. He seemed, at first glance, a man with a low forehead and bright, careless eyes and a body made immobile by flesh and sickness. A man whose spirits despised and defied pain. Yet a second glance showed that the forehead was, after all, a nobly proportioned one, and for all the bulk of that figure, for all the cripple-chair, Donnegan would not have been surprised to see the bulk spring lightly out of the chair to meet him.

For his own part, sitting back on the stool with his cap tucked under his arm and his hands folded about one knee, he met the faint, cold smile of the colonel with a broad grin of his own.

"I can put it in a nutshell," said Donnegan. "I was tired; dead beat; needed a hand-out, and rapped at your door. Along comes a mystery in the shape of an ugly-looking old woman and opens the door to me. Tries to shut me out; I decided to come in. She insists on keeping me outside; all at once I see that I have to get into the house. I am brought in; your daughter tries to steer me off, sees that the job is more than she can get away with, and shelves me off upon you. And that, Colonel Macon, is the pleasant accident which brings you the favor of this call."

It would have been a speech both stupid and pert in the mouth of another; but Donnegan knew how to flavor words with a touch of mockery of himself as well as another. There were two manners in which this speech could have been received—with a wink or with a smile. But it would have been impossible to hear it and grow frigid. As for the colonel, he smiled.

It was a tricky smile, however, as Donnegan felt. It spread easily upon that vast face and again went out and left all to the dominion of the cold, bright eyes.

"A case of curiosity," commented the colonel.

"A case of hunger," said Donnegan.

"My dear Mr. Donnegan, put it that way if you wish!"

"And a case of blankets needed for one night."

"Really? Have you ventured into such a country as this without any equipment?"

"Outside of my purse, my equipment is of the invisible kind."

"Wits," suggested the colonel.

"Thank you."

"Not at all. You hinted at it yourself."

"However, a hint is harder to take than to make."

The colonel raised his faultless right hand—and oddly enough his great corpulence did not extend in the slightest degree to his hand, but stopped short at the wrists—and stroked his immense chin. His skin was like Lou Macon's, except that in place of the white-flower bloom his was a parchment, dead pallor. He lowered his hand with the same slow precision and folded it with the other, all the time probing Donnegan with his difficult eyes.

"Unfortunately—most unfortunately, it is impossible for me to accommodate you, Mr. Donnegan."

The reply was not flippant, but quick. "Not at all. I am the easiest person in the world to accommodate."

The big man smiled sadly.

"My fortune has fallen upon evil days, sir. It is no longer what it was. There are in this house three habitable rooms; this one; my daughter's apartment; the kitchen where old Haggie sleeps. Otherwise you are in a rat trap of a place."

He shook his head, a slow, decisive motion.

"A spare blanket," said Donnegan, "will be enough."

There was another sigh and another shake of the head.

"Even a corner of a rug to roll up in will do perfectly."

"You see, it is impossible for me to entertain you."

"Bare boards will do well enough for me, Colonel Macon. And if I have a piece of bread, a plate of cold beans—anything—I can entertain myself."

"I am sorry to see you so compliant, Mr. Donnegan, because that makes my refusal seem the more unkind. But I cannot have you sleeping on the bare floor. Not on such a night. Pneumonia comes on one like a cat in the dark in such weather. It is really impossible to keep you here, sir."

"H'm-m," said Donnegan. He began to feel that he was stumped, and it was a most unusual feeling for him.

"Besides, for a young fellow like you, with your agility, what is eight miles? Walk down the road and you will come to a place where you will be made at home and fed like a king."

"Eight miles, that's not much! But on such a night as this?"

There was a faint glint in the eyes of the colonel; was he not sharpening his wits for his contest of words, and enjoying it?

"The wind will be at your back and buoy your steps. It will shorten the eight miles to four."

Very definitely Donnegan felt that the other was reading him. What was it that he saw as he turned the pages?

"There is one thing you fail to take into your accounting."

"Ah?"

"I have an irresistible aversion to walking."

"Ah?" repeated Macon.

"Or exercise in any form."

"Then you are unfortunate to be in this country without a horse."

"Unfortunate, perhaps, but the fact is that I'm here. Very sorry to trouble you, though, colonel."

"I am rarely troubled," said the colonel coldly. "And since I have no means of accommodation, the laws of hospitality rest lightly on my shoulders."

"Yet I have an odd thought," replied Donnegan.

"Well? You have expressed a number already, it seems to me."

"It's this: that you've already made up your mind to keep me here."

# CHAPTER VIII

## HE READS THE DEVIL'S MIND

THE colonel stiffened in his chair, and under his bulk even those ponderous timbers quaked a little. Once more Donnegan gained an impression of chained activity ready to rise to any emergency. The colonel's jaw set and the last vestige of the smile left his eyes. Yet it was not anger that showed in its place. Instead, it was rather a hungry searching. He looked keenly into the face and the soul of Donnegan as a searchlight sweeps over waters by night.

"You are a mind reader, Mr. Donnegan."

"No more of a mind reader than a chink is."

"Ah, they are great readers of mind, my friend."

Donnegan grinned, and at this the colonel frowned.

"A great and mysterious people, sir. I keep evidences of them always about me. Look!"

He swept the shaft of the reading light up and it fell upon a red vase against the yellow hangings. Even Donnegan's inexperienced eye read a price into that shimmering vase.

"Queer color," he said.

"Dusty claret. Ah, they have the only names for their colors. Think! Peach bloom—liquid dawn—ripe cherry—oil green—green of powdered tea—blue of the sky after rain—what names for color! What other land possesses such a tongue that goes straight to the heart!"

The colonel waved his faultless hands and then

dropped them back upon the book with the tenderness of a benediction.

"And their terms for texture—pear's rind—lime peel—millet seed! Do not scoff at China, Mr. Donnegan. She is the fairy godmother, and we are the poor children."

He changed the direction of the light; Donnegan watched him, fascinated.

"But what convinced you that I wished to keep you here?"

"To amuse you, Colonel Macon."

The colonel exposed gleaming white teeth and laughed in that soft, smooth-flowing voice.

"Amuse me? For fifteen years I have sat in this room and amused myself by taking in what I would and shutting out the rest of the world. I have made the walls thick and padded them to keep out all sound. You observe that there is no evidence here of the storm that is going on to-night. Amuse me? Indeed!"

And Donnegan thought of Lou Macon in her old, drab dress, huddling the poor cloak around her shoulders to keep out the cold, while her father lounged here in luxury. He could gladly have buried his lean fingers in that fat throat. From the first he had had an aversion to this man.

"Very well, I shall go. It has been a pleasant chat, colonel."

"Very pleasant. And thank you. But before you go, taste this whisky. It will help you when you enter the wind."

He opened a cabinet in the side of the chair and brought out a black bottle and a pair of glasses and put them on the broad arm of the chair. Donnegan sauntered back.

"You see," he murmured, "you will not let me go."

At this the colonel raised his head suddenly and glared into the eyes of his guest, and yet so perfect was his muscular and nerve control that he did not interrupt the thin stream of amber which trickled into one of the glasses. Looking down again, he finished pouring the drinks. They pledged each other with a motion, and drank. It was very old, very oily. And Donnegan smiled as he put down the empty glass.

"Sit down," said the colonel in a new voice.

Donnegan obeyed.

"Fate," went on the colonel, "rules our lives. We give our honest endeavors, but the deciding touch is the hand of Fate."

He garnished this absurd truism with a wave of his hand so solemn that Donnegan was chilled; as though the fat man were actually conversant with the Three Sisters.

"Fate has brought you to me; therefore, I intend to keep you."

"Here?"

"In my service. I am about to place a great mission and a great trust in your hands."

"In the hands of a man you know nothing about?"

"I know you as if I had raised you."

Donnegan smiled, and shaking his head, the red hair flashed and shimmered.

"As long as there is no work attached to the mission, it may be agreeable to me."

"But there is work."

"Then the contract is broken before it is made."

"You are rash. But I had rather begin with a dissent and then work upward."

Donnegan waited.

"To balance against work——"

"Excuse me. Nothing balances against work for me."

"To balance against work," continued the colonel, raising a white hand and by that gesture crushing the protest of Donnegan, "there is a great reward."

"Colonel Macon, I have never worked for money before and I shall not work for it now."

"You trouble me with interruptions. Who mentioned money? You shall not have a penny!"

"No?"

"The reward shall grow out of the work."

"And the work?"

"Is fighting."

At this Donnegan narrowed his eyes and searched the fat man thoroughly. It sounded like the talk of a charlatan, and yet there was a crispness to these sentences that made him suspect something underneath. For that matter, in certain districts his name and his career were known. He had never dreamed that that reputation could have come within a thousand miles of this part of the mountain desert.

"You should have told me in the first place," he said with some anger, "that you knew me."

"Mr. Donnegan, upon my honor, I never heard your name before my daughter uttered it."

Donnegan waited soberly.

"I despise charlatanry as much as the next man. You shall see the steps by which I judged you. When you entered the room I threw a strong light upon you. You did not blanch; you immediately walked straight into the shaft of light although you could not see a foot before you."

"And that proved?"

"A combative instinct, and coolness; not the sort of brute vindictiveness that fights for a rage, for a cool-minded love of conflict. Is that clear?"

Donnegan shrugged his shoulders.

"And above all, I need a fighter. Then I watched your eyes and your hands. The first were direct and yet they were alert. And your hands were perfectly steady."

"Qualifications for a fighter, eh?"

"Do you wish further proof?"

"Well?"

"What of the fight to the death which you went through this same night?"

Donnegan started. It was a small movement, that flinching, and he covered it by continuing the upward gesture of his hand to his coat; he drew out tobacco and cigarette papers and commenced to roll his smoke. Looking up, he saw that the eyes of Colonel Macon were smiling, although his face was grave.

A glint of understanding passed between the two men, but not a spoken word.

"I assure you, there was no death to-night," said Donnegan at length.

"Tush! Of course not! Of course not! But the tear on the shoulder of your coat—ah, that is too smooth edged for a tear, too long for the bite of a scissors. Am I right? Tush! Not a word!"

The colonel beamed with an almost tender pride, and Donnegan, knowing that the fat man looked upon him as a murderer newly come from a death, considered the beaming face and thought many things in silence.

"So it was easy to see that in coolness, courage, fighting instinct, skill, you were probably what I want. Yet something more than all these qualifications is necessary for the task which lies ahead of you."

"You pile up the bad features, eh?"

"To entice you, Donnegan. For one man, paint a rosy beginning, and once under way he will manage the hard parts. For you, show you the hard shell and you will trust that it contains the choice flesh. I was saying, that I waited to see other qualities. in you; qualities of the judgment. And suddenly you flashed upon me a single glance; I felt it clash against my will power. I felt your look go past my guard like a rapier slipping around my blade. I, Colonel Macon, was for the first time outfaced, outmaneuvered. I admit it, for I rejoice in meeting such a man. And the next instant you told me that I should keep you here out of my own wish! Admirable!"

The admiration of the colonel, indeed, almost overwhelmed Donnegan, but he saw that in spite of the genial smile, the face suffused with warmth, the colonel was watching him every instant, flinty-eyed. Donnegan did as he had done on the stairs, he burst into laughter.

When he had done, the colonel was leaning forward in his chair with his fingers interlaced, examining his guest from beneath somber brows. As he sat lurched forward he gave a terrible impression of that reserved energy which Donnegan had sensed before.

"Donnegan," said the colonel, "I shall talk no more nonsense to you. You are a terrible fellow!"

And Donnegan knew that, for the first time in the colonel's life, he was meeting another man upon equal ground.

# CHATER IX

## HE SELLS HIS SOUL

IN a way, it was an awful tribute, for one great fact grew upon him: that the colonel represented almost perfectly the power of absolute evil. Donnegan was not a squeamish sort, but the fat, smiling face of Macon filled him with unutterable aversion. A dozen times he would have left the room, but a silken thread held him back, the thought of Lou.

"I shall be terse and entirely frank," said the colonel, and at once Donnegan reared triple guard and balanced himself for attack or defense.

"Between you and me," went on the fat man, "deceptive words are folly. A waste of energy." He flushed a little. "You are, I believe, the first man who has ever laughed at me." The click of his teeth as he snapped them on this sentence seemed to promise that he should also be the last.

"So I tear away the veils which made me ridiculous, I grant you. Donnegan, we have met each other just in time."

"True," said Donnegan, "you have a task for me that promises a lot of fighting; and in return I get lodgings for the night."

"Wrong, wrong! I offer you much more. I offer you a career of action in which you may forget the great sorrow which has fallen upon you; and in the battles which lie before you, you will find oblivion for the sad past which lies behind you."

Here Donnegan sprang to his feet with his hand

caught at his breast; and he stood quivering, in an agony. Pain worked in him as anger would do; and, his slender frame swelling, his muscles taut, he stood like a panther enduring the torture because it knows it is folly to attempt to escape.

"You are a human devil!" Donnegan said at last, and sank back upon his stool. For the moment he was overcome, his head falling upon his breast, and even when he looked up his face was terribly pale, and his eyes dull. His expression, however, cleared swiftly, and aside from the perspiration which shone on his forehead it would have been impossible ten seconds later to discover that the blow of the colonel had fallen upon him.

All of this the colonel had observed and noted with grim satisfaction. Not once did he speak until he saw that all was well.

"I am sorry," he said at length in a voice almost as delicate as the voice of Lou Macon. "I am sorry, but you forced me to say more than I wished to say."

Donnegan brushed the apology aside.

His voice became low and hurried. "Let us get on in the matter. I am eager to learn from you, colonel."

"Very well. Since it seems that there is a place for both our interests in this matter, I shall run on in my tale and make it, as I promised you before, absolutely frank and curt. I shall not descend into small details. I shall give you a main sketch of the high points; for all men of mind are apt to be confused by the face of a thing, whereas the heart of it is perfectly clear to them."

He settled into his narrative.

"You have heard of The Corner? No? Well,

that is not strange; but a few weeks ago gold was found in the sands where the valleys of Young Muddy and Christobel Rivers join. The Corner is a long, wide triangle of sand, and the sand is filled with a gold deposit brought down from the head-waters of both rivers and precipitated here, where one current meets the other and reduces the resultant stream to sluggishness. The sands are rich—very rich!"

He had become a trifle flushed as he talked, and now, perhaps to cover his emotion, he carefully selected a cigarette from the humidor beside him and lighted it without haste before he spoke another word.

"Long ago I prospected over that valley; a few weeks ago it was brought to my attention again. I determined to stake some claims and work them. But I could not go myself. I had to send a trustworthy man. Whom should I select? There was only one possible. Jack Landis is my ward. A dozen years ago his parents died and they sent him to my care, for my fortune was then comfortable. I raised him with as much tenderness as I could have shown my own son; I lavished on him the affection and——"

Here Donnegan coughed lightly; the fat man paused, and observing that this hypocrisy did not draw the veil over the bright eyes of his guest, he continued: "In a word, I made him one of my family. And when the need for a man came I turned to him. He is young, strong, active, able to take care of himself."

At this Donnegan pricked his ears.

"He went, accordingly, to The Corner and staked the claims and filed them as I directed. I was right. There was gold. Much gold. It panned out in nuggets."

He made an indescribable gesture, and through his strong fingers Donnegan had a vision of yellow gold pouring.

"But there is seldom a discovery of importance claimed by one man alone. This was no exception. A villain named William Lester, known as a scoundrel over the length and breadth of the cattle country, claimed that he had made the discovery first. He even went so far as to claim that I had obtained my information from him and he tried to jump the claims staked by Jack Landis, whereupon Jack, very properly, shot Lester down. Not dead, unfortunately, but slightly wounded.

"In the meantime the rush for The Corner started. In a week there was a village; in a fortnight there was a town; in a month The Corner had become the talk of the ranges. Jack Landis found in the claims a mint. He sent me back a mere souvenir."

The fat man produced from his vest pocket a little chunk of yellow and with a dexterous motion whipped it at Donnegan. It was done so suddenly, so unexpectedly that the wanderer was well-nigh taken by surprise. But his hand flashed up and caught the metal before it struck his face. He found in the palm of his hand a nugget weighing perhaps five ounces, and he flicked it back to the colonel.

"He sent me the souvenir, but that was all. Since that time I have waited. Nothing has come. I sent for word, and I learned that Jack Landis had betrayed his trust, fallen in love with some undesirable woman of the mining camp, denied my claim to any of the gold to which I had sent him. Unpleasant news? Yes. Ungrateful boy? Yes. But my mind is hardened against adversity.

"Yet this blow struck me close to the heart. Because Landis is engaged to marry my daughter, Lou. At first I could hardly believe in his disaffection. But the truth has at length been borne home to me. The scoundrel has abandoned both Lou and me!"

Donnegan repeated slowly: "Your daughter loves this chap?"

The colonel allowed his glance to narrow, and he could do this the more safely because at this moment Donnegan's eyes were wandering into the distance. In that unguarded second Donnegan was defenseless and the colonel read something that set him beaming.

"She loves him, of course," he said, "and he is breaking her heart with his selfishness."

"He is breaking her heart?" echoed Donnegan.

The colonel raised his hand and stroked his enormous chin. Decidedly he believed that things were getting on very well.

"This is the position," he declared. "Jack Landis was threatened by the wretch Lester, and shot him down. But Lester was not single-handed. He belongs to a wild crew, led by a mysterious fellow of whom no one knows very much; a deadly fighter, it is said, and a keen organizer and handler of men. Red-haired, wild, smooth. A bundle of contradictions. They call him 'Lord Nick' because he has the pride of a nobleman and the cunning of the devil. He has gathered a few chosen spirits and cool fighters—'The Pedlar,' Joe Rix, Harry Masters —all celebrated names in the cattle country.

"They worship Lord Nick partly because he is a

genius of crime and partly because he understands how to guide them so that they may rob and even kill with impunity. His peculiarity is his ability to keep within the bounds of the law. If he commits a robbery he always first establishes marvelous alibis and throws the blame toward some one else; if it is the case of a killing, it is always the other man who is the aggressor. He has been before a jury half a dozen times, but the devil knows law and pleads his own case with a tongue that twists the hearts out of the stupid jurors. You see? No common man. And this is the leader of the group of which Lester is one of the most debased members. He had no sooner been shot than Lord Nick himself appeared. He had his followers with him. He saw Jack Landis, threatened him with death, and made Jack swear that he would hand over half of the profits of the mines to the gang—of which, I suppose, Lester gets his due proportion. At the same time, Lord Nick attempted to persuade Jack that I, his adopted father, you might say, was really in the wrong, and that I had stolen the claims from this wretched Lester!"

He waved this disgusting accusation into a mist and laughed with hateful softness.

"The result is this: Jack Landis draws a vast revenue from the mines. Half of it he turns over to Lord Nick, and Lord Nick in return gives him absolute freedom and backing in the camp, where he is, and probably will continue the dominant factor. As for the other half, Landis spends it on this woman with whom he has become infatuated. And not a penny comes through to me!"

Colonel Macon leaned back in his chair and his

eyes became fixed upon a great distance. He smiled, and the blood turned cold in the veins of Donnegan.

"Of course this adventuress, this Nelly Lebrun, plays hand in glove with Lord Nick and his troupe; unquestionably she shares her spoils, so that nine tenths of the revenue from the mines is really flowing back through the hands of Lord Nick and Jack Landis has become a silly figurehead. He struts about the streets of The Corner as a great mine owner, and with the power of Lord Nick behind him, not one of the people of the gambling houses and dance halls dares cross him. So that Jack has come to consider himself a great man. Is it clear?"

Donnegan had not yet drawn his gaze entirely back from the distance.

"This is the possible solution," went on the colonel. "Jack Landis must be drawn away from the influence of this Nelly Lebrun. He must be brought back to us and shown his folly both as regards the adventuress and Lord Nick; for so long as Nelly has a hold on him, just so long Lord Nick will have his hand in Jack's pocket. You see how beautifully their plans and their work dovetails? How, therefore, am I to draw him from Nelly? There is only one way: send my daughter to the camp—send Lou to The Corner and let one glimpse of her beauty turn the shabby prettiness of this woman to a shadow! Lou is my last hope!"

At this Donnegan wakened. His sneer was not a pleasant thing to see.

"Send her to a new mining camp. Colonel Macon, you have the gambling spirit; you are willing to take great chances!"

"So! So!" murmured the colonel, a little taken

aback. "But I should never send her except with an adequate protector."

"An adequate protector even against these celebrated gunmen who run the camp as you have already admitted?"

"An adequate protector—you are the man!"

Donnegan shivered.

"I? I take your daughter to the camp and play her against Nelly Lebrun to win back Jack Landis? Is that the scheme?"

"It is."

"Ah," murmured Donnegan. And he got up and began to walk the room, white-faced; the colonel watched him in a silent agony of anxiety.

"She truly loves this Landis?" asked Donnegan, swallowing.

"A love that has grown out of their long intimacy together since they were children."

"Bah! Calf love! Let the fellow go and she will forget him. Hearts are not broken in these days by disappointments in love affairs."

The colonel writhed in his chair.

"But Lou—you do not know her heart!" he suggested. "If you looked closely at her you would have seen that she is pale. She does not suspect the truth, but I think she is wasting away because Jack hasn't written for weeks."

He saw Donnegan wince under the whip.

"It is true," murmured the wanderer. "She is not like others, Heaven knows!" He turned. "And what if I fail to bring over Jack Landis with the sight of Lou?"

The colonel relaxed; the great crisis was past and Donnegan would undertake the journey.

"In that case, my dear lad, there is an expedient

so simple that you astonish me by not perceiving it. If there is no way to wean Landis away from the woman, then get him alone and shoot him through the heart. In that way you remove from the life of Lou a man unworthy of her and you also make the mines come to the heir of Jack Landis—namely, myself. And in the latter case, Mr. Donnegan, be sure—oh, be sure that I should not forget who brought the mines into my hands!"

# CHAPTER X

## HE TAKES THE NEW TRAIL

FIFTY miles over any sort of going is a stiff march. Fifty miles uphill and down and mostly over districts where there was only a rough cow path in lieu of a road made a prodigious day's work; and certainly it was an almost incredible feat for one who professed to hate work with a consuming passion and who had looked upon an eight-mile jaunt the night before as an insuperable burden. Yet such was the distance which Donnegan had covered, and now he drove the pack mule out on the shoulder of the hill in full view of The Corner with the triangle of the Young Muddy and Christobel Rivers embracing the little town. Even the gaunt, leggy mule was tired to the dropping point, and the tough buckskin which trailed up behind went with downward head. When Louise Macon turned to him, he had reached the point where he swung his head around first and then grudgingly followed the movement with his body. The girl was tired, also, in spite of the fact that she had covered every inch of the distance in the saddle. There was that violet shade of weariness under her eyes and her shoulders slumped forward. Only Donnegan, the hater of labor, was fresh.

They had started in the first dusk of the coming day; it was now the yellow time of the slant afternoon sunlight; between these two points there had been a body of steady plodding. The girl had looked askance at that gaunt form of Donnegan's when they began; but before three hours, seeing that the spring never left his step nor the swinging rhythm his stride, she began to wonder. This afternoon, nothing he did could have surprised her. From the moment he entered the house the night before he had been a mystery. Till her death day she would not forget the fire with which he had stared up at her from the foot of the stairs. But when he came out of her father's room—not cowed and whipped as most men left it—he had looked at her with a veiled glance, and since that moment there had always been a mist of indifference over his eyes when he looked at her.

In the beginning of that day's march all she knew was that her father trusted her to this stranger, Donnegan, to take her to The Corner, where he was to find Jack Landis and bring Jack back to his old allegiance and find what he was doing with his time and his money. It was a quite natural proceeding, for Jack was a wild sort, and he was probably gambling away all the gold that was dug in his mines. It was perfectly natural throughout, except that she should have been trusted so entirely to a stranger. That was a remarkable thing, but, then, her father was a remarkable man, and it was not the first time that his actions had been inscrutable, whether concerning her or the affairs of other people. She had heard men come into their house cursing Colonel Macon with death in their faces; she had seen them sneak out after a soft-voiced interview and never appear again. In her eyes, her father was invincible, all-powerful. When she thought of superlatives, she thought of him. Her conception of mystery was the smile of the colonel, and her conception of tenderness was bounded by the gentle voice of the same man. Therefore, it was entirely sufficient to her that the colonel had said: "Go, and trust everything to Donnegan. He has the power to command you and you must obey—until Jack comes back to you."

That was odd, for, as far as she knew, Jack had never left her. But she had early discarded any will to question her father. Curiosity was a thing which the fat man hated above all else.

Therefore, it was really not strange to her that throughout the journey her guide did not speak half a dozen words to her. Once or twice when she attempted to open the conversation he had replied with crushing monosyllables, and there was an end. For the rest, he was always swinging down the trail ahead of her at a steady, unchanging, rapid stride. Uphill and down it never varied. And so they came out upon the shoulder of the hill and saw the storm center of The Corner. They were in the hills behind the town; two miles would bring them into it. And now Donnegan came back to her from the mule. He took off his hat and shook the dust away; he brushed a hand across his face. He was still unshaven. The red stubble made him hideous, and the dust and perspiration covered his face as with a mask. Only his eyes were rimmed with white skin.

"You'd better get off the horse, here," said Donnegan.

He held her stirrup, and she obeyed without a word.

"Sit down."

She sat down on the flat-topped boulder which he designated, and, looking up, observed the first sign of emotion in his face. He was frowning, and his face was drawn a little.

"You are tired," he stated.

"A little."

"You are tired," said the wanderer in a tone that implied dislike of any denial. Therefore she made no answer. "I'm going down into the town to look things over. I don't want to parade you through the streets until I know where Landis is to be found and how he'll receive you. The Corner is a wild town; you understand?"

"Yes," she said blankly, and noted nervously that the reply did not please him. He actually scowled at her.

"You'll be all right here. I'll leave the pack mule with you; if anything should happen—but nothing is going to happen. I'll be back in an hour or so. There's a pool of water. You can get a cold drink there and wash up if you want to while I'm gone. But don't go to sleep!"

"Why not?"

"A place like this is sure to have a lot of stragglers hunting around it. Bad characters. You understand?"

She could not understand why he should make a mystery of it; but then, he was almost as strange as her father. His careful English and his ragged clothes were typical of him inside and out.

"You have a gun there in your holster. Can you use it?"

"Yes."

"Try it."

It was a thirty-two, a light, woman's weapon. She took it out and balanced it in her hand.

"The blue rock down the hillside. Let me see you chip it."

Her hand went up, and without pausing to sight along the barrel, she fired; fire flew from the rock, and there appeared a white, small scar. Donnegan sighed with relief.

"If you squeezed the butt rather than pulled the trigger," he commented, "you would have made a bull's-eye that time. Now, I don't mean that in any likelihood you'll have to defend yourself. I simply want you to be aware that there's plenty of trouble around The Corner."

"Yes," said the girl.

"You're not afraid?"

"Oh, no."

Donnegan settled his hat a little more firmly upon his head. He had been on the verge of attributing her gentleness to a blank, stupid mind; he began to realize that there was metal under the surface. He felt that some of the qualities of the father were echoed faintly, and at a distance, in the child. In a way, she made him think of an unawakened creature. When she was roused, if the time ever came, it might be that her eye could become a thing alternately of fire and ice, and her voice might carry with a ring.

"This business has to be gotten through quickly," he went on. "One meeting with Jack Landis will be enough."

She wondered why he set his jaw when he said this, but he was wondering how deeply the colonel's ward had fallen into the clutches of Nelly Lebrun. If that first meeting did not bring Landis to his senses, what followed? One of two things. Either the girl must stay on in The Corner and try her hand with her fiancé again, or else the final brutal suggestion of the colonel must be followed; he must kill Landis. It was a cold-blooded suggestion, but Donnegan was a cold-blooded man. As he looked at the girl, where she sat on the boulder, he knew definitely, first and last, that he loved her, and that he would never again love any other woman. Every instinct drew him toward the necessity of destroying Landis. There was his stumblingblock. But what if she truly loved Landis?

He would have to wait in order to find that out. And as he stood there with the sun shining on the red stubble on his face he made a resolution the more profound because it was formed in silence: if she truly loved Landis he would serve her hand and foot until she had her will.

But all he said was simply: "I shall be back before it's dark."

"I shall be comfortable here," replied the girl, and smiled farewell at him.

And while Donnegan went down the slope full of darkness he thought of that smile.

The Corner spread more clearly before him with every step he made. It was a type of the gold-rush town. Of course most of the dwellings were tents —dog tents many of them; but there was a surprising sprinkling of wooden shacks, some of them of considerable size. Beginning at the very edge of the town and spread over the sand flats were the mines and the black sprinkling of laborers. And the town itself was roughly jumbled around one street. Over to the left the main road into The Corner crossed the wide, shallow ford of the Young Muddy River and up this road he saw half a dozen wagons coming, wagons of all sizes; but nothing went out of The Corner. People who came stayed there, it seemed.

He dropped over the lower hills, and the voice of the gold town rose to him. It was a murmur like that of an army preparing for the battle. Now and then a blast exploded, for what purpose he could not imagine in this school of mining. But as a rule the sounds were subdued by the distance. He caught the muttering of many voices, in which laughter and shouts were brought to the level of a whisper at close hand; and through all this there was a persistent clangor of metallic sounds. No doubt from the blacksmith shops where picks and other implements were made or sharpened and all sorts of repairing carried on. But the predominant tone of the voice of The Corner was this persistent ringing of metal. It suggested to Donnegan that here was a town filled with men of iron and all the gentler parts of their natures forgotten. An odd place to bring such a woman as Lou Macon, surely!

He reached the level, and entered the town.

# CHAPTER XI

### HE EATS HUMBLE PIE

HUNTING for news, he went naturally to the news emporium which took the place of the daily paper—namely, he went to the saloons. But on the way he ran through a liberal cross-section of The Corner's populace. First of all, the tents and the ruder shacks. He saw little sheet-iron stoves with the tin dishes piled, unwashed, upon the tops of them when the miners rushed back to their work; broken handles of picks and shovels; worn-out shirts and overalls lay where they had been tossed; here was a flat strip of canvas supported by four four-foot poles and without shelter at the sides, and the belongings of one careless miner tumbled beneath this miserable shelter; another man had striven for some semblance of a home and he had framed a five-foot walk leading up to the closed flap of his tent with stones of a regular size. But nowhere was there a sign of life, and would not be until semidarkness brought the unwilling workers back to the tents.

Out of this district he passed quickly onto the main street, and here there was a different atmosphere. The first thing he saw was a man dressed as a cowpuncher from belt to spurs—spurs on a miner—but above the waist he blossomed in a frock coat and a silk hat. Around the coat he had fastened his belt, and the shirt beneath the coat was common flannel, open at the throat. He walked, or rather staggered, on the arm of an equally strange companion who was arrayed in a white silk shirt, white flannel trousers, white dancing pumps, and a vast sombrero! But as if this was not sufficient protection for his head, he carried a parasol of the most brilliant green silk and twirled it above his head. The two held a wavering course and went blindly past Donnegan.

It was sufficiently clear that the storekeeper had followed the gold.

He noted a cowboy sitting in his saddle while he rolled a cigarette. Obviously he had come in to look things over rather than to share in the mining, and he made the one sane, critical note in the carnival of noise and color. Donnegan began to pass stores. There was the jeweler's; the gent's furnishing; a real estate office—what could real estate be doing on the Young Muddy's desert? Here was the pawnshop, the windows of which were already packed. The blacksmith had a great establishment, and the roar of the anvils never died away; feed and grain and a dozen lunch-counter restaurants. All this had come to The Corner within six weeks.

Liquor seemed to be plentiful, too. In the entire length of the street he hardly saw a sober man, except the cowboy. Half a dozen in one group pitched silver dollars at a mark. But he was in the saloon district now, and dominant among the rest was the big, unpainted front of a building before which hung an enormous sign:

## LEBRUN'S JOY EMPORIUM

Donnegan turned in under the sign.

It was one big room. The bar stretched completely around two sides of it. The floor was dirt, but packed to the hardness of wood. The low roof was supported by a scattering of wooden pillars, and across the floor the gaming tables were spread. At that vast bar not ten men were drinking now; at the crowding tables there were not half a dozen players; yet behind the bar stood a dozen tenders ready to meet the evening rush from the mines. And at the tables waited an equal number of the professional gamblers of the house.

From the door Donnegan observed these things with one sweeping glance, and then proceeded to transform himself. One jerk at the visor of his cap brought it down over his eyes and covered his face with shadow; a single shrug bunched the ragged coat high around his shoulders, and the shoulders themselves he allowed to drop forward. With his hands in his pockets he glided slowly across the room toward the bar, for all the world a picture of the gutter snipe who had been kicked from pillar to post until self-respect is dead in him. And pausing in his advance, he leaned against one of the pillars and looked hungrily toward the bar.

He was immediately hailed from behind the bar with: "Hey, you. No tramps in here. Pay and stay in Lebrun's!"

The command brought an immediate protest. A big fellow stepped from the bar, his sombrero pushed to the back of his head, his shirt sleeves rolled to the elbow away from vast, hairy forearms. One of his long arms swept out and brought Donnegan to the bar.

"I ain't no prophet," declared the giant, "but I can spot a man that's dry. What'll you have, bud?" And to the bartender he added: "Leave him be, pardner, unless you're all set for considerable noise in here."

"Long as his drinks are paid for," muttered the bartender, "here he stays. But these floaters do make me tired!"

He jabbed the bottle acoss the bar at Donnegan and spun a glass noisily at him, and the "floater" observed the angry bartender with a frightened side glance, and then poured his drink gingerly. When the glass was half full he hesitated and sought the face of the bartender again, for permission to go on.

"Fill her up!" commanded the giant. "Fill her up, lad, and drink hearty."

"I never yet," observed the bartender darkly, "seen a beggar that wasn't a hog."

At this Donnegan's protector shifted his belt so that the holster came a little more forward on his thigh.

"Son," he said, "how long you been in these parts?"

"Long enough," declared the other, and lowered his black brows. "Long enough to be sick of it."

"Maybe, maybe," returned the cowpuncher-miner, "meantime you tie to this. We got queer ways out here. When a gent drinks with us he's our friend. This lad here is my pardner, just now. If I was him I would of knocked your head off before now for what you've said——"

"I don't want no trouble," Donnegan said whiningly.

At this the bartender chuckled, and the miner showed his teeth in his disgust.

"Every gent has got his own way," he said sourly. "But while you drink with Hal Stern you drink with your chin up, bud. And don't forget it.

And them that tries to run over you got to run over me."

Saying this, he laid his large left hand on the bar and leaned a little toward the bartender, but his right hand remained hanging loosely at his side. It was near the holster, as Donnegan noticed. And the bartender, having met the boring glance of the big man for a moment, turned surlily away. The giant looked to Donnegan and observed: "Know a good definition of the word skunk?"

"Nope," said Donnegan, brightening now that the stern eye of the bartender was turned away.

"Here's one that might do. A skunk is a critter that bites when your back is turned and runs when you look it in the eye. Here's how!"

He drained his own glass, and Donnegan dexterously followed the example.

"And what might you be doing around these parts?" asked the big man, veiling his contempt under a mild geniality.

"Me? Oh, nothing."

"Looking for a job, eh?"

Donnegan shrugged.

"Work ain't my line," he confided.

"H'm-m," said Hal Stern. "Well, you don't make no bones about it."

"But just now," continued Donnegan, "I thought maybe I'd pick up some sort of a job for a while." He looked ruefully at the palms of his hands which were as tender as the hands of a woman. "Heard a fellow say that Jack Landis was a good sort to work for—didn't rush his men none. They said I might find him here."

The big man grunted.

"Too early for him. He don't circulate around

much till the sun goes down. Kind of hard on his skin, the sun, maybe. So you're going to work for him?"

"I was figuring on it."

"Well, tie to this, bud. If you work for him you won't have him over you."

"No?"

"No, you'll have"—he glanced a little uneasily around him—"Lord Nick."

"Who's he?"

"Who's he?" The big man started in astonishment. "Sufferin' catamounts! Who *is* he?" He laughed in a disagreeable manner. "Well, son, you'll find out, right enough!"

"The way you talk, he don't sound none too good."

Hal Stern grew anxious. "The way I talk? Have I said anything agin' him? Not a word! He's—he's—well, there ain't ever been trouble between us and there never ain't going to be." He flushed and looked steadily at Donnegan. "Maybe he sent you to talk to me?" he asked coldly.

But Donnegan's eyes took on a childish wideness.

"Why, I never seen him," he declared. Hal Stern allowed the muscles of his face to relax. "All right," he said, "they's no harm done. But Lord Nick is a name that ain't handled none too free in these here parts. Remember that!"

"But how," pondered Donnegan, "can I be working for Lord Nick when I sign up to work under Jack Landis?"

"I'll tell you how. Nick and Lebrun work together. Split profits. And Nelly Lebrun works Landis for his dust. So the stuff goes in a circle—Landis to Nelly to Lebrun to Nick. That clear?"

"I don't quite see it," murmured Donnegan.

"I didn't think you would," declared the other, and snorted his disgust. "But that's all I'm going to say. Here come the boys—and dead dry!"

For the afternoon was verging upon evening, and the first drift of laborers fom the mines was pouring into The Corner. One thing at least was clear to Donnegan: that every one knew how infatuated Landis had become with Nelly Lebrun and that Landis had not built up an extraordinarily good name for himself.

# CHAPTER XII

## HE FIGHTS TEMPTATION

BY the time absolute darkness had set in, Donnegan, in the new rôle of lady's chaperon, sat before a dying fire with Louise Macon beside him. He had easily seen from his talk with Stern that Landis was a public figure, whether from the richness of his claims or his relations with Lord Nick and Lebrun, or because of all these things; but as a public figure it would be impossible to see him alone in his own tent, and unless Louise could meet him alone half her power over him—supposing that she still retained any—would be lost. Better by far that Landis should come to her than that she should come to him, so Donnegan had rented two tents by the day at an outrageous figure from the enterprising real estate company of The Corner and to this new home he brought the girl.

She accepted the arrangement with surprising equanimity. It seemed that her father's training had eliminated from her mind any questioning of the motives of others. She became even cheerful as she set about arranging the pack which Donnegan put in her tent. Afterward she cooked their supper over the fire which he built for her. Never was such a quick house-settling. And by the time it was absolutely dark they had washed the dishes and sat before Lou's tent looking over the night lights of The Corner and hearing the voice of its Great White Way opening.

She had not even asked why he did not bring her straight to Jack Landis. She had looked into Donnegan's tent, furnished with a single blanket and his canvas kit, and had offered to share her pack with him. And now they sat side by side before the tent and still she asked no questions about what was to come.

Her silence was to Donnegan the dropping of the water upon the hard rock. He was crumbling under it, and a wild hatred for the colonel rose in him. No doubt that spirit of evil had foreseen all this; and he knew that every moment spent with the girl would drive Donnegan on closer to the accomplishment of the colonel's great purpose—the death of Jack Landis. For the colonel, as Jack's next of kin, would take over all his mining interests and free them at a stroke from the silent partnership which apparently existed with Lord Nick and Lester. One bullet would do all this; and with Jack dead, who else stood close to the girl? It was only necessary that she should not know who sped the bullet home.

A horrible fancy grew up in Donnegan, as he sat there, that between him and the girl lay a dead body.

He was glad when the time came and he could tell her that he was going down to The Corner to find Jack Landis and bring him to her. She rose to watch him go and he heard her say "Come soon!"

It shocked Donnegan into realization that for all her calm exterior she was perfectly aware of the danger of her position in the wild mining camp. She must know, also, that her reputation would be compromised; yet never once had she winced, and Donnegan was filled with wonder as he went down the hill toward the camp which was spread beneath him; for their tents were a little detached from the main body of the town. Behind her gentle eyes, he now felt, and under the softness of her voice, there was the same iron nerve that was in her father. Her hatred could be a deathless passion, and her love also; and the great question to be answered now was, did she truly love Jack Landis?

The Corner at night was like a scene at a circus. There was the same rush of people, the same irregular flush of lights, the same glimmer of lanterns through canvas, the same air of impermanence. Once, in one of those hushes which will fall upon every crowd, he heard a coyote wailing sharply and far away, as though the desert had sent out this voice to mock at The Corner and all it contained.

He had only to ask once to discover where Landis was; Milligan's dance hall. Before Milligan's place a bonfire burned from the beginning of dusk to the coming of day; and until the time when that fire was quenched with buckets of water, it was a sign to all that the merriment was under way in the dance hall. If Lebrun's was the sun of the amusement world in The Corner, Milligan's was the moon. Everybody who had money to lose went to Lebrun's. Every one who was out for gayety went to Milligan's. Milligan was a plunger. He had brought up an orchestra which demanded fifteen dollars a day and he paid them that and more. He not only was able to do this, but he established a bar at the entrance from which all who entered were served with a free drink. The entrance, also, was not subject to charge. The initial drink at the door was spiced to encourage thirst, so Milligan made money as fast, and far more easily, than if he had been digging it out of the ground.

To the door of this pleasure emporium came Donnegan. He had transformed himself into the ragged hobo by the jerking down of his cap again, and the hunching of his shoulders. And shrinking past the bar with a hungry sidewise glance, as one who did not dare present himself for free liquor, he entered Milligan's.

That is, he had put his foot across the threshold when he was caught roughly by the shoulder and dragged to one side. He found himself looking up into the face of a strapping fellow who served Milligan as bouncer. Milligan had an eye for color. Andy Lewis was tolerably well known as a fighting man of parts, who not only wore two guns but could use them both at once, which is much more difficult than is generally understood. But far more than for his fighting parts Milligan hired his bouncer for the sake of his face. It was a countenance made to discourage trouble makers. A mule had kicked Lewis in the chin, and a great white welt deformed his lower lip. Scars of smallpox added to his decorative effect, and he had those extremely bushy brows which for some reason are generally considered to denote ferocity. Now, Donnegan was not above middle height at best, and in his present shrinking attitude he found himself looking up a full head into the formidable face of the bouncer.

"And what are you doing in here?" asked the genial Andy. "Don't you know this joint is for white folks?"

"I ain't colored," murmured Donnegan.

"You look considerable yaller to me," declared Lewis. He straightway chuckled, and his own

keen appreciation of his wit softened his expression.
"What you want?"

Donnegan shivered under his rags.

"I want to see Jack Landis," he said.

It had a wonderful effect upon the doorkeeper.
Donnegan found that the very name of Landis was
a charm of power in The Corner.

"You want to see him?" he queried in amaze-
ment. "You?"

He looked Donnegan over again, and then grinned
broadly, as if in anticipation. "Well, go ahead.
There he sits—no, he's dancing."

The music was in full swing; it was chiefly brass;
but now and then, in softer moments, one could
hear a violin squeaking uncertainly. At least it went
along with a marked, regular rhythm, and the dancers swirled industriously around the floor. A very
gay crowd; color was apparently appreciated in The
Corner. And Donnegan, standing modestly out of
sight behind a pillar until the dance ended, noted
twenty phases of life in twenty faces. And Donnegan saw the flushes of liquor, and heard the loud
voices of happy fellows who had made their
"strikes;" but in all that brilliant crew he had no
trouble in picking out Jack Landis and Nelly Lebrun.

They danced together, and where they passed, the
others steered a little off so as to give them room
on the dance floor, as if the men feared that they
might cross the formidable Landis, and as if the
women feared to be brought into too close comparison with Nelly Lebrun. She was, indeed, a brilliant
figure. She had eyes of the Creole duskiness, a delicate olive skin, with a pastel coloring. The hand
on the shoulder of Landis was a thing of fairy
beauty. And her eyes had that peculiar quality of

seeming to see everything, and rest on every face particularly. So that, as she whirled toward Donnegan, he winced, feeling that she had found him out among the shadows.

She had a glorious partner to set her off. And Donnegan saw bitterly why Lou Macon could love him. Height without clumsiness, bulk and a light foot at once, a fine head, well poised, blond hair and a Grecian profile—such was Jack Landis. He wore a vest of fawn skin; his boots were black in the foot and finished with the softest red leather for the leg. And he had yellow buckskin trousers, laced in a Mexican fashion with silver at the sides; a narrow belt, a long, red silk handkerchief flying from behind his neck in cowboy fashion. So much flashing splendor, even in that gay assembly, would have been childishly conspicuous on another man. But in big Jack Landis there was patently a great deal of the unaffected child. He was having a glorious time on this evening, and his eye roved the room challenging admiration in a manner that was amusing rather than offensive. He was so overflowingly proud of having the prettiest girl in The Corner upon his arm and so conscious of being himself probably the finest-looking man that he escaped conceit, it might almost be said, by his very excess of it.

Upon this splendid individual, then, the obscure Donnegan bent his gaze. He saw the dancers pause and scatter as the music ended, saw them drift to the tables along the edges of the room, saw the scurry of waiters hurrying drinks up in the interval, saw Nelly Lebrun sip a lemonade, saw Jack Landis toss off something stronger. And then Donnegan skirted around the room and came to the table of Jack Landis at the very moment when the latter was tossing a gold piece to the waiter and giving a new order.

Prodigal sons in the distance of thought are apt to be both silly and disgusting, but at close hand they usually dazzle the eye. Even the cold brain of Donnegan was daunted a little as he drew near.

He came behind the chair of the tall master of The Corner, and while Nelly Lebrun stopped her glass halfway to her lips and stared at the ragged stranger, Donnegan was whispering in the ear of Jack Landis: "I've got to see you alone."

Landis turned his head slowly and his eye darkened a little as he met the reddish, unshaven face of the stranger. Then, with a careless shrug of distaste, he drew out a few coins and poured them into Donnegan's palm; the latter pocketed them.

"Lou Macon," said Donnegan.

Jack Landis rose from his chair, and it was not until he stood so close to Donnegan that the latter realized the truly Herculean proportions of the young fellow. He bowed his excuses to Nelly Lebrun, not without grace of manner, and then huddled Donnegan into a corner with a wave of his vast arm.

"Now what do you want? Who are you? Who put that name in your mouth?"

"She's in The Corner," said Donnegan, and he dwelt upon the face of Jack Landis with feverish suspense. A moment later a great weight had slipped from his heart. If Lou Macon loved Landis it was beyond peradventure that Landis was not breaking his heart because of the girl. For at her name he flushed darkly, and then, that rush of color fading, he was left with a white spot in the center of each cheek.

# CHAPTER XIII

### HE EAVESDROPS

FIRST his glance plunged into vacancy; then it flicked over his shoulder at Nelly Lebrun and he bit his lip. Plainly, it was not the most welcome news that Jack Landis had ever heard.

"Where is she?" he asked nervously of Donnegan, and he looked over the ragged fellow again.

"I'll take you to her."

The big man swayed back and forth from foot to foot, balancing in his hesitation. "Wait a moment."

He strode to Nelly Lebrun and bent over her; Donnegan saw her eyes flash up—oh, heart of the south, what eyes of shadow and fire! Jack Landis trembled under the glance; yes, he was deeply in love with the girl. And Donnegan watched her face shade with suspicion, stiffen with cold anger, warm and soften again under the explanations of Jack Landis.

Donnegan, looking from the distance, could read everything; it is nearness that bewitches a man when he talks to a woman. When Odysseus talked to Circe, no doubt he stood on the farther side of the room!

When Landis came again, he was perspiring from the trial of fire through which he had just passed.

"Come," he ordered, and set out at a sweeping stride.

Plainly he was anxious to get this matter done

with as soon as possible. As for Donnegan, he saw a man whom Landis had summoned to take his place sit down at the table with Nelly Lebrun. She was laughing with the newcomer as though nothing troubled her at all, but over his shoulder her glance probed the distance and followed Jack Landis. She wanted to see the messenger again, the man who had called her companion away; but in this it was fox challenging fox. Donnegan took note and was careful to place between him and the girl every pillar and every group of people. As far as he was concerned, her first glance must do to read and judge and remember him by.

Outside Landis shot several questions at him in swift succession; he wanted to know how the girl had happened to make the trip. Above all, what the colonel was thinking and doing and if the colonel himself had come. But Donnegan replied with monosyllables, and Landis, apparently reconciling himself to the fact that the messenger was a fool, ceased his questions. They kept close to a run all the way out of the camp and up the hillside to the two detached tents where Donnegan and the girl slept that night. A lantern burned in both the tents.

"She has made things ready for me," thought Donnegan, his heart opening. "She has kept house for me!"

He pointed out Lou's tent to his companion and the big man, with a single low word of warning, threw open the flap of the tent and strode in.

There was only the split part of a second between the rising and the fall of the canvas, but in that swift interval, Donnegan saw the girl starting up to receive Landis. Her calm was broken at last.

Her cheeks were flushed; and her eyes were starry with what? Expectancy? Love?

It stopped Donnegan like a blow in the face and turned his heart to lead; and then, shamelessly, he glided around the tent and dropped down beside it to eavesdrop. After all, there was some excuse. If she loved the man he, Donnegan, would let him live; if she did not love him, he, Donnegan, would kill him like a worthless rat under heel. That is, if he could. No wonder that the wanderer listened with heart and soul!

He missed the first greeting. It was only a jumble of exclamations, but now he heard: "But, Lou, what a wild idea. Across the mountains—with whom?"

"The man who brought you here."

"Who's he?"

"I don't know."

"You don't know? He looks like a shifty little rat to me."

"He's big enough, Jack."

Such small praise was enough to set Donnegan's heart thumping.

"Besides, father told me to go with him, to trust him."

"Ah!" There was an abrupt chilling and lowering of Landis' voice. "The colonel knows him? He's one of the colonel's men?"

Plainly the colonel was to him as the rod to the child.

"Why didn't you come directly to me?"

"We thought it would be better not to."

"H'm-m. Your guide—well, what was the colonel's idea in sending you here? Heavens above, doesn't he know that a mining camp is no place for a young girl. And you haven't a sign of a chaperon,

Lou! What the devil can I do? What was in his mind?"

"You haven't written for a long time."

"Good Lord! Written! Letters! Does he think I have time for letters?" The lie came smoothly enough. "Working day and night?"

Donnegan smoothed his whiskers and grinned into the night. Landis might prove better game than he had anticipated.

"He worried," said the girl, and her voice was as even as ever. "He worried, and sent me to find out if anything is wrong."

A little pause. Donnegan would have given much to see how the big man met this sentence.

Then: "Nonsense! What is there to worry about? Lou, I'm half inclined to think that the colonel doesn't trust me!"

She did not answer. Was she reading beneath the boisterous assurance of Landis?

"One thing is clear to me—and to you, too, I hope. The first thing is to send you back in a hurry."

Still no answer.

"Lou, do you distrust me?"

At length she managed to speak, but it was with some difficulty: "There is another reason for sending me."

"Tell me."

"Can't you guess, Jack?"

"I'm not a mind reader."

"The cad," said Donnegan through his teeth.

"It's the old reason."

"Money?"

"Yes."

A shadow swept across the side of the tent; it was Landis waving his arm carelessly.

"If that's all, I can fix you up and send you back with enough to carry the colonel along. Look here—why, I have five hundred with me. Take it, Lou. There's more behind it, but the colonel mustn't think that there's as much money in the mines as people say. No idea how much living costs up here. Heavens, no! And the prices for labor! And then they shirk the job from dawn to dark. I have to watch 'em every minute, I tell you!"

He sighed noisily.

"But the end of it is, dear"—how that small word tore into the heart of Donnegan, who crouched outside—"that you must go back to-morrow morning. I'd send you to-night, if I could. As a matter of fact, I don't trust the red-haired rat who——"

The girl interrupted while Donnegan still had control of his hair-trigger temper.

"You forget, Jack. Father sent me here, but he did not tell me to come back."

At this Jack Landis burst into an enormous laughter.

"You don't mean, Lou, that you actually intend to stay on?"

"What else can I mean?"

"Of course it makes it awkward if the colonel didn't expressly tell you just what to do. I suppose he left it to my discretion, and I decide definitely that you must go back at once."

"I can't do it."

"Lou, don't you hear me saying that I'll take the responsibility? If your father blames you let him tell me——"

He broke down in the middle of his sentence and

another of those uncomfortable little pauses ensued. Donnegan knew that their eyes were miserably upon each other; the man tongue-tied by his guilt; the girl wretchedly guessing at the things which lay behind her fiancé's words.

"I'm sorry you don't want me here."

"It isn't that, but——"

He apparently expected to be interrupted, but she waited coolly for him to finish the sentence, and, of course, he could not. After all, for a helpless girl she had a devilish effective way of muzzling Landis. Donnegan chuckled softly in admiration.

All at once she broke through the scene; her voice did not raise or harden, but it was filled with finality, as though she were weary of the interview.

"I'm tired out; it's been a hard ride, Jack. You go home now and look me up again any time to-morrow."

"I—Lou—I feel mighty bad about having you up here in this infernal tent, when the camp is full, and——"

"You can't lie across the entrance to my tent and guard me, Jack. Besides, I don't need you for that. The man who's with me will protect me."

"He doesn't look capable of protecting a cat!"

"My father said that in any circumstances he would be able to take care of me."

This reply seemed to overwhelm Landis.

"The colonel trusts him as far as all that?" he muttered. "Then I suppose you're safe enough. But what about comfort, Lou?"

"I've done without comfort all my life. Run along, Jack. And take this money with you. I can't have it."

"But, didn't the colonel send——"

"You can express it through to him. To me it's—not pleasant to take it."

"Why, Lou, you don't mean——"

"Good night, Jack. I don't mean anything, except that I'm tired."

The shadow swept along the wall of the tent again. Donnegan, with a shaking pulse, saw the profile of the girl and the man approach as he strove to take her in his arms and kiss her good night. And then one slender bar of shadow checked Landis.

"Not to-night."

"Lou, you aren't angry with me?"

"No. But you know I have queer ways. Just put this down as one of them. I can't explain."

There was a muffled exclamation and Landis went from the tent and strode down the hill; he was instantly lost in the night. But Donnegan, turning to the entrance flap, called softly. He was bidden to come in, and when he raised the flap he saw her sitting with her hands clasped loosely and resting upon her knees. Her lips were a little parted, and colorless; her eyes were dull with a mist; and though she rallied herself a little, the wanderer could see that she was only half aware of him.

The face which he saw was a milestone in his life. For he had loved her jealously, fiercely before; but seeing her now, dazed, hurt, and uncomplaining, tenderness came into Donnegan. It spread to his heart with a strange pain and made his hands tremble.

All that he said was: "Is there anything you need?"

"Nothing," she replied, and he backed out and away.

But in that small interval he had turned out of the course of his gay, selfish life. If Jack Landis had hurt her like this—if she loved him so truly—then Jack Landis she should have.

There was an odd mixture of emotions in Donnegan; but he felt most nearly like the poor man from whose hand his daughter tugs back and looks wistfully, hopelessly, into the bright window at all the toys. What pain is there greater than the pain that comes to the poor man in such a time? He huddles his coat about him, for his heart is as cold as a Christmas day; and if it would make his child happy, he would pour out his heart's blood on the snow.

Such was the grief of Donnegan as he backed slowly out into the night. Though Jack Landis were fixed as high as the moon he would tear him out of his place and give him to the girl.

# CHAPTER XIV

### DONNEGAN FINDS A PLAN

THE lantern went out in the tent; she was asleep; and when he knew that, Donnegan went down into The Corner. He had been trying to think out a plan of action, and finding nothing better than to trust a gun stupidly under Landis' nose and make him mark time, Donnegan went into Lebrun's place. As if he hoped the bustle there would supply him with ideas.

Lebrun's was going full blast. It was not filled with the shrill mirth of Milligan's. Instead, all voices were subdued to a point here. The pitch was never raised. If a man laughed, he might show his teeth but he took good care that he did not break into the atmosphere of the room. For there was a deadly undercurrent of silence which would not tolerate more than murmurs on the part of others. Men sat grim-faced over the cards, the man who was winning, with his cold, eager eye; the chronic loser of the night with his iron smile; the professional, ever debonair, with the dull eye which comes from looking too often and too closely into the terrible face of chance. A very keen observer might have observed a resemblance between those men and Donnegan.

Donnegan roved swiftly here and there. The calm eye and the smooth play of an obvious professional in a linen suit kept him for a moment at one table, looking on; then he went to the games, and after changing the gold which Jack Landis had given as alms to silver dollars, he lost it with precision upon the wheel.

He went on, from table to table, from group to group. In Lebrun's his clothes were not noticed. It was no matter whether he played or did not play, whether he won or lost; they were too busy to notice. But he came back, at length, to the man who wore the linen coat and who won so easily. Something in his method of dealing appeared to interest Donnegan greatly.

It was jack pot; the chips were piled high; and the man in the linen coat was dealing again. How deftly he mixed the cards!

Indeed, all about him was elegant, from the turn of his black cravat to the cut of the coat. An inebriate passed, shouldered and disturbed his chair, and rising to put it straight again, the gambler was seen to be about the height and build of Donnegan.

Donnegan studied him with the interest of an artist. Here was a man, harking back to Nelly Lebrun and her love of brilliance, who would probably win her preference over Jack Landis for the simple reason that he was different. That is, there was more in his cravat to attract astonished attention in The Corner than there was in all the silver lace of Landis. And he was a man's man, no doubt of that. On the inebriate he had flashed one glance of fire, and his lean hand had stirred uneasily toward the breast of his coat. Donnegan, who missed nothing, saw and understood.

Interested? He was fascinated by this man because he recognized the kinship which existed between them. They might almost have been blood brothers, except for differences in the face. He knew, for instance, just what each glance of the man in the linen coat meant, and how he was weighing his antagonists. As for the others, they were cool players themselves, but here they had met their master. It was the difference between the amateur and the professional. They played good chancey poker, but the man in the linen coat did more—he stacked the cards!

For the first moment Donnegan was not sure; it was not until there was a slight faltering in the deal—an infinitely small hesitation which only a practiced eye like that of Donnegan's could have noticed—that he was sure. The winner was crooked. Yet the hand was interesting for all that. He had done the master trick, not only giving himself the winning hand but also giving each of the others a fine set of cards.

And the betting was wild on that historic pot! To begin with the smallest hand was three of a kind; and after the draw the weakest was a straight. And they bet furiously. The stranger had piqued them with his consistent victories. Now they were out for blood. Chips having been exhausted, solid gold was piled up on the table—a small fortune!

The man in the linen coat, in the middle of the hand, called for drinks. They drank. They went on with the betting. And then at last came the call.

Donnegan could have clapped his hands to applaud the smooth rascal. It was not an affair of breaking the others who sat in. They were all prosperous mine owners, and probably they had been carefully selected according to the size of purse, in preparation for the sacrifice. But the stakes were swept into the arms and then the canvas bag of the winner. If it was not enough to ruin the miners it was at least enough to clean them out of ready cash and discontinue the game on that basis. They rose; they went to the bar for a drink; but while the winner led the way, two of the losers dropped back a trifle and fell into earnest conversation, frowning. Donnegan knew perfectly what the trouble was. They had noticed that slight faltering in the deal; they were putting their mental notes on the game together.

But the winner, apparently unconscious of suspicion, lined up his victims at the bar. The first drink went hastily down; the second was on the way—it was standing on the bar. And here he excused himself; he broke off in the very middle of a story, and telling them that he would be back any moment, stepped into a crowd of newcomers.

The moment he disappeared, Donnegan saw the other four put their heads close together, and saw a sudden darkening of faces; but as for the genial winner, he had no sooner passed to the other side of the crowd and out of view, than he turned directly toward the door. His careless saunter was exchanged for a brisk walk; and Donnegan, without making himself conspicuous, was hard pressed to follow that pace.

At the door he found that the gambler, with his canvas sack under his arm, had turned to the right toward the line of saddle horses which stood in the shadow; and no sooner did he reach the gloom at the side of the building than he broke into a soft, swift run. He darted down the line of horses until he came to one which was already mounted. This Donnegan saw as he followed somewhat more leisurely and closer to the horses to avoid observance. He made out that the man already on horseback

was a big negro and that he had turned his own
mount and a neighboring horse out from the rest
of the horses, so that they were both pointing down
the street of The Corner. Donnegan saw the negro
throw the lines of his lead horse into the air. In
exchange he caught the sack which the runner tossed
to him, and then the gambler leaped into his saddle.

It was a simple but effective plan. Suppose he
were caught in the midst of a cheat; his play would
be to break away to the outside of the building,
shooting out the lights, if possible—trusting to the
confusion to help him—and there he would find his
horse held ready for him at a time when a second
might be priceless. On this occasion no doubt the
clever rascal had sensed the suspicion of the others.

At any rate, he lost no time. He waited neither
to find his stirrups nor grip the reins firmly, but
the same athletic leap which carried him into the
saddle set the horse in motion, and from a standing
start the animal broke into a headlong gallop. He
received, however, an additional burden at once.

For Donnegan, from the second time he saw the
man of the linen coat, had been revolving a daring plan, and during the poker game the plan had
slowly matured. The moment he made sure that
the gambler was heading for a horse, he increased
his own speed. Ordinarily he would have been
noted, but now, no doubt, the gambler feared no
pursuit except one accompanied by a hue and cry.
He did not hear the shadow-footed Donnegan rac-
ing over the soft ground behind him; but when he
had gained the saddle, Donnegan was close behind
with the impetus of his run to aid him. It was
comparatively simple, therefore, to spring high in the
air, and he struck fairly and squarely behind the

saddle of the man in the linen coat. When he landed his revolver was in his hand and the muzzle jabbed into the back of the gambler.

The other made one frantic effort to twist around, then recognized the pressure of the revolver and was still. The horses, checking their gallops in unison, were softly dog-trotting down the street.

"Call off your boy!" warned Donnegan, for the big negro had reined back; the gun already gleamed in his hand.

A gesture from the master sent the gun into obscurity, yet still the fellow continued to fall back.

"Tell him to ride ahead."

"Keep in front, George."

"And not too far."

"Very well. And now?"

"We'll talk later. Go straight on, George, to the clump of trees beyond the end of the street. And ride straight. No dodging!"

"It was a good hand you played," continued Donnegan, taking note that of the many people who were now passing them none paid the slightest attention to two men riding on one horse and chatting together as they rode. "It was a good hand, but a bad deal. Your thumb slipped on the card, eh?"

"You saw, eh?" muttered the other.

"And two of the others saw it. But they weren't sure till afterward."

"I know. The blockheads! But I spoiled their game for them. Are you one of us, pal?"

But Donnegan smiled to himself. For once at least the appeal of gambler to gambler should fail.

"Keep straight on," he said. "We'll talk later on."

# CHAPTER XV

## HE STEALS A MAN

BEFORE Donnegan gave the signal to halt in a clear space where the starlight was least indistinct, they reached the center of the trees.

"Now, George," he said to the negro, "drop your gun to the ground."

There was a flash and faint thud.

"Now the other gun."

"They ain't any more, sir."

"Your other gun," repeated Donnegan.

A little pause. "Do what he tells you, George," said the gambler at length, and a second weapon fell.

"Now keep on your horse and keep a little off to the side," went on Donnegan, "and remember that if you try to give me the jump I might miss you in this light, but I'd be sure to hit your horse. So don't take chances, George. Now, sir, just hold your hands over your head and then dismount."

He had already gone through the gambler and taken his weapons; he was now obeyed. The man of the linen coat tossed up his arms, flung his right leg over the horn of the saddle, and slipped to the ground.

Donnegan joined his captive. "I warn you first," he said gently, "that I am quite expert with a revolver, and that it will be highly dangerous to attempt to trick me. Lower your arms if you wish, but please be careful of what you do with your hands. There are such things as knife throwing, I know, but it takes a fast wrist to flip a knife faster than a bullet. We understand each other?"

"Perfectly," agreed the other. "By the way, my name is Godwin. And suppose we become frank. You are in temporary distress. It was impossible for you to make a loan at the moment and you are driven to this forced—touch. Now, if half——"

"Hush," said Donnegan. "You are too generous. But the present question is not one of money. I have long since passed over that. The money is now mine. Steady!" This to the negro, who lurched in the saddle; but the master was calm as stone. "It is not the question of the money that troubles me, but the question of the men. I could easily handle one of you. But I fear to allow both of you to go free. You would return on my trail; there are such things as waylayings by night, eh? And so, Mr. Godwin, I think my best way out is to shoot you through the head. When your body is found it will be taken for granted that the servant killed the master for the sake of the money which he won by crooked card play. I think that's simple. Put your hands up, George, or, by heck, I'll let the starlight shine through you!"

The huge arms of George were raised above his head; Godwin, in the meantime, had not spoken.

"I almost think you mean it," he said after a short pause.

"Good," said Donnegan, "I do not wish to kill you unprepared."

There was a strangled sound deep in the throat of Godwin; then he was able to speak again, but now his voice was made into a horrible jumble by fear.

"Pal," he said, "you're dead wrong. The coon—
he's a devil. If you let him live he'll kill you—
as sure as you're standing here. You don't know
him. He's George Green. He's got a record as
long as my arm and as bad as the devil's name.
He—he's the man to get rid of. Me? Why, man,
you and I could team it together. But the nigger
—not——"

Donnegan began to laugh, and the gambler stammered to a halt.

"I knew you when I laid eyes on you for the first
time," said Donnegan. "You have the hands of a
craftsman, but your eyes are put too close together.
A coward's eyes—a cur's face, Godwin. But you,
George—have you heard what he said?"

No answer from George but a snarl.

"It sounds logical what he said, eh, George?"

Dead silence.

"But," said Donnegan, "there are flaws in the
plan. Godwin, get out of your clothes."

The other fell on his knees.

"For Heaven's sake," he pleaded.

"Shut up," commanded Donnegan. "I'm not
going to shoot you. I never intended to, you fool.
But I wanted to see if you were worth splitting the
coin with. You're not. Now get out of your
clothes."

He was obeyed in fumbling haste, and while that
operation went on, he succeeded in jumping out of
his own rags and still kept the two fairly steadily
under the nose of his gun. He tossed this bundle
to Godwin, who accepted it with a faint oath; and
Donnegan stepped calmly and swiftly into the clothes
of his victim.

"A perfect fit," he said at length, "and to show

that I'm pleased, here's your purse back. Must be close to two hundred in that, from the weight."

Godwin muttered some intelligible curse.

"Tush. Now, get out! If you show your face in The Corner again, some of those miners will spot you, and they'll dress you in tar and feathers."

"You fool. If they see you in my clothes?"

"They'll never see these after to-night, probably. You have other clothes in your packs, Godwin. Lots of 'em. You're the sort who knows how to dress, and I'll borrow your outfit. Get out!"

The other made no reply; a weight seemed to have fallen upon him along with his new outfit, and he slunk into the darkness. George made a move to follow; there was a muffled shriek from Godwin, who fled headlong; and then a sharp command from Donnegan stopped the negro.

"Come here," said Donnegan.

George Washington Green rode slowly closer.

"If I let you go what would you do?"

There was a glint of teeth.

"I'd find him."

"And break him in two, eh? Instead, I'm going to take you home, where you'll have a chance of breaking me in two instead. There's something about the cut of your shoulders and your head that I like, Green; and if you don't murder me in the first hour or so, I think we'll get on very well together. You hear?"

The silence of George Washington Green was a tremendous thing.

"Now ride ahead of me. I'll direct you how to go."

He went first straight back through the town and up the hill to the two tents. He made George go before him into the tent and take up the roll of bedding; and then, with George and the bedding leading the way, and Donnegan leading the two horses behind, they went across the hillside to a shack which he had seen vacated that evening. It certainly could not be rented again before morning, and in the meantime Donnegan would be in possession, which was a large part of the law in The Corner, as he knew.

A little lean-to against the main shack served as a stable; the creek down the hillside was the watering trough. And Donnegan stood by while the big negro silently tended to the horses—removing the packs and preparing them for the night. Still in silence he produced a small lantern and lighted it. It showed his face for the first time—the skin ebony black and polished over the cheekbones, but the rest of the face almost handsome, except that the slight flare of his nostrils gave him a cast of inhuman ferocity. And the fierceness was given point by a pair of arms of gorilla length; broad shoulders padded with rolling muscles, and the neck of a bull. On the whole, Donnegan, a connoisseur of fighting men, had never such promise of strength.

At his gesture, the negro led the way into the house. It was more commodious than most of the shacks of The Corner. In place of a single room this had two compartments—one for the kitchen and another for the living room. In vacating the hut, the last occupants had left some of the furnishings behind them. There was a mirror, for instance, in the corner; and beneath the mirror a cheap table in whose open drawer appeared a tumble of papers. Donnegan dropped the heavy sack of the Godwin's winnings to the floor, and while the negro hung

the lantern on a nail on the wall, Donnegan crossed
to the table and appeared to run through the papers.

He was humming carelessly while he did it, but
all the time he watched with catlike intensity the
reflection of George in the mirror above him.  He
saw—rather dimly, for the cheap glass showed all
its images in waves—that George turned abruptly
after hanging up the lantern, paused, and then
whipped a hand into his coat pocket and out again.

Donnegan leaped lightly to one side, and the
knife, hissing past his head, buried itself in the wall,
and its vibrations set up a vicious humming.  As
for Donnegan, the leap that carried him to one side
whirled him about also; he faced the big negro who
was now crouched in the very act of following the
knife cast with the lunge of his powerful body.
There was no weapon in the hand of the white
man, and yet George hesitated, balanced—and then
slowly drew himself erect.

He was puzzled.  An outburst of oaths, the flash
of a gun. and he would have been at home in the
brawl, but the silence, the smile of Donnegan and
the steady glance were too much for him.  Presently
his eyes rolled white, the certain sign of fear; he
moistened his lips, and yet he could not speak.  And
Donnegan knew that what paralyzed the negro was
the manner in which the white man had received
warning.  Evidently the simple explanation of the
mirror did not occur to the fellow; and the whole
incident took on supernatural colorings.  A phrase
of explanation and Donnegan would become again
an ordinary human being; but while the small link
was a mystery the brain and body of George were
numb.  It was necessary above all to continue unex-
plainable.  Donnegan, turning, drew the knife from

the wall with a jerk. Half the length of the keen blade had sunk into the wood—a mute tribute to the force and speed of George's hand—and now the master took the bright little weapon by the point and gave it back to the other.

"If you throw for the body instead of the head," said Donnegan, "you have a better chance of sending the point home."

He turned his back again upon the gaping negro, and drawing up a broken box before the open door he sat down to contemplate the night. Not a sound behind him. It might be that the big fellow had regained his nerve and was stealing up for a second attempt; but Donnegan would have wagered his soul that George Washington Green had his first and last lesson and that he would rather play with bare lightning than ever again cross his new master.

At length: "When you make down the bunks," said Donnegan, "put mine farthest from the kitchen. You had better do that first."

"Yes—sir," came the deep bass murmur behind him.

And the heart of Donnegan stirred, for that "sir" meant many things.

Presently George crossed the floor with a burden; there was the "whish" of the blankets being unrolled —and then a slight pause. It seemed to him that he could hear a heavier breathing. Why? And searching swiftly back through his memory he recalled that his other gun, a stub-nosed thirty-eight, was in the center of his blanket roll.

And he knew that George had the weapon in his big hand. One pressure of the trigger would put an end to Donnegan; one bullet would give George the canvas sack and its small treasure.

"When you clean my gun," said Donnegan, "take the action to pieces and go over every part."

He could actually feel the start of George.

Then: "Yes, sir," in a subdued whisper.

If the escape from the knife had startled George, this second incident had convinced him that his new master possessed eyes in the back of his head.

And Donnegan, paying no further heed to him, looked steadily across the hillside to the white tent of Lou Macon, fifty yards away.

# CHAPTER XVI

### HE MAKES A NEW SCHEME

HIS plan, grown to full stature so swiftly, and springing out of nothing, well nigh, had come out of his first determination to bring Jack Landis back to Lou Macon; for he could interpret those blank, misty eyes with which she had sat after the departure of Landis in only one way. Yet to rule even the hand of big Jack Landis would be hard enough and to rule his heart was quite another story. Remembering Nelly Lebrun, he saw clearly that the only way in which he could be brought back to Lou was first to remove Nelly as a possibility in his eyes. But how remove Nelly as long as it was her cue from her father to play Landis for his money? How remove her, unless it were possible to sweep Nelly off her feet with another man? She might, indeed, be taken by storm, and if she once slighted Landis for the sake of another, his boyish pride would probably do the rest, and his next step would be to return to Lou Macon.

All this seemed logical, but where find the man to storm the heart of Nelly and dazzle her bright, clever eyes? His own rags had made him shrug his shoulders; and it was the thought of clothes which had made him fasten his attention so closely on the man of the linen suit in Lebrun's. Donnegan with money, with well-fitted clothes, and with a few notorious escapades behind him—yes, Donnegan with such a flying start might flutter the heart of Nelly

Lebrun for a moment. But he must have the money, the clothes, and then he must deliberately set out to startle The Corner, make himself a public figure, talked of, pointed at, known, feared, respected, and even loved by at least a few. He must accomplish all these things beginning at a literal zero.

It was the impossible nature of this that tempted Donnegan. But the paradoxical picture of the ragged skulker in Milligan's actually sitting at the same table with Nelly Lebrun and receiving her smiles stayed with him. He intended to rise, literally Phœnixlike, out of ashes. And the next morning, in the red time of the dawn, he sat drinking the coffee which George Washington Green had made for him and considering the details of the problem. Clothes, which had been a main obstacle, were now accounted for, since, as he had suspected, the packs of Godwin contained a luxurious wardrobe of considerable compass. At that moment, for instance, Donnegan was wrapped in a dressing gown of padded silk and his feet were encased in slippers.

But clothes were the least part of his worries. To startle The Corner, and thereby make himself attractive in the eyes of Nelly Lebrun, overshadowing Jack Landis—that was the thing! But to startle The Corner, where gold strikes were events of every twenty-four hours, just now—where robberies were common gossip, and where the killings now averaged nearly three a day—to startle The Corner was like trying to startle the theatrical world with a sensational play. Indeed, this parallel could have been pursued, for Donnegan was the nameless actor and the mountain desert was the stage on which he intended to become a headliner. No wonder, then, that his lean face was compressed in thought. Yet no one could have guessed it by his conversation. At the moment he was interrupted, his talk ran somewhat as follows.

"George, Godwin taught you how to make coffee?"

"Yes, sir," from George. Since the night before the negro had appeared totally subdued. Never once did he venture a comment. And ever Donnegan was conscious of big, bright eyes watching him in a reverent fear not untinged by superstition. Once, in the middle of the night, he had wakened and seen the vast shadow of George's form leaning over the sack of money. Murder by stealth in the dark had been in the negro's mind, no doubt. But when, after that, he came and leaned over Donnegan's bunk, the master closed his eyes and kept on breathing regularly, and finally the negro returned to his own place—softly as a gigantic cat. Even in the master's sleep he found something to be dreaded, and Donnegan knew that he could now trust the fellow through anything. In the morning, at the first touch of light, he had gone to the stores and collected provisions. And a comfortable breakfast followed.

"Godwin," resumed Donnegan, "was talented in many ways."

The negro showed his teeth in silence; for since Godwin proposed the sacrifice of the servant to preserve himself, George had aparently altered his opinion of the gambler.

"A talented man, George, but he knew nothing about coffee. It should never boil. It should only begin to cream through the crust. Let that happen; take the pot from the fire; put it back and let the surface cream again. Do this three times, and then pour the liquor from the grounds and you have the right strength and the right heating. You understand?"

"Yes, sir."

"And concerning the frying of bacon——"

At this point the interruption came in the shape of four men at the open door; and one of these Donnegan recognized as the real estate dealer, who had shrewdly set up tents and shacks on every favorable spot in The Corner and was now reaping a rich harvest. Gloster was his name. It was patent that he did not see in the man in the silk dressing robe the unshaven miscreant of the day before who had rented the two tents.

"How'dee," he said, standing on the threshold, with the other three in the background.

Donnegan looked at him and through him.

"My name is Gloster. I own this shack and I've come to find out why you're in it."

"George," said Donnegan, "speak to him. Tell him that I know houses are scarce in The Corner; that I found this place by accident vacant; that I intend to stay in it on purpose."

George Washington Green instantly rose to the situation; he swallowed a vast grin and strode to the door. And though Mr. Gloster's face crimsoned with rage at such treatment he controlled his voice. In The Corner manhood was apt to be reckoned by the pound, and George was a giant.

"I heard what your boss said, buddie," said Gloster. "But I've rented this cabin and the next one to these three gents and their party, and they want a home. Nothing to do but vacate. Which speed is the thing I want. Thirty minutes will——"

"Thirty minutes don't change nothing," declared George in his deep, soft voice.

The real estate man choked. Then: "You tell your boss that jumping a cabin is like jumping a claim. They's a law in The Corner for gents like him."

George made a gesture of helplessness; but Gloster turned to the three.

"Both shacks or none at all," said the spokesman. "One ain't big enough to do us any good. But if this bird won't vamose——"

He was a tolerably rough appearing sort and he was backed by two of a kind. No doubt dangerous action would have followed had not George shown himself capable of rising to a height. He stepped from the door; he approached Gloster and said in a confidential whisper that reached easily to the other three: "They ain't any call for a quick play, mister. Watch yo'selves. Maybe you don't know who the boss is?"

"And what's more, I don't care," said Gloster defiantly but with his voice instinctively lowered. He stared past George, and behold, the man in the dressing gown still sat in quiet and sipped his coffee.

"It's Donnegan," whispered George.

"Don—who's he?"

"You don't know Donnegan?"

The mingled contempt and astonishment of George would have moved a thing of stone. It certainly troubled Gloster. And he turned to the three.

"Gents," he said, "they's two things we can do. Try the law—and law's a lame lady in these parts —or throw him out. Say which?"

The three looked from Gloster to the shack; from the shack to Donnegan, absently sipping his coffee; from Donnegan to George, who stood exhibiting a broad grin of anticipated delight. The contrast was too much for them.

There is one great and deep-seated terror in the mountain desert, and that is for the man who may be other than he seems. The giant with the rough voice and the boisterous ways is generally due for a stormy passage west of the Rockies; but the silent man with the gentle manners receives respect. Traditions live of desperadoes with exteriors of womanish calm and the action of devils. And Donnegan sipping his morning coffee fitted into the picture which rumor had painted. The three looked at one another, declared that they had not come to fight for a house but to rent one, that the real estate agent could go to the devil for all of them, and that they were bound elsewhere. So they departed and left Gloster both relieved and gloomy.

. "Now," said Donnegan to George, "tell him that we'll take both the shacks, and he can add fifty per cent to his old price."

The bargain was concluded on the spot; the money was paid by George. Gloster went down the hill to tell The Corner that a mystery had hit the town and George brought the canvas bag back to Donnegan with the top still untied—as though to let it be seen that he had not pocketed any of the gold.

"I don't want to count it," said Donnegan. "Keep the bag, George. Keep money in your pocket. Treat both of us well. And when that's gone I'll get more."

If the manner in which Donnegan had handled the renting of the cabins had charmed George, he was wholly entranced by this last touch of free spending. To serve a man who was his master was one thing; to serve one who trusted him so completely was quite another. To live under the same roof with a man who was a riddle was sufficiently delightful; but to be allowed actually to share in the mystery was a super-happiness. He was singing when he started to wash the dishes, and Donnegan went across the hill to the tent of Lou Macon.

She was laying the fire before the tent; and the morning freshness had cleared from her face any vestige of the trouble of the night before; and in the slant light her hair was glorious, all ruffling gold, semitransparent. She did not smile at him; but she could give the effect of smiling while her face remained grave; it was her inward calm content of which people were aware.

"You missed me?"

"Yes."

"You were worried?"

"No."

He felt himself put quietly at a distance. So he took her up the hill to her new home—the shack beside his own; and George cooked her breakfast. When she had been served, Donnegan drew the negro to one side.

"She's your mistress," said Donnegan. "Everything you do for her is worth two things you do for me. Watch her as if she were in your eye. And if a hair of her head is ever harmed—you see that fire burning yonder—the bed of coals?"

"Sir?"

"I'll catch you and make a fire like that and feed you into it—by inches!"

And the pale face of Donnegan became for an instant the face of a demon. George Washington Green saw, and never forgot.

Afterward, in order that he might think, Donnegan got on one of the horses he had taken from Godwin and rode over the hills. They were both leggy chestnuts, with surprising signs of blood and all the earmarks of sprinters; but in Godwin's trade sharp get-aways were probably often necessary. The pleasure he took in the action of the animal kept him from getting into his problem.

How to startle The Corner? How follow up the opening gun which he had fired at the expense of Gloster and the three miners?

He broke off, later in the day, to write a letter to Colonel Macon, informing him that Jack Landis was tied hard and fast by Nelly Lebrun and that for the present nothing could be done except wait, unless the colonel had suggestions to offer.

The thought of the colonel, however, stimulated Donnegan. And before midafternoon he had thought of a thing to do.

# CHAPTER XVII

## HE STEPS ON THE STAGE

THE bar in Milligan's was not nearly so pretentious an affair as the bar in Lebrun's, but it was of a far higher class. Milligan had even managed to bring in a few bottles of wine, and he had dispensed cheap claret at two dollars a glass when the miners wished to celebrate a rare occasion. There were complaints, not of the taste, but of the lack of strength. So Milligan fortified his liquor with pure alcohol and after that the claret went like a sweet song in The Corner. Among other things, he sold mint juleps; and it was the memory of the big sign proclaiming this fact that furnished Donnegan with his idea.

He had George Washington Green put on his town clothes—a riding suit in which Godwin had had him dress for the sake of formal occasions. Resplendent in black boots, yellow riding breeches, and blue silk shirt, the big negro came before Donnegan for instructions.

"Go down to Milligan's," said the master. "They don't allow colored people to enter the door, but you go to the door and start for the bar." George turned green, but said nothing. "They won't let you go very far. When they stop you, tell them you come from Donnegan and that you have to get me some mint for a julep. Insist. The bouncer will start to throw you out."

George showed his teeth.

"No fighting back. Don't lift your hand. When you find that you can't get in, come back here. Now, ride."

So George mounted the horse and went. It was not a task to his liking. With the exception of the quiet-voiced fiend Donnegan, who had eyes in the back of his head, George was quite willing to face any man in the world, white or black, so long as he could choose his own ground, but he knew that there are certain things which it is ill for one of his color to do, and that is to enter precincts set apart for the whites.

Straight to Milligan's he rode and dismounted; and half of The Corner's scant daytime population came into the street to see the brilliant horseman pass.

"Scar-faced" Lewis met the giant negro at the door. And size meant little to Andy, except an easier target.

"Well, confound my soul," said Lewis, blocking the way. "A nigger in Milligan's? Get out!"

Big George did not move.

"I been sent, mister," he said mildly. "I been sent for enough mint to make a julep."

"You been sent to the wrong place," declared Andy, hitching at his cartridge belt. "Ain't you seen that sign?"

And he pointed to the one which eliminated colored patrons.

"Signs don't mean nothin' to my boss," said George.

"Who's he?"

"Donnegan."

"And who's Donnegan?"

It puzzled George. He scratched his head in bewilderment seeking for an explanation. "Donnegan is—Donnegan," he explained.

"I heard Gloster talk about him," offered some one in the rapidly growing group. "He's the gent that rented the two places on the hill."

"Tell him to come himse'f," said Andy Lewis. "We don't play no favorites at Milligan's."

"Mister," said big George, "I don't want to bring no trouble on this heah place, but—don't make me go back and bring Donnegan."

Even Andy Lewis was staggered by this assurance.

"Rules is rules," he finally decided. "And out you go."

Big George stepped from the doorway and mounted his horse.

"I call on all you gen'lemen," he said to the assembled group, "to say that I done tried my best to do this peaceable. It ain't me that's sent for Donnegan; it's him!"

He rode away, leaving Scar-faced Lewis biting his long mustaches in anxiety. He was not exactly afraid, but he waited in the suspense which comes before a battle. Moreover, an audience was gathering. The word went about as only a rumor of mischief can travel. New men had gathered. The few day gamblers tumbled out of Lebrun's across the street to watch the fun. The storekeepers were in their doors. Lebrun himself, withered and dark and yellow of eye, came to watch. And here and there through the crowd there was a spot of color where the women of the town appeared. And among others, Nelly Lebrun with Jack Landis beside her. On the whole it was not a large crowd, but what it lacked in size it made up in intense interest.

For though The Corner had had its share of troubles of fist and gun, most of them were entirely impromptu affairs. Here was a fight in the offing for which the stage was set, the actors set in full view of a conveniently posted audience, and all the suspense of a curtain rising. The waiting bore in upon Andy Lewis. Without a doubt he intended to kill his man neatly and with dispatch, but the possibility of missing before such a crowd as this sent a chill up and down his spine. If he failed now his name would be a sign for laughter ever after in The Corner.

A hum passed down the street; it rose to a chuckle, and then fell away to sudden silence, for Donnegan was coming.

He came on a prancing chestnut horse which sidled uneasily on a weaving course, as though it wished to show off for the benefit of the rider and the crowd at once. It was a hot afternoon and Donnegan's linen riding suit shone an immaculate white. He came straight down the street, as unaware of the audience which awaited him as though he rode in a park where crowds were the common thing. Behind him came George Green, just a careful length back. Rumor went before the two with a whisper on either side.

"That's Donnegan. There he comes!"

"Who's Donnegan?"

"Gloster's man. The one who bluffed out Gloster and three others."

"He pulled his shooting iron and trimmed the whiskers of one of 'em with a chunk of lead."

"D'you mean that?"

"What's *that* kind of a gent doing in The Corner?"

"Come to buy, I guess. He looks like money."

"Looks like a confounded dude."

"We'll see his hand in a minute."

Donnegan was now opposite the dance hall, and Andy Lewis had his hand touching the butt of his gun, but though Donnegan was looking straight at him, he kept his reins in one hand and his heavy riding crop in the other. And without a move toward his own gun, he rode straight up to the door of the dance hall, with Andy in front of it. The negro drew rein behind him and turned upon the crowd one broad, superior grin.

As who should say: "I promised you lightning; now watch it strike!"

If the crowd had been expectant before, it was now reduced to wire-drawn tenseness.

"Are you the fellow who turned back my man?" asked Donnegan.

His quiet voice fell coldly upon the soul of Andy. He strove to warm himself by an outbreak of temper.

"They ain't any poor fool dude can call me a 'fellow!'" he shouted.

The crowd blinked; but when it opened its eyes the gunplay had not occurred. The hand of Andy was relaxing from the butt of his gun and an expression of astonishment and contempt was growing upon his face.

"I haven't come to curse you," said the rider, still occupying his hands with crop and reins. "I've come to ask you a question and get an answer. Are you the fellow who turned back my man?"

"I guess you ain't the kind I was expectin' to call on me," drawled Andy, his fear gone, and he winked at the crowd. But the others were not yet ready to laugh. Something about the calm face of Donnegan had impressed them. "Sure, I'm the one that kicked the coon out. Niggers ain't allowed in there."

"It's the last of my thoughts to break in upon a convention in your city," replied the grave rider, "but my man did not come to use the place as a dance hall. He was sent on an errand—as a servant —and therefore he had a right to expect a servant's courtesy. George, get off your horse and go into Milligan's place. I want that mint!"

For a moment Andy was too stunned to answer. Then his voice came harshly and he swayed from side to side, gathering and summoning his wrath.

"Keep out, nigger! Keep out, or you're buzzard meat. I'm warnin'——"

For the first time his glance left the rider to find George, and that instant was fatal. The hand of Donnegan licked out as the snake's tongue darts— the loaded quirt slipped over in his hand, and holding it by the lash he brought the butt of it thudding on the head of Andy.

Even then the instinct to fight remained in the stunned man; while he fell, he was drawing the revolver; he lay in a crumpling heap at the feet of Donnegan's horse with the revolver shoved muzzle first into the sand.

Donnegan's voice did not rise.

"Go in and get that mint, George," he ordered. "And hurry. This rascal has kept me waiting until I'm thirsty."

Big George hesitated only one instant—it was to sweep the crowd for the second time with his confident grin—and he strode through the door of the dance hall. As for Donnegan, his only movement was to swing his horse around and shift riding crop and reins into the grip of his left hand. His other hand was dropped carelessly upon his hip. Now, both these things were very simple maneuvers, but The Corner noted that his change of face had enabled Donnegan to bring the crowd under his eye, and that his right hand was now ready for a more serious bit of work if need be. Moreover, he was probing faces with his glance. And every armed man in that group felt that the eye of the rider was directed particularly toward him.

There had been one brief murmur; then the silence lay heavily again, for it was seen that Andy had been only slightly stunned—knocked out, as a boxer might be. Now his sturdy brains were clearing. His body stiffened into a human semblance once more; he fumbled, found the butt of his gun with his first move. He pushed his hat straight, and so doing he raked the welt which the blow had left on his head. The pain finished clearing the mist from his mind; in an instant he was on his feet, maddened with shame. He saw the semicircle of white faces, and the whole episode flashed back on him. He had been knocked down like a dog.

For a moment he looked into the blank faces of the crowd; some one noted that there was no gun strapped at the side of Donnegan. A voice shouted a warning.

"Stop, Lewis. The dude ain't got a gun. It's murder!"

It was now that Lewis saw Donnegan sitting the saddle directly behind him, and he whirled with a moan of fury. It was a twist of his body—in his eagerness—rather than a turning upon his feet. And he was half around before the rider moved.

Then he conjured a gun from somewhere in his clothes. There was the flash of the steel, an explosion, and Scarfaced Lewis was on his knees with a scream of pain holding his right forearm with his left hand.

The crowd hesitated still for a second, as though it feared to interfere; but Donnegan had already put up his weapon. A wave of the curious spectators rushed across the street and gathered around the injured man. They found that he had been shot through the fleshy part of the thumb, and the bullet, ranging down the arm, had sliced a furrow to the bone all the way to the elbow. It was a grisly wound.

Big George Washington Green came running to the door of the dance hall with a sprig of something green in his hand; one glance assured him that all was well; and once more that wide, confident grin spread upon his face. He came to the master and offered the mint; and Donnegan, raising it to his face, inhaled the scent deeply.

"Good," he said. "And now for a julep, George! Let's go home!"

Across the street a dark-eyed girl had clasped the arm of her companion in hysterical excitement.

"Did you see?" she asked of her tall companion.

"I saw a murderer shoot down a man; he ought to be hung for it!"

"But the mint! Did you see him smile over it? Oh, what a devil he is; and what a man!"

Jack Landis flashed a glance of suspicion down at her, but her dancing eyes had quite forgotten him. They were following the progress of Donnegan down the street. He rode slowly, and the negro kept that formal distance, just a length behind.

# CHAPTER XVIII

### HE CALLS FOR THE SPOTLIGHT

BEFORE Milligan's the crowd began to buzz like murmuring hornets around a nest that has been tapped, when they pour out and cannot find the disturber. It was a rather helpless milling around the wounded man, and Nelly Lebrun was the one who worked her way through the crowd and came to Andy Lewis. She did not like Andy. She had been known to refer to him as a cowardly hawk of a man; but now she bullied the crowd in a shrill voice and made them bring water and cloth. Then she cleansed and bandaged the wound in Andy Lewis' arm and had some of them take him away.

By this time the outskirts of the crowd had melted away; but those who had really seen all parts of the little drama remained to talk. The subject was a real one. Had Donnegan aimed at the hand of Andy and risked his own life on his ability to disable the other without killing him? Or had he fired at Lewis' body and struck the hand and arm only by a random lucky chance?

If the second were the case, he was only a fair shot with plenty of nerve and a great deal of luck. If the first were true, then his was a nerve of ice-tempered steel, an eye vulture-sharp, and a hand, miraculous, fast, and certain. To strike that swinging hand with a snap shot, when a miss meant a bullet fired at his own body at deadly short range—truly it would take a credulous man to believe that

Donnegan had coldly planned to disable his man without killing him.

"A murderer by intention," exclaimed Milligan. He had hunted long and hard before he found a man with a face like that of Lewis, capable of maintaining order by a glance; now he wanted revenge. Also, a negro had entered his place and for the first time one of his laws had been broken. "A murderer by intention!" he cried to the crowd, standing beside the place where the imprint of Andy's knees was still in the sand. "And like a murderer he ought to be treated. He aimed to kill Andy; he had luck and only broke his hand. Now, boys, I say it ain't so much what he's done as the way he's done it. He's given us the laugh. He's come in here in his dude clothes and tried to walk over us. But it don't work. Not in The Corner. If Andy was dead I'd say lynch the dude. But he ain't, and all I say is: Run him out of town."

Here there was a brief outburst of applause, but when it ended, it was observed that there was a low, soft laughter. The crowd gave way between Milligan and the mocker. It was seen that he who laughed was old Lebrun, rubbing his olive-skinned hands together and showing his teeth in his mirth. There was no love lost between Lebrun and Milligan, even if Nelly was often in the dance hall and the center of its merriment.

"It takes a thief to catch a thief," said Lebrun enigmatically, when he saw that he had the ear of the crowd, "and it takes a man to catch a man."

"What the devil do you mean by that?" a dozen voices asked.

"I mean, that if you got men enough to run out

this man Donnegan, The Corner is a better town than I think."

It brought a growl, but no answer. Lebrun had never been seen to lift his hand, but he was more dreaded than a rattler.

"We'll try," said Milligan dryly. "I ain't much of a man myself"—there were dark rumors about Milligan's past, and the crowd chuckled at this modesty—"but I'll try my hand agin' him with a bit of backing. And first I want to tell you boys that they ain't any danger of him having aimed at Andy's hand. I tell you, it ain't possible, hardly, for him to have planned to hit a swingin' target like that. Maybe some could do it. I dunno."

"How about Lord Nick?"

"Sure, Lord Nick might do anything. But Donnegan ain't Lord Nick."

"Not by twenty pounds and three inches."

This brought a laugh. And by comparison with the terrible and familiar name of Lord Nick, Donnegan became a smaller danger. Besides, as Milligan said, it was undoubtedly luck. And when he called for volunteers, three or four stepped up at once. The others made a general milling, as though each were trying to get forward and each were prevented by the crowd in front. But in the background big Jack Landis was seriously trying to get to the firing line. He was encumbered with the clinging weight of Nelly Lebrun.

"Don't go, Jack," she pleaded. "Please! Please! Be sensible. For my sake!"

She backed this appeal with a lifting of her eyes and a parting of her lips, and Jack Landis paused.

"You won't go, dear Jack?"

Now, Jack knew perfectly well that the girl was

only half sincere. It is the peculiar fate of men that they always know when a woman is playing with them, but, from Samson down, they always go to the slaughter with open eyes, hoping each moment that the girl has been seriously impressed at last. As for Jack Landis, his slow mind did not readily get under the surface of the arts of Nelly, but he knew now that there was at least a tinge of real concern in the girl's desire to keep him from the posse which Milligan was raising.

"But they's something about him that I don't like, Nelly. Something sort of familiar that I don't like." For naturally enough he did not recognize the transformed Donnegan, and the name he had never heard before. "A gun-fighter, that's what he is!"

"Why, Jack, sometimes they call you the same thing; say that you hunt for trouble now and then!"

"Do they say that?" asked the young chap quickly, flushing with vanity. "Oh, I aim to take care of myself. And I'd like to take a hand with this murdering Donnegan."

"Jack, listen! Don't go; keep away from him!"

"Why do you look like that? As if I was a dead one already."

"I tell you, Jack, he'd kill you!"

Something in her terrible assurance whitened the cheeks of Landis, but he was also angered. When a very young man becomes both afraid and angry he is apt to be dangerous. "What do you know of him?" he asked suspiciously.

"You silly! But I saw his face when he lifted that mint. He'd already forgotten about the man he had just shot down. He was thinking of nothing but the scent of the mint. And did you notice the negro? The big negro? He never had a moment's doubt of his master's ability to handle the entire crowd. I tell you, it gave me a chill of ghosts to see the big black fellow's eyes. He knew that Donnegan would win. And Donnegan won! Jack, you're a big man and a strong man and a brave man, and we all know it. But don't be foolish. Stay away from Donnegan!"

He wavered just an instant. If she could have sustained her pleading gaze a moment longer she would have won him, but at the critical instant her gaze became distant. She was seeing the calm face of Donnegan as he raised the mint. And as though he understood, Jack Landis hardened.

"I'm glad you don't want me shot up, Nelly," he said coldly. "Mighty good of you to watch out for me. But—I'm going to run this Donnegan out of town!"

"He's never harmed you; why——"

"I don't like his looks. For a man like me that's enough!"

And he strode away toward Milligan. He was greeted by a cheer just as the girl reached the side of her father.

"The big fellow is going," she said. "Make him come back!"

But the old man was still rubbing his hands; there seemed to be a perpetual chill in the tips of the fingers.

"He is a jackass. The moment I first saw his face I knew that he was meant for gun fodder— buzzard food! Let him go. Bah!"

The girl shivered. "And then the mines?" she asked, changing her tactics.

"Ah, yes. The mines! But leave that to Lord Nick. He'll handle it well enough!"

So Jack Landis strode up the hill first and foremost of the six stalwart men who wished to correct the stranger's apparent misunderstandings of the status of The Corner. They were each armed to the teeth and each provided with enough bullets to disturb a small city. All this in honor of Donnegan.

They found the shack wrapped in the warm, mellow light of the late afternoon; and on a flat-topped rock outside it big George sat whittling a stick into a grotesque imitation of a snake coiled. He did not rise when the posse approached. He merely rocked back upon the rock, embraced his knees in both of his enormous arms, and, in a word, transformed himself into a round ball of mirth. But having hugged away his laughter he was able to convert his joy into a vast grin. That smile stopped the posse. When a mob starts for a scene of violence the least exhibition of fear incenses it, but mockery is apt to pour water on its flames of anger.

Decidedly the fury of the posse was chilled by the grin of George. Milligan, who had lived south of the Mason-Dixon line, stepped up to impress George properly.

"Niggah," he said, frowning, "go in and tell your man that we've come for him. Tell him to step right out here and get ready to talk. We don't mean him no harm less'n he can't explain one or two things. Hop along, niggah!"

The "niggah" did not stir. Only he shifted his eyes from face to face and his grin broadened. Ripples of mirth waved along his chest and convulsed his face, but still he did not laugh. "Go in and tell them things to Donnegan," he said. "But don't ask me to wake up the master. He's sleepin' soun' an' fas.' Like a baby; mostly, he sleeps every day to get rested up for the night. Now, can't you-all wait till Donnegan wakes up to-night? No? Then step right in, gen'lemen; but if you-all is set on wakin' him up now, George will jus' step over the hill, because he don't want to be near the explosion."

At this, he allowed his mirth free rein. His laughter shook up to his throat, to his enormous mouth; it rolled and bellowed across the hillside; and the posse stood, each man in his place, and looked frigidly upon one another. But having been laughed at, they felt it necessary to go on, and do or die. So they strode across the hill and were almost to the door when another phenomenon occurred. A girl in a cheap calico dress of blue was seen to run out of a neighboring shack and spring up before the door of Donnegan's hut. When she faced the crowd it stopped again.

The soft wind was blowing the blue dress into lovely, long, curving lines; about her throat a white collar of some sheer stuff was being lifted into waves, or curling against her cheek; and the golden hair, in disorder, was tousled low upon her forehead. Whirling thus upon the crowd, she shocked them to a pause, with her parted lips, her flare of delicate color.

"Have you come here," she cried, "for—for Donnegan?"

"Lady," began some one, and then looked about for Jack Landis, who was considered quite a hand with the ladies. But Jack Landis was discovered fading out of view down the hillside. One glance at that blue dress had quite routed him, for now he remembered the red-haired man who had escorted Lou Macon to The Corner—and the colonel's singular trust in this fellow. It explained much, and he fled before he should be noted.

Before the spokesman could continue his speech, the girl had whipped inside the door. And the posse was dumbfounded. Milligan saw that the advance was ruined. "Boys," he said, "we came to fight a man; not to storm a house with a woman in it. Let's go back. We'll tend to Donnegan later on."

"We'll drill him clean!" muttered the others furiously, and straightway the posse departed down the hill.

But inside the girl had found, to her astonishment, that Donnegan was stretched upon his bunk wrapped again in the silken dressing gown and with a smile upon his lips. He looked much younger, as he slept, and perhaps it was this that made the girl steal forward upon tiptoe and touch his shoulder so gently.

He was up on his feet in an instant. 'Alas, vanity, vanity! Donnegan in shoes was one thing, for his shoes were of a particular kind; but Donnegan in his slippers was a full two inches shorter. He was hardly taller than the girl; he was, if the bitter truth must be known, almost a small man. And Donnegan was furious at having been found by her in such careless attire—and without those dignity-building shoes. First he wanted to cut the throat of big George.

"What have you done, what have you done?" cried the girl, in one of those heart-piercing whispers of fear. "They have come for you—a whole crowd —of armed men—they're outside the door! What have you done? It was something done for me, I know!"

Donnegan suddenly transferred his wrath from big George to the mob.

"Outside my door?" he asked. And as he spoke he slipped on a belt at which a heavy holster tugged down on one side, and buckled it around him.

"Oh, no, no, no!" she pleaded, and caught him in her arms.

Donnegan allowed her to stop him with that soft power for a moment, until his face went white—as if with pain. Then he adroitly gathered both her wrists into one of his bony hands; and having rendered her powerless, he slipped by her and cast open the door.

It was an empty scene upon which they looked, with big George rocking back and forth upon a rock, convulsed with silent laughter. Donnegan looked sternly at the girl and swallowed. He was fearfully susceptible to mockery.

"There seems to have been a jest?" he said.

But she lifted to him a happy, tearful face.

"Ah, thank Heaven!" she cried gently.

Oddly enough, Donnegan at this set his teeth and turned upon his heel, and the girl stole out the door again, and closed it softly behind her. As a matter of fact, not even the terrible colonel inspired in her quite the fear which Donnegan instilled.

# CHAPTER XIX

### HE GIVES ALMS

"BIG Landis lost his nerve and sidestepped at the last minute, and then the whole gang faded."
That was the way the rumors of the affair always ended at each repetition in Lebrun's and Milligan's that night. The Corner had many things to talk about during its brief existence, but nothing to compare with a man who entered a shooting scrape with such a fellow as Scar-faced Lewis all for the sake of a spray of mint. And the main topic of conversation was: Did Donnegan aim at the body or the hand of the bouncer?

On the whole, it was an excellent thing for Milligan's. The place was fairly well crowded, with a few vacant tables. For every one wanted to hear Milligan's version of the affair. He had a short and vigorous one, trimmed with neat oaths. It was all the girl in the blue calico dress, according to him. The posse couldn't storm a house with a woman in it or even conduct a proper lynching in her presence. And no one was able to smile when Milligan said this. Neither was any one nervy enough to question the courage of Landis. It looked strange, that sudden flight of his, but then, he was a proven man. Every one remembered the affair of Lester. It had been a clean-cut fight, and Jack Landis had won cleanly on his merits.

Nevertheless some of the whispers had not failed to come to the big man, and his brow was black.

The most terribly heartless and selfish passion of all is shame in a young man. To repay the sidelong glances which he met on every side, Jack Landis would have willingly crowded every living soul in The Corner into one house and touched a match to it. And chiefly because he felt the injustice of the suspicion. He had no fear of Donnegan.

He had a theory that little men had little souls. Not that he ever formulated the theory in words, but he vaguely felt it and adhered to it. He had more fear of one man of six two than of a dozen under five ten. He reserved in his heart of hearts a place of awe for one man whom he had never seen. That was for Lord Nick, for that celebrated character was said to be as tall and as finely built as Jack Landis himself. But as for Donnegan— Landis' wished there were three Donnegans instead of one.

To-night his cue was surly silence. For Nelly Lebrun had been warned by her father, and she was making desperate efforts to recover any ground she might have lost. Besides, to lose Jack Landis would be to lose the most spectacular fellow in The Corner, to say nothing of the one who held the largest and the choicest of the mines. The blond, good looks of Landis made a perfect background for her dark beauty. With all these stakes to play for, Nelly outdid herself. If she were attractive enough ordinarily, when she exerted herself to fascinate, Nelly was intoxicating. What chance had poor Jack Landis against her? He did not call for her that night but went to play gloomily at Lebrun's until Nelly walked into Lebrun's and drew him away from a table. Half an hour later she had him whirling through a dance in Milligan's and had danced the gloom out of his mind for the moment. Before the evening was well under way, Landis was making love to her openly, and Nelly was in the position of one who had roused the bear.

It was a dangerous flirtation and it was growing clumsy. In any place other than The Corner it would have been embarrassing long ago; and when Jack Landis, after a dance, put his one big hand over both of Nelly's and held her moveless while he poured out a passionate declaration, Nelly realized that something must be done. Just what she could not tell.

And it was at this very moment that a wave of silence, beginning at the door, rushed across Milligan's dance floor. It stopped the bartenders in the act of mixing drinks; it put the musicians out of key, and in the midst of a waltz phrase they broke down and came to a discordant pause.

What was it?

The men faced the door, wondering, and then the swift rumor passed from lip to lip—almost from eye to eye, so rapidly it sped—Donnegan is coming! Donnegan, and the negro with him.

"Some one tell Milligan!"

But Milligan had already heard; he was back of the bar giving directions; guns were actually unlimbering. What would happen?

"Shall I get you out of this?" Landis asked the girl.

"Leave now?" She laughed fiercely and silently. "I'm just beginning to live! Miss Donnegan in action? No, sir!"

She would have given a good deal to retract that sentence, for it washed the face of Landis white with jealousy.

Surely Donnegan had built greater than he knew. And suddenly he was there in the midst of the house. No one had stopped him—at least, no one had interfered with his negro. Big George had on a white suit and a dappled green necktie; he stood directly behind his master and made him look like a small boy. For Donnegan was in black, and he had a white neckcloth wrapped as high and stiffly as an old-fashioned stock. Altogether he was a queer, drab figure compared with the brilliant Donnegan of that afternoon. He looked older, more weary. His lean face was pale; and his hair flamed with redoubled ardor on that account. Never was hair as red as that, not even the hair of Lord Nick, said the people in Milligan's this night.

He was perfectly calm even in the midst of that deadly silence. He stood looking about him. He saw Gloster, the real estate man, and bowed to him deliberately.

For some reason that drew a gasp.

Then he observed a table which was apparently to his fancy and crossed the floor with a light, noiseless step, big George padding heavily behind him. At the little round table he waited until George had drawn out the chair for him and then he sat down. He folded his arms lightly upon his breast and once more surveyed the scene, and big George drew himself up behind his master. Just once his eyes rolled and flashed savagely in delight at the sensation they were making, then the face of George was once again impassive.

If Donnegan had not carried it off with a certain air, the whole entrance would have seemed decidedly stagey, but The Corner, as it was, found much to wonder at and little to criticize. And in the West grown men are as shrewd judges of affectation as children are in other places.

"Putting on a lot of style, eh?" said Jack Landis, and with fierce intensity he watched the face of Nelly Lebrun.

For once she was unguarded.

"He's superb!" she exclaimed. "The big negro is going to bring a drink for his master."

She looked up, surprised by the silence of Landis, and found that his face was actually yellow.

"I'll tell you something. Do you remember the little red-headed tramp who came in here the other night and spoke to me?"

"Very well. You seemed to be bothered."

"Maybe. I dunno. But that's the man—the one who's sitting over there now all dressed up—the man The Corner is talking about—Donnegan! A tramp!"

She caught her breath.

"Is that the one?" A pause. "Well, I believe it. He's capable of anything!"

"I think you like him all the better for knowing that."

"Jack, you're angry."

"Why should I be? I hate to see you fooled by the bluff of a tramp, though."

"Tush! Do you think I'm fooled by it? But it's an interesting bluff, Jack, don't you think?"

"Nelly, he's interesting enough to make you blush; by Heaven, the houn' is lookin' right at you now, Nelly!"

He had pressed her suddenly against the wall and she struck back desperately in self-defense.

"By the way, what did he want to see you about?"

It spiked the guns of Landis for the time being, at least. And the girl followed by striving to prove that her interest in Donnegan was purely impersonal.

"He's clever," she ran on, not daring to look at the set face of her companion. "See how he fails to notice that he's making a sensation? You'd think he was in a big restaurant in a city. He takes the drink off the tray from the negro as if it were a common thing to be waited on by a body-servant in The Corner. Jack, I'll wager that there's something crooked about him. A professional gambler, say!"

Jack Landis thawed a little under this careless chatter. He still did not quite trust her.

"Do you know what they're whispering? That I was afraid to face him!"

She tilted her head back, so that the light gleamed on her round throat, and she broke into laughter.

"Why, Jack, that's foolish. You proved yourself when you first came to The Corner. Maybe some of the newcomers may have said something, but all the old-timers know you had some different reason for leaving the rest of them. By the way, what was the reason?"

She sent a keen little glance at him from the corner of her eyes, but the moment she saw that he was embarrassed and at sea because of the query she instantly slipped into a fresh tide of careless chatter and covered up his confusion for him.

"See how the girls are making eyes at him."

"I'll tell you why," Jack replied. "A girl likes to be with the man who's making the town talk." He added pointedly: "Oh, I've found that out!"

She shrugged that comment away.

"He isn't paying the slightest attention to any of them," she murmured. "He's queer! Has he just come here hunting trouble?"

# CHAPTER XX

## HE DANCES

IT should be understood that before this the men in Milligan's had reached a subtly unspoken agreement that red-haired Donnegan was not one of them. In a word, they did not like him because he made a mystery of himself. And, also, because he was different. Yet there was a growing feeling that the shooting of Lewis through the hand had not been an accident, for the whole demeanor of Donnegan composed the action of a man who is a professional trouble maker. There was no reason why he should go to Milligan's and take his negro with him unless he wished a fight. And why a man should wish to fight the entire Corner was something no one could guess.

That he should have done all this merely to focus all eyes upon him, and particularly the eyes of a girl, did not occur to any one. It looked rather like the bravado of a man who lived for the sake of fighting. Now, men who hunt trouble in the mountain desert generally find all that they may desire, but for the time being every one held back, wolfishly, waiting for another to take the first step toward Donnegan. Indeed, there was an unspoken conviction that the man who took the first step would probably not live to take another. In the meantime both men and women gave Donnegan the lion's share of their attention. There was only one who was clever enough to conceal it, and that one was the pair of eyes to which the red-haired man was playing—Nelly Lebrun. She confined herself strictly to Jack Landis.

So it was that when Milligan announced a tag dance and the couples swirled onto the floor gayly, Donnegan decided to take matters into his own hands and offer the first overt act. It was clumsy; he did not like it; but he hated this delay. And he knew that every moment he stayed on there with big George behind his chair was another red rag flaunted in the face of The Corner. Of course George was entirely in the rôle of a servant, but that did not lessen the insolence of Donnegan.

He saw the men who had no girl with them brighten at the announcement of the tag dance. And when the dance began he saw the prettiest girls tagged quickly, one after the other. All except Nelly Lebrun. She swung securely around the circle in the big arms of Jack Landis. She seemed to be set apart and protected from the common touch by his size, and by his formidable, challenging eye. Donnegan felt as never before the unassailable position of this fellow; not only from his own fighting qualities, but because he had behind him the whole unfathomable power of Lord Nick and his gang.

Nelly approached in the arms of Landis in making the first circle of the dance floor; her eyes, grown dull as she surrendered herself wholly to the rhythm of the waltz, saw nothing. They were blank as unlighted charcoal. She came opposite Donnegan; her back was toward him; she swung in the arms of Landis, and then, past the shoulder of her partner, she flashed a glance at Donnegan. The spark had fallen on the charcoal, and her eyes were aflame.

Aflame to Donnegan; the next instant the veil had dropped across her face once more.

She was carried on, leaving Donnegan tingling. A wise man upon whom that look had fallen might have seen, not Nelly Lebrun in the cheap dance hall, but Helen of Sparta and all Troy's dead. But Donnegan was clever, not wise. And he saw only Nelly Lebrun and the broad shoulders of Jack Landis.

Let the critic deal gently with Donnegan. He loved Lou Macon with all his heart and his soul, and yet because another beautiful girl had looked at him, there he sat at his table with his jaw set and the devil in his eye. And while she and Landis were whirling through the next circumference of the room, Donnegan was seeing all sides of the problem. If he tagged Landis it would be casting the glove in the face of the big man—and in the face of old Lebrun—and in the face of that mysterious and evil power, Lord Nick himself. And consider, that besides these he had already insulted all of The Corner.

Why not let things go on as they were? Suppose he were to allow Landis to plunge deeper into his infatuation? Suppose he were to bring Lou Macon to this place and let her see Landis sitting with Nelly, making love to her with every tone in his voice, every light in his eye? Would not that cure Lou? And would not that open the door to Donnegan?

And remember, in considering how Donnegan was tempted, that he was not a conscientious man. He was in fact what he seemed to me—a wanderer, a careless vagrant, living by his wits. For all this, he had been touched by the divine fire—a love that is

greater than self. And the more deeply he hated
Landis, the more profoundly he determined that he
should be discarded by Nelly and forced back to
Lou Macon. In the meantime Nelly and Jack were
coming again. They were close; they were passing;
and this time her eye had no spark for Donnegan.

Yet he rose from his table, reached the floor with
a few steps, and touched Landis lightly on the
shoulder. The challenge was passed. Landis stopped
abruptly and turned his head; his face showed merely
dull astonishment. The current of dancers split and
washed past on either side of the motionless trio,
and on every face there was a glittering curiosity.
What would Landis do?

Nothing. He was too stupefied to act. He, Jack
Landis, had actually been tagged while he was
dancing with the woman which all The Corner
knew to be his girl! And before his befogged senses
cleared the girl was in the arms of the red-haired
man and was lost in the crowd.

What a buzz went around the room! For a moment Landis could no more move than he could
think; then he sent a sullen glance toward the girl
and retreated to their table. A childish sullenness
clouded his face while he sat there; only one decision came clearly to him: he must kill Donnegan!

In the meantime people noted two things. The
first was that Donnegan danced very well with Nelly
Lebrun; and his red hair beside the silken black of
the girl's was a startling contrast. It was not a
common red. It flamed, as though with phosphoric
properties of its own. But they danced well; and
the eyes of both of them were gleaming. Another
thing: men did not tag Donnegan any more than
they had offered to tag Landis. One or two slipped

out from the outskirts of the floor, but something in the face of Donnegan discouraged them and made them turn elsewhere as though they had never started for Nelly Lebrun in the first place. Indeed, to a two-year-old child it would have been apparent that Nelly and the red-headed chap were interested in each other.

As a matter of fact they did not speak a single syllable until they had gone around the floor one complete turn and the dance was coming toward an end.

It was he who spoke first, gloomily: "I shouldn't have done it; I shouldn't have tagged him!"

At this she drew back a little so that she could meet his eyes.

"Why not?"

"The whole crew will be on my trail."

"What crew?"

"Beginning with Lord Nick!"

This shook her completely out of the thrall of the dance.

"Lord Nick? What makes you think that?"

"I know he's thick with Landis. It'll mean trouble."

He was so simple about it that she began to laugh. It was not such a voice as Lou Macon's. It was high and light, and one could suspect that it might become shrill under a stress.

"And yet it looks as though you've been hunting trouble," she said.

"I couldn't help it," said Donnegan naïvely.

It was a very subtle flattery, this frankness from a man who had puzzled all The Corner. Nelly Lebrun felt that she was about to look behind the scenes and she tingled with delight.

"Tell me," she said. "Why not?"

"Well," said Donnegan, "I had to make a noise because I wanted to be noticed."

She glanced about her; every eye was upon them.

"You've made your point," she murmured. "The whole town is talking of nothing else."

"I don't care an ounce of lead about the rest of the town."

"Then——"

She stopped abruptly, seeing toward what he was tending. And the heart of Nelly Lebrun fluttered for the first time in many a month. She believed him implicitly. It was for her sake that he had made all this commotion; to draw her attention. For every lovely girl, no matter how cool-headed, has a foolish belief in the power of her beauty. As a matter of fact Donnegan had told her the truth. It had all been to win her attention, from the fight for the mint to the tagging for the dance. How could she dream that it sprang out of anything other than a wild devotion to her? And while Donnegan coldly calculated every effect, Nelly Lebrun began to see in him the man of a dream, a spirit out of a dead age, a soul of knightly, reckless chivalry. In that small confession he cast a halo about himself which no other hand could ever remove entirely so far as Nelly Lebrun was concerned.

"You understand?" he was saying quietly.

She countered with a question as direct as his confession.

"What are you, Mr. Donnegan?"

"A wanderer," said Donnegan instantly, "and an avoider of work."

At that they laughed together. The strain was broken and in its place there was a mutual excitement. She saw Landis in the distance watching their laughter with a face contorted with anger, but it only increased her unreasoning happiness.

"Mr. Donnegan, let me give you friendly advice. I like you; I know you have courage; and I saw you meet Scar-faced Lewis. But if I were you I'd leave The Corner to-night and never come back. You've set every man against you. You've stepped on the toes of Landis and he's a big man here. And even if you were to prove too much for Jack you'd come against Lord Nick, as you say yourself. Do you know Nick?"

"No."

"Then, Mr. Donnegan, leave The Corner!"

The music, ending, left them face to face as he dropped his arm from about her. And she could appreciate now, for the first time, that he was smaller than he had seemed at a distance, or while he was dancing. He seemed a frail figure indeed to face the entire banded Corner—and Lord Nick.

"Don't you see," said Donnegan, "that I can't stop now?"

There was a double meaning that sent her color flaring.

He added in a low, tense voice. "I've gone too far. Besides, I'm beginning to hope!"

She paused, then made a little gesture of abandon.

"Then stay, stay!" she whispered with eyes on fire. "And good luck to you, Mr. Donnegan!"

# CHAPTER XXI

### HE STANDS IN PERIL

AS they went back, toward Nelly's table, where Jack Landis was trying to appear carelessly at ease, the face of Donnegan was pale. One might have thought that excitement and fear caused his pallor; but as a matter of fact it was in him an unfailing sign of happiness and success. Landis had manners enough to rise as they approached. He found himself being presented to the smaller man. He heard the cool, precise voice of Donnegan acknowledging the introduction; and then the red-headed man went back to his table and his negro; and Jack Landis was alone with Nelly Lebrun again.

He scowled at her, and she tried to look repentant; but since she could not keep the dancing light out of his eyes, she compromised by looking steadfastly down at the table. Which convinced Landis that she was thinking of her late partner. He made a great effort, swallowed, and was able to speak smoothly enough.

"Looked as if you were having a pretty good time with that—tramp."

The color in her cheeks was anger; Landis took it for shame.

"He dances beautifully," she replied.

"Yeh; he's pretty smooth. Take a gent like that, it's hard for a girl to see through him."

"Let's not talk about him, Jack."

"All right. Is he going to dance with you again?"

"I promised him the third dance after this."

For a time Landis could not trust his voice.

Then: "Kind of sorry about that. Because I'll be going home before then."

At this she raised her eyes for the first time. He was astonished and a little horrified to see that she was not in the least flustered, but very angry.

"You'll go home before I have a chance for that dance?" she asked. "You're acting like a two-year-old, Jack. You are!"

He flushed. Burning would be too easy a death for Donnegan.

"He's making a laughingstock out of me; look around the room!"

"Nobody's thinking about you at all, Jack. You're just self-conscious."

Of course, it was pouring acid upon an open wound. But she was past the point of caution.

"Maybe they ain't," said Landis, controlling his rage. "I don't figure that I amount to much. But I rate myself as high as a skunk like him!"

It may have been a smile that she gave him. At any rate, he caught the glint of teeth, and her eyes were as cold as steel points. If she had actually defended the stranger she would not have infuriated Landis so much.

"Well, what does he say about himself?"

"He says frankly that he's a vagrant."

"And you don't believe him?"

She did not speak.

"Makin' a play for sympathy. Confound a man like that, I say!"

Still she did not answer; and now Landis became alarmed.

"D'you really like him, Nelly?"

"I liked him well enough to introduce him to you, Jack."

"I'm sorry I talked so plain if you put it that way," he admitted heavily. "I didn't know you picked up friends so fast as all that!" He could not avoid adding this last touch of the poison point.

His back was to Donnegan, and consequently the girl, facing him, could look straight across the room at the red-headed man. She allowed herself one brief glance, and she saw that he was sitting with his elbow on the table, his chin in his hand, looking fixedly at her. It was the gaze of one who forgets all else and wraps himself in a dream. Other people in the room were noting that changeless stare and the whisper buzzed more and more loudly, but Donnegan had forgotten the rest of the world, it seemed. It was a very cunning piece of acting, not too much overdone, and once more the heart of Nelly Lebrun fluttered.

She remembered that in spite of his frankness he had not talked with insolent presumption to her. He had merely answered her individual questions with an astonishing, childlike frankness. He had laid his heart before her, it seemed. And now he sat at a distance looking at her with the white, intense face of one who sees a dream.

Nelly Lebrun was recalled by the heavy breathing of Jack Landis and she discovered that she had allowed her eyes to rest too long on the red-headed stranger. She had forgotten; her eyes had widened; and even Jack Landis was able to look into her mind and see things that startled him. For the first time he sensed that this was more than a careless flirtation. And he sat stiffly at the table, looking at her and through her with a fixed smile. Nelly, horrified, strove to cover her tracks.

"You're right, Jack," she said. "I—I think there

was something brazen in the way he tagged you.
And—let's go home together!"

Too late. The mind of Landis was not oversharp,
but now jealousy gave it a point. He nodded his
assent, and they got up, but there was no increase
in his color. She read as plain as day in his face
that he intended murder this night and Nelly was
truly frightened.

So she tried different tactics. All the way to
the substantial little house which Lebrun had built
at a little distance from the gambling hall, she kept
up a running fire of steady conversation. But when
she said good night to him, his face was still set.
She had not deceived him. When he turned, she
saw him go back into the night with long strides,
and within half an hour she knew, as clearly as if
she were remembering the picture instead of fore-
seeing it, that Jack and Donnegan would face each
other gun in hand on the floor of Milligan's dance
hall.

Still, she was not foolish enough to run after
Jack, take his arm, and make a direct appeal. It
would be too much like begging for Donnegan, and
even if Jack forgave her for this interest in his rival,
she had sense enough to feel that Donnegan himself
never would. Something, however, must be done to
prevent the fight, and she took the straightest course.

She went as fast as a run would carry her straight
behind the intervening houses and came to the back
entrance to the gaming hall. There she entered and
stepped into the little office of her father. "Black"
Lebrun was not there. She did not want him. In
his place there sat The Pedlar and Joe Rix; they
were members of Lord Nick's chosen crew, and since
Nick's temporary alliance with Lebrun for the sake

of plundering Jack Landis, Nick's men were Nelly's men. Indeed, this was a formidable pair. They were the kind of men about whom many whispers and no facts circulate; and yet the facts are far worse than the whispers. It was said that Joe Rix. who was a fat little man with a great aversion to a razor and a pair of shallow, pale blue eyes, was in reality a merciless fiend. He was; and he was more than that, if there be a stronger superlative. If Lord Nick had dirty work to be done, there was the man who did it with a relish. The Pedlar, on the other hand, was an exact opposite. He was long, lean, raw-boned, and prodigiously strong in spite of his lack of flesh. He had vast hands, all loose skin and outstanding tendons; he had a fleshless face over which his smile was capable of extending limitlessly. He was the sort of a man from whom one would expect shrewdness, some cunning, stubbornness, a dry humor, and many principles. All of which, except the last, was true of The Pedlar.

There was this peculiarity about The Pedlar. In spite of his broad grins and his wise, bright eyes, none, even of Lord Nick's gang, extended a friendship or familiarity toward him. When they spoke of The Pedlar they never used his name. They referred to him as "him" or they indicated him with gestures. If he had a fondness for any living creature it was for fat Joe Rix.

Yet on seeing this ominous pair, Nelly Lebrun cried out softly in delight. She ran to them, and dropped a hand on the bony shoulder of The Pedlar and one on the plump shoulder of Joe Rix, whose loose flesh rolled under her finger tips.

"It's Jack Landis!" she cried. "He's gone to Milligan's to fight the new man. Stop him!"

"Donnegan?" said Joe, and did not rise.

"Him?" said The Pedlar, and moistened his broad lips like one on the verge of starvation.

"Are you going to sit here?" she cried. "What will Lord Nick say if he finds out you've let Jack get into a fight."

"We ain't nursin' mothers," declared The Pedlar. "But I'd kind of like to look on!"

And he rose. Unkinking joint after joint, straightening his legs, his back, his shoulders, his neck, he soared up and up until he stood a prodigious height. The girl controlled a shudder of disgust.

"Joe!" she appealed.

"You want us to clean up Donnegan?" he asked, rising, but without interest in his voice.

To his surprise, she slipped back to the door and blocked it with her outcast arms.

"Not a hair of his head!" she said fiercely. "Swear that you won't harm him, boys!"

"What the devil!" ejaculated Joe, who was a blunt man in spite of his fat. "You want us to keep Jack from fightin', but you don't want us to hurt the other gent. What you want? Hog-tie 'em both?"

"Yes, yes; keep Jack out of Milligan's; but for Heaven's sake don't try to put a hand on Donnegan."

"Why not?"

"For your sakes; he'd kill you, Joe!"

At this they both gaped in unison, and as one man they drawled in vast admiration: "Good heavens!"

"But go, go, go!" cried the girl.

And she shoved them through the door and into the night.

# CHAPTER XXII

## HE RECEIVES A BLOW

TO the people in Milligan's it had been most inchedible that Jack Landis should withdraw from a competition of any sort. And though the girls were able to understand his motives in taking Nelly Lebrun away they were not able to explain this fully to their men companions. For one and all they admitted that Jack was imperiling his hold on the girl in question if he allowed her to stay near this red-headed fiend. But one and all they swore that Jack Landis had ruined himself with her by taking her away. And this was a paradox which made masculine heads in The Corner spin. The main point was that big Jack Landis had backed down before a rival; and this fact was stunning enough. Donnegan, however, was not confused. He sent big George to ask Milligan to come to him for a moment.

Milligan, at this, cursed George for a "no-good nigger," but he was drawn by curiosity to consent. A moment later he was seated at Donnegan's table, drinking his own liquor as it was served to him from the hands of the negro. If the first emotion of the dance-hall proprietor were anger and intense curiosity, his second emotion was that never-failing surprise, which all who came close to the wanderer felt. For he had that rare faculty of seeming larger when in action, even when actually near much bigger men. Only when one came close to Donnegan one stepped, as it were, through a veil, and saw the almost fragile reality. When Milligan had caught his breath and adjusted himself, he began as follows:

"Now, Bud," he said, "you've made a pretty play. Not bad at all. But no more bluffs in Milligan's."

"Bluff!" Donnegan repeated gently.

"About the nigger. I let it pass for one night, but not for another."

"My dear Mr. Milligan! However"—changing the subject easily—"what I wish to speak to you about is a bit of trouble which I foresee. I think, sir, that Jack Landis is coming back."

"What makes you think that?"

"It's a feeling I have. I have queer premonitions, Mr. Milligan. I'm sure he's coming and I'm sure he's going to attempt a murder."

Milligan's thick lips framed his question but he did not speak; fear made his face ludicrous.

"Right here?"

"Yes."

"A shootin' scrape here! You?"

"He has me in mind. That's why I'm speaking to you."

"Don't wait to speak to me about it. Get up and get out!"

"Mr. Milligan, you're wrong. I'm going to stay here and you're going to protect me."

"Well, confound your soul! They ain't much nerve about you, is there?"

"You run a public place. You have to protect your patrons from insult."

"And who began it, then? Who started walkin' on Jack's toes? Now you come whinin' to me! By heck, I hope Jack gets you!"

"You're a genial soul," said Donnegan. "Here's to you!"

But something in his smile as he sipped his liquor made Milligan sit straighter in his chair.

As for Donnegan, he was thinking hard and fast. If there were a shooting affair and he won, he would nevertheless run a close chance of being hung by a mob. He must dispose that mob to look upon him as the defendant and Landis as the aggressor. He had foreseen the crisis until it was fairly upon him. He had thought of Nelly playing Landis along more gradually and carefully, so that, while he was slowly learning that she was growing cold to him, he would have a chance to grow fond of Lou Macon once more. But even across the width of the room he had seen the girl fire up, and from that moment he knew the result. Landis already suspected him; Landis, with the feeling that he had been robbed, would do his best to kill the thief. He might take a chance with Landis, if it came to a fight, just as he had taken a chance with Lewis. But how different this case would be! Landis was no dull-nerved ruffian and drunkard. He was a keen boy with a hair-trigger balance, and in a gunplay he would be apt to beat the best of them all. Of all this Donnegan was fully aware. Either he must place his own life in terrible hazard or else he must shoot to kill; and if he killed, what of Lou Macon?

While he smiled into the face of Milligan, perspiration was bursting out under his armpits.

"Mr. Milligan, I implore you to give me your aid."

"What's the difference?" Milligan asked in a changed tone. "If he don't fight you here he'll fight you later."

"You're wrong, Mr. Milligan. He isn't the sort

to hold malice.  He'll come here to-night and try to
get at me like a bulldog straining on a leash.  If
he is kept away he'll get over his bad temper."

Milligan pushed back his chair.

"You've tried to force yourself down the throat
of The Corner," he said, "and now you yell for
help when you see the teeth."

He had raised his voice.  Now he got up and
strode noisily away.  Donnegan waited until he was
halfway across the dance floor and then rose in turn.

"Gentlemen," he said.

The quiet voice cut into every conversation; the
musicians lowered the instruments.

"I have just told Mr. Milligan that I am sure
Jack Landis is coming back here to try to kill me.
I have asked for his protection.  He has refused it.
I intend to stay here and wait for him, Jack Landis.
In the meantime I ask any able-bodied man who will
do so, to try to stop Landis when he enters."

He sat down, raised his glass, and sipped the
drink.  Two hundred pairs of eyes were fastened
with hawklike intensity upon him, and they could
perceive no quiver of his hand.

The sipping of his liquor was not an affectation.
For he was drinking, at incredible cost, liquors from
Milligan's bootlegged store of rareties.  They had
traveled an underground route to come to Milligan's
and he put a comfortable tax upon the prohibited
liquor.

The effect of Donnegan's announcement was first
a silence, then a hum, then loud voices of protest,
curiosity—and finally a scurrying toward the doors.

Yet really very few, outside of women, left.  The
rest valued a chance to see the fight beyond fear of
random slugs of lead which might fly their way.

Besides, where such men as Donnegan and big Jack Landis were concerned, there was not apt to be much wild shooting. The dancing stopped, of course. The music was ordered by Milligan to play, in a frantic endeavor to rouse custom again; but the music of its own accord fell away in the middle of the piece. For the musicians could not watch the notes and the door at the same time.

As for Donnegan, he found that it was one thing to wait and another to be waited for. He, too, wished to turn and watch that door until it should be filled by the bulk of Jack Landis. Yet he fought the desire.

And in the midst of this torturing suspense an idea came to him, and at the same instant Jack Landis entered the doorway. He stood there looking vast against the night. One glance around was sufficient to teach him the meaning of the silence. The stage was set, and the way opened to Donnegan. Without a word, big George stole to one side.

Straight to the middle of the dance floor went Jack Landis, red-faced, with long, heavy steps. He faced Donnegan.

"You skunk!" shouted Landis. "I've come for you!"

And he went for his gun. Donnegan, too, stirred. But when the revolver leaped into the hand of Landis, it was seen that the hands of Donnegan rose past the line of his waist, past his shoulders, and presently locked easily behind his head. A terrible chance, for Landis had come within a breath of shooting. So great was the impulse that, as he checked the pressure of his forefinger, he stumbled a whole pace forward. He walked on.

"You need cause to fight?" he cried, striking Donnegan across the face with the back of his left hand, jerking up the muzzle of the gun in his right.

Now a dark trickle was seen to come from the broken lips of Donnegan, yet he was smiling faintly.

Jack Landis muttered a curse and said sneeringly: "Are you afraid?"

There were sick faces in that room; men turned their heads, for nothing is so ghastly as the sight of a man who is taking water.

"Hush," said Donnegan. "I'm going to kill you, Jack. But I want to kill you fairly and squarely. There's no pleasure, you see, in beating a youngster like you to the draw. I want to give you a fighting chance. Besides"—he removed one hand from behind his head and waved it carelessly to where the men of The Corner crouched in the shadow—"you people have seen me drill one chap already, and I'd like to shoot you in a new way. Is that agreeable?"

Two terrible, known figures detached themselves from the gloom near the door.

"Hark to this gent sing," said one, and his name was The Pedlar. "Hark to him sing, Jack, and we'll see that you get fair play."

"Good," said his friend, Joe Rix. "Let him take his try, Jack."

As a matter of fact, had Donnegan reached for a gun, he would have been shot before even Landis could bring out a weapon, for the steady eye of Joe Rix, hidden behind The Pedlar, had been looking down a revolver barrel at the forehead of Donnegan, waiting for that first move. But something about the coolness of Donnegan fascinated them.

"Don't shoot, Joe," The Pedlar had said. "That bird is the chief over again. Don't plug him!"

And that was why Donnegan lived.

# CHAPTER XXIII

### HE FIGHTS

IF he had taken the eye of the hardened Rix and the still harder Pedlar, he had stunned the men of The Corner. And breathlessly they waited for his proposal to Jack Landis.

He spoke with his hands behind his head again, after he had slowly taken out a handkerchief and wiped his chin.

"I'm a methodical fellow, Landis," he said. "I hate to do an untidy piece of work. I have been disgusted with myself since my little falling out with Lewis. I intended to shoot him cleanly through the hand, but instead of that I tore up his whole forearm. Sloppy work, Landis. I don't like it. Now, in meeting you. I want to do a clean, neat, precise job. One that I'll be proud of."

A moaning voice was heard faintly in the distance. It was The Pedlar, who had wrapped himself in his gaunt arms and was crooning softly, with unspeakable joy: "Hark to him sing! Hark to him sing! A ringer for the chief!"

"Why should we be in such a hurry?" continued Donnegan. "You see that clock in the corner? Tut, tut! Turn your head and look. Do you think I'll drop you while you look around?"

Landis flung one glance over his shoulder at the big clock, whose pendulum worked solemnly back and forth.

"In five minutes," said Donnegan, "it will be

eleven o'clock. And when it's eleven o'clock the clock will chime. Now, Landis, you and I shall sit down here like gentlemen and drink our liquor and think our last thoughts. Heavens, man, is there anything more disagreeable than being hurried out of life? But when the clock chimes, we draw our guns and shoot each other through the heart—the brain —wherever we have chosen. But, Landis, if one of us should inadvertently—or through nervousness— beat the clock's chime by the split part of a second, the good people of The Corner will fill that one of us promptly full of lead."

He turned to the crowd.

"Gentlemen, is it a good plan?"

As well as a Roman crowd if it wanted to see a gladiator die, the frayed nerves of The Corner responded to the stimulus of this delightful entertainment. There was a joyous chorus of approval.

"When the clock strikes, then," said Landis, and flung himself down in a chair, setting his teeth over his rage.

Donnegan smiled benevolently upon him; then he turned again and beckoned to the negro. Big George strode closer and leaned.

"George," he said, "I'm not going to kill this fellow."

"No, sir; certainly, sir," whispered the other. "George can kill him for you, sir."

Donnegan smiled wanly.

"I'm not going to kill him, George, on account of the girl on the hill. You know? And the reason is that she's fond of the lubber. I'll try to break his nerve, George, and drill him through the arm, say. No, I can't take chances like that. But if I have him shaking in time, I'll shoot him through the right shoulder, George.

"But if I miss and he gets me instead, mind you, never raise a hand against him. If you so much as touch his skin, I'll rise out of my grave and haunt you white. You hear? Good-by, George."

But big George withdrew without a word, and the reason for his speechlessness was the glistening of his eyes.

"If I live," said Donnegan, "I'll show that George that I appreciate him."

He went on aloud to Landis: "So glum, my boy? Tush! We have still four minutes left. Are you going to spend your last four minutes hating me?"

He turned: "Another liqueur, George. Two of them."

The negro brought the drinks, and having put one on the table of Donnegan, he was directed to take the other to Landis.

"It's really good stuff," said Donnegan. "I'm not an expert on these matters; but I like the taste. Will you try it?"

It seemed that Landis dared not trust himself to speech. As though a vast and deadly hatred were gathered in him, and he feared lest it should escape in words the first time he parted his teeth.

He took the glass of liqueur and slowly poured it upon the floor. From the crowd there was a deep murmur of disapproval. And Landis, feeling that he had advanced the wrong foot in the matter, glowered scornfully about him and then stared once more at Donnegan.

"Just as you please," said Donnegan, sipping his glass. "But remember this, my young friend, that a fool is a fool, drunk or sober."

Landis showed his teeth, but made no other answer. And Donnegan anxiously flashed a glance at the clock. He still had three minutes. Three minutes in which he must reduce this stalwart fellow to a trembling, nervous wreck. Otherwise, he must shoot to kill, or else sit there and become a certain sacrifice for the sake of Lou Macon. Yet he controlled the muscles of his face and was still able to smile as he turned again to Landis.

"Three minutes left," he said. "Three minutes for you to compose yourself, Landis. Think of it, man! All the good life behind you. Have you nothing to remember? Nothing to soften your mind? Why die, Landis, with a curse in your heart and a scowl on your lips?"

Once more Landis stirred his lips; but there was only the flash of his teeth; he maintained his resolute silence.

"Ah," murmured Donnegan, "I am sorry to see this. And before all your admirers, Landis. Before all your friends. Look at them scattered there under the lights and in the shadows. No farewell word for them? Nothing kindly to say? Are you going to leave them without a syllable of goodfellowship?"

"Confound you!" muttered Landis.

There was another hum from the crowd; it was partly wonder, partly anger. Plainly they were not pleased with Jack Landis on this day.

Donnegan shook his head sadly.

"I hoped," he said, "that I could teach you how to die. But I fail. And yet you should be grateful to me for one thing, Jack. I have kept you from being a murderer in cold blood. I kept you from killing a defenseless man as you intended to do when you walked up to me a moment ago."

He smiled genially in mockery, and there was a scowl on the face of Landis.

"Two minutes," said Donnegan.

Leaning back in his chair, he yawned. For a whole minute he did not stir.

"One minute?" he murmured inquisitively.

And there was a convulsive shudder through the limbs of Landis. It was the first sign that he was breaking down under the strain. There remained only one minute in which to reduce him to a nervous wreck!

The strain was telling in other places. Donnegan turned and saw in the shadow and about the edges of the room a host of drawn, tense faces and burning eyes. Never while they lived would they forget that scene.

"And now that the time is close," said Donnegan, "I must look to my gun."

He made a gesture; how it was, no one was swift enough of eye to tell, but a gun appeared in his hand. At the flash of it, Landis' weapon leaped up to the mark and his face convulsed. But Donnegan calmly spun the cylinder of his revolver and held it toward Landis, dangling from his forefinger under the guard.

"You see?" he said to Landis. "Clean as a whistle, and easy as a girl's smile. I hate a stiff action, Jack."

And Landis slowly allowed the muzzle of his own gun to sink. For the first time his eyes left the eyes of Donnegan, and sinking, inch by inch, stared fascinated at the gun in the hand of the enemy.

"Thirty seconds," said Donnegan by way of conversation.

Landis jerked up his head and his eyes once

more met the eyes of Donnegan, but this time they were wide, and the pointed glance of Donnegan sank into them. The lips of Landis parted. His tongue tremblingly moistened them.

"Keep your nerve," said Donnegan in an undertone.

"You hound!" gasped Landis.

"I knew it," said Donnegan sadly. "You'll die with a curse on your lips."

He added: "Ten seconds, Landis!"

And then he achieved his third step toward victory, for Landis jerked his head around, saw the minute hand almost upon its mark, and swung back with a shudder toward Donnegan. From the crowd there was a deep breath.

And then Landis was seen to raise the muzzle of his gun again, and crouch over it, leveling it straight at Donnegan. He, at least, would send his bullet straight to the mark when that first chime went humming through the big room.

But Donnegan? He made his last play to shatter the nerve of Landis. With the minute hand on the very mark, he turned carelessly, the revolver still dangling by the trigger guard, and laughed toward the crowd.

And out of the crowd there came a deep, sobbing breath of heart-breaking suspense.

It told on Landis. Out of the corner of his eye Donnegan saw the muscles of the big man's face sag and tremble; saw him allow his gun to fall, in imitation of Donnegan to his side; and saw the long arm quivering.

And then the chime rang, with a metalic, sharp click and then a long and reverberant clanging.

With a gasp Landis whipped up his gun and fired.

Once, twice, again, the weapon crashed. And, to
the eternal wonder of all who saw it, at a distance
of five paces Landis three times missed his man.
But Donnegan, sitting back with a smile, raised his
own gun almost with leisure, unhurried, dropped it
upon the mark, and sent a forty-five slug through
the right shoulder of Jack Landis.

The blow of the slug, lke the punch of a strong
man's fist, knocked the victim out of his chair to the
floor. He lay clutching at his shoulder.

"Gentlemen," said Donnegan, rising, "is there a
doctor here?"

# CHAPTER XXIV

### HE SEES THE DEVIL AGAIN

THAT was the signal for the rush that swept across the floor and left a flood of marveling men around the fallen Landis. On the outskirts of this tide, Donnegan stepped up to two men, Joe Rix and The Pedlar. They greeted him with expectant glances.

"Gentlemen," said Donnegan, "will you step aside?"

They followed him to a distance from the clamoring group.

"I have to thank you," said Donnegan.

"For what?"

"For changing your minds," said Donnegan, and left them.

And afterward The Pedlar murmured with an oddly twisted face: "Cat-eye, Joe. He can see in the dark! But I told you he was worth savin'."

"Speakin' in general," said Joe, "which you ain't hardly ever wrong when you get stirred up about a thing."

"He's something new," The Pedlar said wisely.

"Ay, he's rare."

"But talkin' aside, suppose he was to meet up with Lord Nick?"

The smile of Joe Rix was marvelously evil.

"You got a great mind for great things," he declared. "You ought to of been in politics."

In the meantime the doctor had been found. The

wound had been cleansed. It was a cruel one, for the bullet had torn its way through flesh and sinew, and for many a week the fighting arm of Jack Landis would be useless. It had, moreover, carried a quantity of cloth into the wound, and it was almost impossible to cleanse the hole satisfactorily. As for the bullet itself, it had whipped cleanly through, at that short distance making nothing of its target.

A door was knocked off its hinges. But before the wounded man was placed upon it, Lebrun appeared at the door into Milligan's. He was never a very cheery fellow in appearance, and now he looked like a demoniac. He went straight to Joe Rix and the skeleton form of The Pedlar. He raised one finger as he looked at them.

"I've heard," said Lebrun. "Lord Nick likewise shall hear."

Joe Rix changed color. He bustled about, together with The Pedlar, and lent a hand in carrying the wounded man to the house of Lebrun, for Nelly Lebrun was to be the nurse of Landis.

In the meantime, Donnegan went up the hill with big George behind him. Already he was a sinisterly marked man. Working through the crowd near Lebrun's gambling hall, a drunkard in the midst of a song stumbled against him. But the sight of the man with whom he had collided, sobered him as swiftly as the lash of a whip across his face. It was impossible for him, in that condition, to grow pale. But he turned a vivid purple.

"Sorry, Mr. Donnegan."

Donnegan, with a shrug of his shoulders, passed on. The crowd split before him, for they had heard his name. There were brave men, he knew, among them. Men who would fight to the last drop of blood rather than be shamed, but they shrank from Donnegan without shame, as they would have shrunk from the coming of a rattler had their feet been bare. So he went easily through the crowd with big George in his wake, walking proudly.

For George was making large discoveries, among which not the least was the fact that it might be a far prouder thing to be the servant of one man than to be free himself. He had stood to one side and watched Donnegan indomitably beat down the will of Jack Landis, and the sight would live in the mind of George forever. Indeed, if his master had bidden the sun to stand in the heavens, the big negro would have looked for obedience. That the forbearance of Donnegan should have been based on a desire to serve a girl certainly upset the mind of George, but it taught him an amazing thing—that Donnegan was capable of affection.

The terrible Donnegan went on. In his wake the crowd closed slowly, for many had paused to look after the little man. Until they came to the outskirts of the town and climbed the hill toward the two shacks. The one was, of course, dark. But the shack in which Lou Macon lived burst with light. Donnegan paused to consider this miracle. He listened, and he heard voices—the voice of a man, laughing loudly. Thinking something was wrong, he hurried forward and called loudly.

What he saw when he was admitted made him speechless. Colonel Macon, ensconced in his invalid chair, faced the door, and near him was Lou Macon. Lou rose, half frightened by the unexpected interruption, but the liquid laughter of the colonel set all to rights at once.

"Come in, Donnegan. Come in, lad," said the colonel.

"I heard a man's voice," Donnegan said half apologetically. The sick color began to leave his face, and relief swept over it slowly. "I thought something might be wrong. I didn't think of you." And looking down, as all men will in moments of relaxation from a strain, he did not see the eyes of Lou Macon grow softly luminous as they dwelt upon him.

"Come in, George," went on the colonel, "and make yourself comfortable in the kitchen. Close the door. Sit down, Donnegan. When your letter came I saw that I was needed here. Lou, have you looked into our friend's cabin? No? Nothing like a woman's touch to give a man the feeling of home-liness, Lou. Step over to Donnegan's cabin and put it to rights. Yes, I know that George takes care of it, but George is one thing, and your care will be another. Besides, I must be alone with him for a moment. Man talk confuses a girl, Lou. You shouldn't listen to it."

She withdrew with that faint, dreamy smile with which she so often heard the instructions of her father; as though she were only listening with half of her mind. When she was gone, though the door to the kitchen stood wide open, and big George was in it, the colonel lowered his bass voice so success-fully that it was as safe as being alone with Donne-gan.

"And now for facts," he began.

"But," said Donnegan, "how—that chair—how in the world have you come here?"

The colonel shook his head.

"My dear boy, you grieve and disappoint me. The

manner in which a thing is done is not important. Mysteries are usually simply explained. As for my small mystery—a neighbor on the way to The Corner with a wagon stopped in, and I asked him to take me along. So here I am. But now for your work here, lad?"

"Bad," said Donnegan.

"I gathered you had been unfortunate. And now you have been fighting?"

"You have heard?"

"I see it in your eye, Donnegan. When a man has been looking fear in the face for a time, an image of it remains in his eyes. They are wider, glazed with the other thing."

"It was forced on me," said Donnegan. "I have shot Landis."

He was amazed to see the colonel was vitally affected. His lips remained parted over his next word, and one eyelid twitched violently. But the spasm passed over quickly. When he raised his perfect hands and pressed them together just under his chin. He smiled in a most winning manner that made the blood of Donnegan run cold.

"Donnegan," he said softly, "I see that I have misjudged you. I underestimated you. I thought, indeed, that your rare qualities were qualified by painful weaknesses. But now I see that you are a man, and from this moment we shall act together with open minds. So you have done it? Tush, then I need not have taken my trip. The work is done; the mines come to me as the heir of Jack. And yet, poor boy, I pity him! He misjudged me; he should not have ventured to this deal with Lord Nick and his compatriots!"

"Wait," exclaimed Donnegan. "You're wrong; Landis is not dead."

Once more the colonel was checked, but this time the alteration in his face was no more than a comma's pause in a long balanced sentence. It was impossible to obtain more than one show of emotion from him in a single conversation.

"Not dead? Well, Donnegan, that is unfortunate. And after you had punctured him you had no chance to send home the finishing shot?"

Donnegan merely watched the colonel and tapped his bony finger against the point of his chin.

"Ah," murmured the colonel, "I see another possibility. It is almost as good—it may even be better than his death. You have disabled him, and having done this you at once take him to a place where he shall be under your surveillance—this, in fact, is a very comfortable outlook—for me and my interests. But for you, Donnegan, how the devil do you benefit by having Jack flat on his back, sick, helpless, and in a perfect position to excite all the sympathies of Lou?"

Now, Donnegan had known cold-blooded men in his day, but that there existed such a man as the colonel had never come into his mind. He looked upon the colonel, therefore, with neither disgust nor anger, but with a distant and almost admiring wonder. For perfect evil always wins something akin to admiration from more common people.

"Well," continued the colonel, a little uneasy under this silent scrutiny—silence was almost the only thing in the world that could trouble him—"well, Donnegan, my lad, this is your plan, is it not?"

"To shoot down Landis, then take possession of him and while I nurse him back to health hold a gun—metaphorically speaking—to his head and make him do as I please: sign some lease, say, of the mines to you?"

The colonel shifted himself to a more comfortable position in his chair, brought the tips of his fingers together under his vast chin, and smiled benevolently upon Donnegan.

"It is as I thought," he murmured. "Donnegan, you are rare; you are exquisite!"

"And you," said Donnegan, "are a scoundrel."

"Exactly. I am very base." The colonel laughed. "You and I alone can speak with intimate knowledge of me." His chuckle shook all his body, and set the folds of his face quivering. His mirth died away when he saw Donnegan come to his feet.

"Eh?" he called.

"Good-by," said Donnegan.

"But where—Landis—— Donnegan, what devil is in your eye?"

"A foolish devil, Colonel Macon. I surrender the benefits of all my work for you and go to make sure that you do not lay your hands upon Jack Landis."

The colonel opened and closed his lips foolishly like a fish gasping silently out of water. It was rare indeed for the colonel to appear foolish.

"In Heaven's name, Donnegan!"

The little man smiled. He had a marvelously wicked smile, which came from the fact that his lips could curve while his eyes remained bright and straight, and malevolently unwrinkled. He laid his hand on the knob of the door.

"Donnegan," cried the colonel, gray of face, "give me one minute."

## CHAPTER XXV

### HE PASSES THROUGH THE FIRE

DONNEGAN stepped to a chair and sat down. He took out his watch and held it in his hand, studying the dial, and the colonel knew that his time limit was taken literally.

"I swear to you," he said, "that if you can help me to the possession of Landis while he is ill, I shall not lay a finger upon him or harm him in any way."

"You swear?" said Donnegan with that ugly smile.

"My dear boy, do you think I am reckless enough to break a promise I have given to *you?*"

The cynical glance of Donnegan probed the colonel to the heart, but the eyes of the fat man did not wince. Neither did he speak again, but the two calmly stared at each other. At the end of the minute, Donnegan slipped the watch into his pocket.

"I am ready to listen to reason," he said. And the colonel passed one of his strong hands across his forehead.

"Now," and he sighed, "I feel that the crisis is passed. With a man of your caliber, Donnegan, I fear a snap judgment above all things. Since you give me a chance to appeal to your reason I feel safe. As from the first, I shall lay my cards upon the table. You are fond of Lou. I took it for granted that you would welcome a chance to brush Landis out of your path. It appears that I am wrong. I admit my error. Only fools cling to convictions; wise men are ready to meet new viewpoints. Very well. You wish to spare Landis for reasons of your own which I do not pretend to fathom. Perhaps, you pity him; I cannot tell. Now, you wonder why I wish to have Landis in my care if I do not intend to put an end to him and thereby become owner of his mines? I shall tell you frankly. I intend to own the mines, if not through the death of Jack, then through a legal act signed by the hand of Jack."

"A willing signature?" asked Donnegan, calmly.

A shadow came and went across the face of the colonel, and Donnegan caught his breath. There were times when he felt that if the colonel possessed strength of body as well as strength of mind even he, Donnegan, would be afraid of the fat man.

"Willing or unwilling," said the colonel, "he shall do as I direct!"

"Without force?"

"Listen to me," said the colonel. "You and I are not children, and therefore we know that ordinary men are commanded rather by fear of what may happen to them than by being confronted with an actual danger. I have told you that I shall not so much as raise the weight of a finger against Jack Landis. I shall not. But a whisper adroitly put in his ear may accomplish the same ends." He added with a smile. "Personally, I dislike physical violence. In that, Mr. Donnegan, we belong to opposite schools of action."

The picture came to Donnegan of Landis, lying in the cabin of the colonel, his childish mind worked upon by the devilish insinuation of the colonel.

Truly, if Jack did not go mad under the strain he would be very apt to do as the colonel wished.

"I have made a mess of this from the beginning," said Donnegan, quietly. "In the first place, I intended to play the rôle of the self-sacrificing. You don't understand? I didn't expect that you would. In short, I intended to send Landis back to Lou by making a flash that would dazzle The Corner, and dazzle Nelly Lebrun as well—win her away from Landis, you see? But the fool, as soon as he saw that I was flirting with the girl, lowered his head and charged at me like a bull. I had to strike him down in self-defense.

"But now you ask me to put him wholly in your possession. Colonel, you omit one link in your chain of reasoning. The link is important—to me. What am I to gain by placing him within the range of your whispering?"

"Tush! Do I need to tell you? I still presume you are interested in Lou, though you attempted to do so much to give Landis back to her. Well, Donnegan, you must know that when she learns it was a bullet from your gun that struck down Landis, she'll hate you, my boy, as if you were a snake. But if she knows that after all you were forced into the fight, and that you took the first opportunity to bring Jack into my—er—paternal care—her sentiments may change. No, they *will* change."

Donnegan left his chair and began to pace the floor. He was no more self-conscious in the presence of the colonel than a man might be in the presence of his own evil instincts. And it was typical of the colonel's insight that he made no attempt to influence the decision of Donnegan after this point was reached. He allowed him to work out the matter in his own way. At length, Donnegan paused.

"What's the next step?" he asked.

The colonel sighed, and by that sigh he admitted more than words could tell.

"A reasonable man," he said, "is the delight of my heart. The next step, Donnegan, is to bring Jack Landis to this house."

"Tush!" said Donnegan. "Bring him away from Lebrun? Bring him away from the tigers of Lord Nick's gang? I saw them at Milligan's place to-night. A bad shot, Colonel Macon."

"A set you can handle," said the colonel, calmly.

"Ah?"

"The danger will in itself be the thing that tempts you," he went on. "To go among those fellows, wild as they are, and bring Jack Landis away to this house."

"Bring him here," said Donnegan with indescribable bitterness, "so that she may pity his wounds? Bring him here where she may think of him and tend him and grow to hate me?"

"Grow to fear you," said the colonel.

"An excellent thing to accomplish," said Donnegan coldly.

"I have found it so," remarked the colonel, and lighted a cigarette.

He drew the smoke so deep that when it issued again from between his lips it was a most transparent, bluish vapor. Fear came upon Donnegan. Not fear, surely, of the fat man, helpless in his invalid's chair, but fear of the mind working ceaselessly behind those hazy eyes. He turned without a word and went to the door. The moment it opened under his hand, he felt an hysterical impulse

to leap out of the room swiftly and slam the door
behind him—to put a bar between him and the eye
of the colonel, just as a child leaps from the dark
room into the lighted and closed the door quickly to
keep out the following night. He had to compel
himself to move with proper dignity.

When outside, he sighed; the quiet of the night
was like a blessing compared with the ordeal of the
colonel's devilish coldness. Macon's advice had
seemed almost logical the moment before. Win Lou
Macon by the power of fear, well enough, for was
not fear the thing which she had followed all her
life? Was it not through fear that the colonel himself had reduced her to such abject, unquestioning
obedience?

He went thoughtfully to his own cabin, and, down-
headed in his musings, he became aware with a
start of Lou Macon in the hut. She had changed
the room as her father had bidden her to do. Just
wherein the difference lay, Donnegan could not tell.
There was a touch of evergreen in one corner; she
had laid a strip of bright cloth over the rickety little
table, and in ten minutes she had given the hut a
semblance of permanent livableness. Donnegan saw
her now, with some vestige of the smile of her art
upon her face; but she immediately smoothed it to
perfect gravity. He had never seen such perfect
self-command in a woman.

"Is there anything more that I can do?" she
asked, moving toward the door.

"Nothing."

"Good night."

"Wait."

She still seemed to be under the authority which
the colonel had delegated to Donnegan when they

started for The Corner. She turned, and without a word came back to him. And a pang struck through Donnegan. What would he not have given if she had come at his call not with these dumb eyes, but with a spark of kindliness? Instead, she obeyed him as a soldier obeys a commander.

"There has been trouble," said Donnegan.

"Yes?" she said, but there was no change in her face.

"It was forced upon me." Then he added: "It amounted to a shooting affair."

There was a change in her face now, indeed. A glint came in her eyes, and the suggestion of the colonel which he had once or twice before sensed in her, now became more vivd than ever before. The same contemptuous heartlessness, which was the colonel's most habitual expression, now looked at Donnegan out of the lovely face of the girl.

"They were fools to press you to the wall," she said. "I have no pity for them."

For a moment Donnegan only stared at her; on what did she base her confidence in his prowess as a fighting man?

"It was only one man," he said huskily.

Ah, there he had struck her home! As though the words were a burden, she shrank from him; then she slipped suddenly close to him and caught both his hands. Her head was raised far back; she had pressed close to him; she seemed in every line of her body to plead with him against himself, and all the veils which had curtained her mind from him dropped away. He found himself looking down into eyes full of fire and shadow; and eager lips; and the fiber of her voice made her whole body tremble.

"It isn't Jack?" she pleaded. "It isn't Jack that you've fought with?"

And he said to himself: "She loves him with all her heart and soul!"

"It is he," said Donnegan in an agony. Pain may be like a fire that tempers some strong men; and now Donnegan, because he was in torment, smiled, and his eye was as cold as steel.

The girl flung away his hands.

"You bought murderer!" she cried at him.

"He is not dead."

"But you shot him down!"

"He attacked me; it was self-defense."

She broke into a low-pitched, mirthless laughter. Where was the filmy-eyed girl he had known? The laughter broke off short—like a sob.

"Don't you suppose I've known?" she said. "That I've read my father? That I knew he was sending a bloodhound when he sent you? But, oh, I thought you had a touch of the other thing!"

He cringed under her tone.

"I'll bring him to you," said Donnegan desperately. "I'll bring him here so that you can take care of him."

"You'll take him away from Lord Nick—and Lebrun—and the rest?" And it was the cold smile of her father with which she mocked him.

"I'll do it."

"You play a deep game," said the girl bitterly. "Why would you do it?"

"Because," said Donnegan faintly, "I love you."

Her hand had been on the knob of the door; now she twitched it open and was gone; and the last that Donnegan saw was the width of the startled eyes.

"As if I were a leper," muttered Donnegan. "By Heaven, she looked at me as if I were unclean!"

But once outside the door, the girl stood with both hands pressed to her face, stunned. When she dropped them, they folded against her breast, and her face tipped up.

Even by starlight, had Donnegan been there to look, he would have seen the divinity which comes in the face of a woman when she loves.

# CHAPTER XXVI

## HE HUNTS TROUBLE

HAD he been there to see, even in the darkness he would have known, and he could have crossed the distance between their lives with a single step, and taken her into his heart. But he did not see. He had thrown himself upon his bunk and lay face down, his arms stretched rigidly out before him, his teeth set, his eyes closed.

For what Donnegan had wanted in the world, he had taken; by force when he could, by subtlety when he must. And now, what he wanted most of all was gone from him, he felt, forever. There was no power in his arms to take that part of her which he wanted; he had no craft which could encompass her.

Big George, stealing into the room, wondered at the lithe, slender form of the master in the bed. Seeing him thus, it seemed that with the power of one hand, George could crush him. But George would as soon have closed his fingers over a rattler. He slipped away into the kitchen and sat with his arms wrapped around his body, as frightened as though he had seen a ghost.

But Donnegan lay on the bed without moving for hours and hours, until big George, who sat wakeful and terrified all that time, was sure that the master slept. Then he stole in and covered Donnegan with a blanket, for it was the chill, gray time of the night.

But Donnegan was not asleep, and when George rose in the morning, he found the master sitting at the table with his arms folded tightly across his breast and his eyes burning into vacancy.

He spent the day in that chair.

It was the middle of the afternoon when George came with a scared face and a message that a "gen'-leman who looks riled, sir," wanted to see him. There was no answer, and George perforce took the silence as acquiescence. So he opened the door and announced: "Mr. Lester to see you, sir."

Into the fiery haze of Donnegan's vision stepped a raw-boned fellow with sandy hair and a disagreeably strong jaw.

"You're the gent that's here with the colonel, ain't you?" said Lester.

Donnegan did not reply.

"You're the gent that cleaned up on Landis, ain't you?" continued the sandy-haired man.

There was still the same silence, and Lester burst out: "It don't work, Donnegan. You've showed you're man-sized several ways since you been in The Corner. Now I come to tell you to get out from under Colonel Macon. Why? Because he's crooked, because we know he's crooked; because he played crooked with me. You hear me talk?"

Still Donnegan considered him without a word.

"We're goin' to run him out, Donnegan. We want you on our side if we can get you; if we can't get you, then we'll run you out along with the colonel."

He began to talk with difficulty, as though Donnegan's stare unnerved him. He even took a step back toward the door.

"You can't bluff me out, Donnegan. I ain't alone.

They's others behind me. I don't need to name no names. Here's another thing: you ain't alone yourself. You got a woman and a cripple on your hands. Now, Donnegan, you're a fast man with a gun and you're a fast man at thinkin', but I ask you personal: have you got a chance runnin' under that weight?"

He added fiercely: "I'm through. Now, talk turkey, Donnegan, or you're done!"

For the first time Donnegan moved. It was to make to big George a significant signal with his thumb, indicating the visitor. However, Lester did not wait to be thrown bodily from the cabin. One enormous oath exploded from his lips, and he backed sullenly through the door and slammed it after him.

"It kind of looks," said big George, "like a war, sir."

And still Donnegan did not speak, until the afternoon was gone, and the evening, and the full black of the night had swallowed up the hills around The Corner.

Then he left the chair, shaved, and dressed carefully, looked to his revolver, stowed it carefully and invisibly away among his clothes, and walked leisurely down the hill. An outbreak of cursing, stamping, hair-tearing, shooting could not have affected big George as this quiet departure did. He followed, unordered, but as he stepped across the threshold of the hut he rolled up his eyes to the stars.

"Oh, heavens above," muttered George, "have mercy on Mr. Donnegan. He ain't happy."

And he went down the hill, making sure that he was fit for battle with knife and gun.

He had sensed Donnegan's mental condition accurately enough. The heart of the little man was swelled to the point of breaking. A twenty-hour vigil had whitened his face, drawn in his cheeks, and painted his eyes with shadow; and now he wanted action. He wanted excitement, strife, competition; something to fill his mind. And naturally enough he had two places in mind—Lebrun's and Milligan's.

It is hard to replace the state of Donnegan's mind at this time. Chiefly, he was conscious of a peculiar and cruel pain that made him hollow; it was like homesickness raised to the $n$th degree. Vaguely he realized that in some way, somehow, he must fulfill his promise to the girl and bring Jack Landis home. The colonel dared not harm the boy for fear of Donnegan; and the girl would be happy. For that very reason Donnegan wanted to tear Landis to shreds.

It is not extremely heroic for a man tormented with sorrow to go to a gambling hall and then to a dance hall to seek relief. But Donnegan was not a hero. He was only a man, and, since his heart was empty, he wanted something that might fill it. Indeed, like most men, suffering made him a good deal of a boy.

So the high heels of Donnegan tapped across the floor of Lebrun's. A murmur went before him whenever he appeared now, and a way opened for him. At the roulette wheel he stopped, placed fifty on the red, and watched it double three times. George, at a signal from the master, raked in the winnings. And Donnegan sat at a faro table and won again, and again rose disconsolately and went on. For when men do not care how luck runs it never fails to favor them. The devotees of fortune are the ones she punishes.

In the meantime the whisper ran swiftly through The Corner.

"Donnegan is out hunting trouble."

About the good that is in men rumor often makes mistakes, but for evil she has an infallible eye and at once sets all of her thousand tongues wagging. Indeed, any man with half an eye could not fail to get the meaning of his fixed glance, his hard set jaw, and the straightness of his mouth. If he had been a ghost, men could not have avoided him more sedulously, and the giant negro who stalked at his back. Not that The Corner was peopled with cowards. The true Westerner avoids trouble, but cornered, he will fight like a wild cat.

So people watched from the corner of their eyes as Donnegan passed.

He left Lebrun's. There was no competition. Luck blindly favored him, and Donnegan wanted contest, excitement. He crossed to Milligan's. Rumor was there before him. A whisper conveyed to a pair of mighty-limbed cow-punchers that they were sitting at the table which Donnegan had occupied the night before, and they wisely rose without further hint and sought other chairs. Milligan, anxious-eyed, hurried to the orchestra, and with a blast of sound they sought to cover up the entry of the gun man.

As a matter of fact that blare of horns only served to announce him. Something was about to happen; the eyes of men grew shadowy; the eyes of women brightened. And then Donnegan appeared, with George behind him, and crossed the floor straight to his table of the night before. Not that he had forethought in going toward it, but he was moving absent-mindedly.

Indeed, he had half forgotten that he was a public figure in The Corner, and sitting sipping the cordial which the negro brought him at once, he let his glance rove swiftly around the room. The eye of more than one brave man sank under that glance; the eye of more than one woman smiled back at him; but where the survey of Donnegan halted was on the face of Nelly Lebrun.

She was crossing the farther side of the floor alone, unescorted except for the whisper about her, but seeing Donnegan she stopped abruptly. Donnegan instantly rose. She would have gone on again in a flurry; but that would have been too pointed.

A moment later Donnegan was threading his way across the dance floor to Nelly Lebrun, with all eyes turned in his direction. He had his hat under his arm; and in his black clothes, with his white stock, he made an old-fashioned figure as he bowed before the girl and straightened again.

"Did you send for me?" Donnegan inquired.

Nelly Lebrun was frankly afraid; and she was also delighted. She felt that she had been drawn into the circle of intense public interest which surrounded the red-headed stranger; she remembered on the other hand that her father would be furious if she exchanged two words with the man. And for that very reason she was intrigued. Donnegan, being forbidden fruit, was irresistible. So she let the smile come to her lips and eyes, and then laughed outright in her excitement.

"No," she said with her lips, while her eyes said other things.

"I've come to ask a favor; to talk with you one minute."

"If I should—what would people say?"

"Let's find out."

"It would be—daring," said Nelly Lebrun. "After last night."

"It would be delightful," said Donnegan. "Here's a table ready for us."

She went a pace closer to it with him.

"I think you've frightened the poor people away from it. I mustn't sit down with you, Mr. Donnegan."

And she immediately slipped into a chair.

# CHAPTER XXVII

### HE TALKS OF LOVE

SHE qualified her surrender, of course, by sitting on the very edge of the chair. She had on a wine-colored dress, and, with the excitement whipping color into her cheeks and her eyes dancing, Nelly Lebrun was a lovely picture.

"I must go at once," said Nelly.

"Of course, I can't expect you to stay."

She dropped one hand on the edge of the table. One would have thought that she was in the very act of rising.

"Do you know that you frighten me?"

"I?" said Donnegan, with appropriate inflection.

"As if I were a man and you were angry."

"But you see?" And he made a gesture with both of his palms turned up. "People have slandered me. I am harmless."

"The minute is up, Mr. Donnegan. What is it you wish?"

"Another minute."

"Now you laugh at me."

"No, no!"

"And in the next minute?"

"I hope to persuade you to stay still the third minute."

"Of course, I can't."

"I know; it's impossible."

"Quite." She settled into the chair. "See how

people stare at me! They remember poor Jack Landis and they think—the whole crowd——"

"A crowd is always foolish. In the meantime, I'm happy."

"You?"

"To be here; to sit close to you; to watch you."

Her glance was like the tip of a rapier, searching him through for some iota of seriousness under this banter.

"Ah?" and Nelly Lebrun laughed.

"Don't you see that I mean it?"

"You can watch me from a distance, Mr. Donnegan."

"May I say a bold thing?"

"You have said several."

"No one can really watch you from a distance."

She canted her head a little to one side; such an encounter of personal quips was a seventh heaven to her.

"That's a riddle, Mr. Donnegan."

"A simple one. The answer is, because there's too much to watch."

He joined her when she laughed, but the laughter of Donnegan made not a sound, and he broke in on her mirth suddenly.

"Ah, don't you see I'm serious?"

Her glance flicked on either side, as though she feared some one might have read his lips.

"Not a soul can hear me," murmured Donnegan, "and I'm going to be bolder still, and tell you the truth."

"It's the last thing I dare stay to hear."

"You are too lovely to watch from a distance, Nelly Lebrun."

He was so direct that even Nelly Lebrun, expert

in flirtations, was given pause, and became sober. She shook her head and raised a cautioning finger. But Donnegan was not shaken.

"Because there is a glamour about a beautiful girl," he said gravely. "One has to step into the halo to see her, to know her. Are you contented to look at a flower from a distance? That's an old comparison, isn't it? But there is something like a fragrance about you, Nelly Lebrun. Don't be afraid. No one can hear; no one shall ever dream I've said such bold things to you. In the meantime, we have a truth party. There is a fragrance, I say. It must be breathed. There is a glow which must touch one. As it touches me now, you see?"

Indeed, there was a faint color in his cheeks. And the girl flushed more deeply; her eyes were still bright, but they no longer sharpened to such a penetrating point. She was believing at least a little part of what he said, and her disbelief only heightened her joy in what was real in this strangest of love-makings.

"I shall stay here to learn one thing," she said. "What deviltry is behind all this talk, Mr. Donnegan?"

"Is that fair to me? Besides, I only follow a beaten trail in The Corner."

"And that?"

"Toward Nelly Lebrun."

"A beaten trail? You?" she cried, with just a touch of anger. "I'm not a child, Mr. Donnegan!"

"You are not; and that's why I am frank."

"You have done all these things—following this trail you speak of?"

"Remember," said Donnegan soberly. "What have I done?"

"Shot down two men; played like an actor on a stage a couple of times at least, if I must be blunt; hunted danger like—like a reckless madman; dared all The Corner to cross you; flaunted the red rag in the face of the bull. Those are a few things you have done, sir! And all on one trail? That trail you spoke of?"

"Nelly Lebrun——"

"I'm listening; and do you know I'm persuading myself to believe you?"

"It's because you feel the truth before I speak it. Truth speaks for itself, you know."

"I have closed my eyes—you see? I have stepped into a masquerade. Now you can talk."

"Masquerades are exciting," murmured Donnegan.

"And they are sometimes beautiful."

"But this sober truth of mine——"

"Well?"

"I came here unknown—and I saw you, Nelly Lebrun."

He paused; she was looking a little past him.

"I came in rags; no friends; no following. And I saw that I should have to make you notice me."

"And why? No, I shouldn't have asked that."

"You shouldn't ask that," agreed Donnegan. "But I saw you the queen of The Corner, worshiped by all men? What could I do? I am not rich. I am not gay. I am not big. You see?"

He drew her attention to his smallness with a flush which never failed to touch the face of Donnegan when he thought of his size; and he seemed to swell and grow greater in the very instant she glanced at him.

"What could I do? One thing; fight. I have

fought. I fought to get the eye of The Corner, but most of all to attract your attention. I came closer to you. I saw that one man blocked the way—mostly. I decided to brush him aside. How?"

"By fighting?" She had not been carried away by his argument. She was watching him like a lynx every moment.

"Not by that. By bluffing. You see, I was not fool enough to think that you would—particularly notice a fighting bully."

He laid his open hand on the table. It was like exposing both strength and weakness; and into such a trap it would have been a singularly hard-minded woman who might not have stepped. Nelly Lebrun leaned a little closer. She forgot to criticize.

"It was bluff. I saw that Landis was big and good-looking. And what was I beside him? Nothing. I could only hope that he was hollow; yellow—you see? So I tried the bluff. You know about it. The clock, and all that clap-trap. But Landis wasn't yellow. He didn't crumble. He lasted long enough to call my bluff, and I had to shoot in self-defense. And then, when he lay on the floor, I saw that I had failed."

"Failed?"

He lowered his eyes for fear that she would catch the glitter of them.

"I knew that you would hate me for what I had done because I had only proved that Landis was a brave youngster with enough nerve for nine out of ten. And I came to-night—to ask you to forgive me. No, not that—only to ask you to understand. Do you?"

He raised his glance suddenly at that, and their eyes met with one of those electric shocks which will go tingling through two people. And when the lips of Nelly Lebrun parted a little, he knew that she was in the trap. He closed his hand that lay on the table—curling the fingers slowly. In that way he expressed all his exultation.

"There is something wrong," said the girl, in a tone of one who argues with herself. "It's all too logical to be real."

"Ah?"

"Was that your only reason for fighting Jack Landis?"

"Do I have to confess even that?"

She smiled in the triumph of her penetration, but it was a brief, unhappy smile. One might have thought that she would have been glad to be deceived.

"I came to serve a girl who was unhappy," said Donnegan. "Her fiancé had left her; her fiancé was Jack Landis. And she's now in a hut up the hill waiting for him. And I thought that if I ruined him in your eyes he'd go back to a girl who wouldn't care so much about bravery. Who'd forgive him for having left her. But you see what a fool I was and how clumsily I worked? My bluff failed, and I only wounded him, put him in your house, under your care, where he'll be happiest, and where there'll never be a chance for this girl to get him back."

Nelly Lebrun, with her folded hands under her chin, studied him.

"Mr. Donnegan," she said, "I wish I knew whether you are the most chivalrous, self-sacrificing of men, or simply the most gorgeous liar in the desert."

"And it's hardly fair," said Donnegan, "to expect me to tell you that."

# CHAPTER XXVIII

### HE STEALS HIS SECOND MAN

IT gave them both a welcome opportunity to laugh, welcome to the girl because it broke into an excitement which was rapidly telling upon her, and welcome to Donnegan because the strain of so many malversations of the truth was telling upon him as well. They laughed together. One hasty glance told Donnegan that half the couples in the room were whispering about Donnegan and Nelly Lebrun; but when he looked across the table he saw that Nelly Lebrun had not a thought for what might be going on in the minds of others. She was quite content.

"And the girl?" she said.

Donnegan rested his forehead upon his hand in thought. He dared not let Nelly see his face at this moment, for the mention of Lou Macon had poured the old flood of sorrow back upon him. And therefore, when he looked up, he was sneering.

"You know these blond, pretty girls?" he said.

"Oh, they are adorable!"

"With dull eyes," said Donnegan coldly, and a twinkle came in the responsive eye of Nelly Lebrun. "The sort of a girl who sees a hero in such a fellow as Jack Landis."

"And Jack *is* brave."

"I shouldn't have said that."

"Never mind. Brave, but such a *boy*."

"Are you serious?"

She looked questionably at Donnegan and they smiled together, slowly.

"I—I'm glad it's that way," and Donnegan sighed.

"And did you really think it could be any other way?"

"I didn't know. I'm afraid I was blind."

"But the poor girl on the hill; I wish I could see her."

She was watching Donnegan very sharply again.

"A good idea. Why don't you?"

"You seem to like her?"

"Yes," said Donnegan judiciously. "She has an appealing way; I'm very sorry for her. But I've done my best; I can't help her."

"Isn't there some way?"

"Of what?"

"Of helping her."

Donnegan laughed. "Go to your father and persuade him to send Landis back to her."

She shook her head.

"Of course, that wouldn't do. There's business mixed up in all this, you know."

"Business? Well, I guessed at that."

"My part in it wasn't very pleasant," she remarked sadly.

Donnegan was discreetly silent, knowing that silence extracts secrets.

"They made me—flirt with poor Jack. I really liked him!"

How much the past tense may mean!

"Poor fellow," murmured the sympathetic Donnegan. "But why," with gathering heat, "couldn't you help me to do the thing I can't do alone? Why couldn't you get him away from the house?"

"With Joe Rix and The Pedlar guarding him?"

"They'll be asleep in the middle of the night."

"But Jack would wake up and make a noise."

"There are things that would make him sleep through anything."

"But how could he be moved?"

"On a horse litter kept ready outside."

"And how carried to the litter?"

"I would carry him." The girl looked at him with a question and then with a faint smile beginning. "Easily," said Donnegan, stiffening in his chair. "Very easily."

It pleased her to find this weakness in the pride of the invincible Donnegan. It gave her a secure feeling of mastery. So she controlled her smile and looked with a sort of superior kindliness upon the red-headed little man.

"It's no good," Nelly Lebrun said with a sigh. "Even if he were taken away—and then it would get you into a bad mess."

"Would it? Worse than I'm in?"

"Hush! Lord Nick is coming to The Corner; and no matter what you've done so far—I think I could quiet him. But if you were to take Landis away—then nothing could stop him."

Donnegan sneered.

"I begin to think Lord Nick is a bogie," he said. "Every one whispers when they speak of him." He leaned forward. "I should like to meet him, Nelly Lebrun!"

It staggered Nelly. "Do you mean that?" she cried softly.

"I do."

She caught her breath and then a spark of deviltry gleamed. "I wonder!" said Nelly Lebrun, and her glance weighed Donnegan.

"All I ask is a fair chance," he said.

"He is a big man," said the girl maliciously.

The never failing blush burned in the face of Donnegan.

"A large target is more easily hit," he said through his teeth.

Her thoughts played back and forth in her eyes.

"I can't do it," she said.

Donnegan played a random card.

"I was mistaken," he said darkly. "Jack was not the man I should have faced. Lord Nick!"

"No, no, no, Mr. Donnegan!"

"You can't persuade me. Well, I was a fool not to guess it!"

"I really think," said the girl gloomily, "that as soon as Lord Nick comes, you'll hunt him out!"

He bowed to her with cold politeness. "In spite of his size," said Donnegan through his teeth once more.

And at this the girl's face softened and grew merry.

"I'm going to help you to take Jack away," she said, "on one condition."

"And that?"

"That you won't make a step toward Lord Nick when he comes."

"I shall not avoid him," said Donnegan.

"You're unreasonable! Well, not avoid him, but simply not provoke him. I'll arrange it so that Lord Nick won't come hunting trouble."

"And he'll let Jack stay with the girl and her father?"

"Perhaps he'll persuade them to let him go of their own free will."

Donnegan thought of the colonel and smiled.

"In that case, of course, I shouldn't care at all." He added: "But do you mean all this?"

"You shall see."

They talked only a moment longer and then Donnegan left the hall with the girl on his arm. Certainly the thoughts of all in Milligan's followed that pair; and it was seen that Donnegan took her to the door of her house and then went away through the town and up the hill. And big George followed him like a shadow cast from a lantern behind a man walking in a fog.

In the hut on the hill, Donnegan put George quickly to work, and with a door and some bedding, a litter was hastily constructed and swung between the two horses. In the meantime, Donnegan climbed higher up the hill and watched steadily over the town until, in a house beneath him, two lights were shown. He came back at that and hurried down the hill with George behind and around the houses until they came to the pretentious cabin of the gambler, Lebrun.

Once there, Donnegan went straight to an unlighted window, tapped; and it was opened from within, softly. Nelly Lebrun stood within.

"It's done," she said. "Joe and The Pedlar are sound asleep. They drank too much."

"Your father."

"Hasn't come home."

"And Jack Landis?"

"No matter what you do, he won't wake up; but be careful of his shoulder. It's badly torn. How can you carry him?"

She could not see Donnegan's flush, but she heard his teeth grit. And he slipped through the window, gesturing to George to come close. It was still darker inside the room—far darker than the starlit night outside. And the one path of lighter gray was the bed of Jack Landis. His heavy breathing was the only sound. Donnegan kneeled beside him and worked his arms under the limp figure.

And while he kneeled there a door in the house was opened and closed softly. Donnegan stood up.

"Is the door locked?"

"No," whispered the girl.

"Quick!"

"Too late. It's father, and he'd hear the turning of the key."

They waited, while the light, quick step came down the hall of the cabin. It came to the door, it went past; and then the steps retraced and the door was opened gently.

There was a light in the hall; the form of Lebrun was outlined black and distinct.

"Jack!" he whispered.

No sound; he made as if to enter, and then he heard the heavy breathing of the sleeper, apparently.

"Asleep, poor fool," murmured the gambler, and closed the door.

The door was no sooner closed than Donnegan had raised the body of the sleeper. Once, as he rose, straining, it nearly slipped from his arms; and when he stood erect he staggered. But once he had gained his equilibrium, he carried the wounded man easily enough to the window through which George reached his gorilla arms and lifted out the burden.

"You see?" said Donnegan, panting, to the girl.

"Yes; it was really wonderful!"

"You are laughing, now."

"I? But hurry. My father has a fox's ear for noises."

"He will not hear this, I think." There was a swift scuffle, very soft of movement.

"Nelly!" called a far-off voice.

"Hurry, hurry! Don't you hear?"

"You forgive me?"

"No—yes—but hurry!"

"You will remember me?"

"Mr. Donnegan!"

"Adieu!"

She caught a picture of him sitting in the window for the split part of a second, with his hat off, bowing to her. Then he was gone. And she went into the hall, panting with excitement.

"Heavens!" Nelly Lebrun murmured. "I feel as if I had been hunted, and I must look it. What if he——" Whatever the thought was she did not complete it. "It may have been for the best," added Nelly Lebrun.

# CHAPTER XXIX

## HIS ARCH ENEMY APPEARS

IT is your phlegmatic person who can waken easily in the morning, but an active mind readjusts itself slowly to the day. So Nelly Lebrun roused herself with an effort and scowled toward the door at which the hand was still rapping.

"Yes?" she called drowsily.

"This is Nick. May I come in?"

"This is who?"

The name had brought her instantly into complete wakefulness; she was out of the bed, had slipped her feet into her slippers and whipped a dressing gown around her while she was asking the question. It was a luxurious little boudoir which she had managed to equip. Skins of the lynx, cunningly matched, had been sewn together to make her a rug, and the soft fur of the wild cat was the outer covering of her bed. She threw back the tumbled bed-clothes, tossed half a dozen pillows into place, transforming it into a day couch, and ran to the mirror.

And in the meantime, the deep voice outside the door was saying: "Yes, Nick. May I come in?"

She gave a little ecstatic cry, but while it was still tingling on her lips, she was winding her hair into shape with lightning speed; had dipped the tips of her fingers in cold water and rubbed her eyes awake and brilliant, and with one circular rub had brought the color into her cheeks.

Scarcely ten seconds from the time when she first answered the knock, Nelly was opening the door and peeping out into the hall.

The rest was done by the man without; he cast the door open with the pressure of his foot, caught the girl in his arms, and kissed her; and while he closed the door the girl slipped back and stood with one hand pressed against her face, and her face held that delightful expression halfway between laughter and embarrassment. As for Lord Nick, he did not even smile. He was not, in fact, a man who was prone to gentle expressions, but having been framed by nature for a strong dominance over all around him, his habitual expression was a proud self-containment. It would have been insolence in another man; in Lord Nick it was rather leonine.

He was fully as tall as Jack Landis, but he carried his height easily, and was so perfectly proportioned that unless he was seen beside another man he did not look large. The breadth of his shoulders was concealed by the depth of his chest; and the girth of his throat was made to appear quite normal by the lordly size of the head it supported. To crown and set off his magnificent body there was a handsome face; and he had the combination of active eyes and red hair, which was noticeable in Donnegan, too. In fact, there was a certain resemblance between the two men; in the set of the jaw for instance, in the gleam of the eye, and above all in an indescribable ardor of spirit, which exuded from them both. Except, of course, that in Donnegan, one was conscious of all spirit and very little body, but in Lord Nick hand and eye were terribly mated. Looking upon so splendid a figure, it was no wonder that the mountain desert had forgiven the crimes of Lord Nick because of the careless insolence with which he treated the law. It requires an exceptional man to make a legal life attractive and respected; it takes a genius to make law-breaking glorious.

No wonder that Nelly Lebrun stood with her hand against her cheek, looking him over, smiling happily at him, and questioning him about his immediate past all in the same glance. He waved her back to her couch, and she hesitated. Then, as though she remembered that she now had to do with Lord Nick in person, she obediently curled up on the lounge, and waited expectantly.

"I hear you've been raising the devil," said this singularly frank admirer.

The girl merely looked at him.

"Well?" he insisted.

"I haven't done a thing," protested Nelly rather childishly.

"No?" One felt that he could have crushed her with evidence to the contrary but that he was restraining himself—it was not worth while to bother with such a girl seriously. "Things have fallen into a tangle since I left, old Satan Macon is on the spot and your rat of a father has let Landis get away. What have you been doing, Nelly, while all this was going on? Sitting with your eyes closed?"

He took a chair and lounged back in it gracefully.

"How could I help it? I'm not a watchdog."

He was silent for a time. "Well," he said, "if you told me the truth I suppose I shouldn't love you, my girl. But this time I'm in earnest. Landis is a mint, silly child. If we let him go we lose the mint."

"I suppose you'll get him back?"

"First, I want to find out how he got away."

"I know how."

"Ah?"

"Donnegan."

"Donnegan, Donnegan, Donnegan!" burst out Lord Nick, and though he did not raise the pitch of his voice, he allowed its volume to swell softly so that it filled the room like the humming of a great, angry tiger. "Nobody says three words without putting in the name of Donnegan as one of them! You, too!"

She shrugged her shoulders.

"Donnegan thrills The Corner!" went on the big man in the same terrible voice. "Donnegan wears queer clothes; Donnegan shoots Scar-faced Lewis; Donnegan pumps the nerve out of poor Jack Landis and then drills him. Why, Nelly, it looks as though I'll have to kill this intruding fool!"

She blanched at this, but he did not appear to notice.

"It's a long time since you've killed a man, isn't it?" she asked coldly.

"It's an awful business," declared Lord Nick. "Always complications; have to throw the blame on the other fellow. And even these blockheads are beginning to get tired of my self-defense pleas."

"Well," murmured the girl, "don't cross that bridge until you come to it; and you'll never come to it."

"Never. Because I don't want him killed."

"Ah," Lord Nick murmured. "And why?"

"Because he's in love—with me."

"Tush!" said Lord Nick. "I see you, my dear. Donnegan seems to be a rare fellow, but he couldn't have gotten Landis out of this house without help.

Rix and The Pedlar may have been a bit sleepy, but Donnegan had to find out when they fell asleep. He had a confederate. Who? Not Rix; not The Pedlar; not Lebrun. They all know me. It had to be some one who doesn't fear me. Who? Only one person in the world. Nelly, you're the one!"

She hesitated a breathless instant.

"Yes," she said, "I am."

She added, as he stared calmly at her, considering: "There's a girl in the case. She came up here to get Landis; seems he was in love with her once. And I pitied her. I sent him back to her. Suppose he is a mint; haven't we coined enough money out of him? Besides, I couldn't have kept on with it."

"No?"

"He was getting violent, and he talked marriage all day, every day. I haven't any nerves, you say, but he began to put me on edge. So I got rid of him."

"Nelly, are you growing a conscience?"

She flushed and then set her teeth.

"But I'll have to teach you business methods, my dear. I have to bring him back."

"You'll have to go through Donnegan to do it."

"I suppose so."

"You don't understand, Nick. He's different."

"Eh?"

"He's like you."

"What are you driving at?"

"Nick, I tell you upon my word of honor, no matter what a terrible fighter you may be, Donnegan will give you trouble. He has your hair and your eyes, and he moves like a cat. I've never seen such a man—except you. I'd rather see you fight the plague than fight Donnegan!"

For the first time Lord Nick showed real emotion; he leaned a little forward.

"Just what does he mean to you?" he asked. "I've stood for a good deal, Nelly; I've given you absolute freedom, but if I ever suspect you——"

The lion was up in him unmistakably now. And the girl shrank.

"If it were serious, do you suppose I'd talk like this?"

"I don't know. You're a clever little devil, Nell. But I'm clever, too. And I begin to see through you. Do you still want to save Donnegan?"

"For your own sake."

He stood up.

"I'm going up the hill to-day. If Donnegan's there, I'll go through him; but I'm going to have Landis back!"

She, also, rose.

"There's only one way out and I'll take that way. I'll get Donnegan to leave the house."

"I don't care what you do about that."

"And if he isn't there, will you give me your word that you won't hunt him out afterward?"

"I never make promises, Nell."

"But I'll trust you, Nick."

"Very well. I start up the hill in an hour. You have that long."

# CHAPTER XXX

## HE IS LURED FROM DANGER

THE air was thin and chilly; snow had fallen in the mountains to the north, and the wind was bringing the cold down to The Corner. Nelly Lebrun noted this as she dressed and made up her mind accordingly. She sent out two messages: one to the cook to send breakfast to her room, which she ate while she finished dressing with care; and the other to the gambling house, summoning one of the waiters. When he came, she gave him a note for Donnegan. The fellow flashed a glance at her as he took the envelope. There was no need to give that name and address in The Corner, and the girl tingled under the glance.

She finished her breakfast and then concentrated in polishing up her appearance. From all of which it may be gathered that Nelly Lebrun was in love with Donnegan, but she really was not. But he had touched in her that cord of romance which runs through every woman; whenever it is touched the vibration is music, and Nelly was filled with the sound of it. And except for Lord Nick, there is no doubt that she would have really lost her head; for she kept seeing the face of Donnegan, as he had leaned toward her across the little table in Milligan's. And that, as any one may know, is a dangerous symptom.

Her glances were alternating between her mirror and her watch, and the hands of the latter pointed to the fact that fifty minutes of her hour had elapsed when a message came up that she was waited for in the street below. So Nelly Lebrun went down in her riding costume, the corduroy swishing at each step, and tapping her shining boots with the riding crop. Her own horse she found at the hitching rack, and beside it Donnegan was on his chestnut horse. It was a tall horse, and he looked more diminutive than ever before, pitched so high in the saddle.

He was on the ground in a flash with the reins tucked under one arm and his hat under the other; she became aware of gloves and white-linen stock, and pale, narrow face. Truly Donnegan made a natty appearance.

"There's no day like a cool day for riding," she said, "and I thought you might agree with me."

He untethered her horse while he murmured an answer. But for his attitude she cared little so long as she had him riding away from that house on the hill where Lord Nick in all his terror would appear in some few minutes. Besides, as they swung up the road—the chestnut at a long-strided canter and Nelly's black at a soft and choppy pace—the wind of the gallop struck into her face and Nelly was made to enjoy things one by one and not two by two. They hit over the hills, and when the first impulse of the ride was done they were a mile or more away from The Corner—and Lord Nick.

The resemblance between the two men was less striking now that she had Donnegan beside her. He seemed more weazened, paler, and intense as a violin string screwed to the snapping point; there was none of the lordly tolerance of Nick about him; he was like a bull terrier compared with a stag hound. And only the color of his eyes and his hair made her make the comparison at all.

"What could be better?" she said when they checked their horses on a hilltop to look over a gradual falling of the ground below. "What could be better?" The wind flattened a loose curl of hair against her cheek, and overhead the wild geese were flying and crying, small and far away.

"One thing better," said Donnegan, "and that is to sit in a chair and see this."

She frowned at such frankness; it was almost blunt discourtesy.

"You see, I'm a lazy man."

"How long has it been," the girl asked sharply, "since you have slept?"

"Two days, I think."

"What's wrong?"

He lifted his eyes slowly from a glittering, distant rock, and brought his glance toward her by degrees. He had a way of exciting people even in the most commonplace conversation, and the girl felt a thrill under his look.

"That," said Donnegan, "is a dangerous question."

And he allowed such hunger to come into his eye that she caught her breath. The imp of perversity made her go on.

"And why dangerous?"

It was an excellent excuse for an outpouring of the heart from Donnegan, but, instead, his eyes twinkled at her.

"You are not frank," he remarked.

She could not help laughing, and her laughter trailed away musically in her excitement.

"Having once let down the bars I cannot keep you at arm's length. After last night I suppose I should never have let you see me for—days and days."

"That's why I'm curious," said Donnegan, "and not flattered. I'm trying to find what purpose you have in taking me riding."

"I wonder," she said thoughtfully, "if you will."

And since such fencing with the wits delighted her, she let all her delight come with a sparkle in her eyes.

"I have one clew."

"Yes?"

"And that is that you may have the old-woman curiosity to find out how many ways a man can tell her that he's fond of her."

Though she flushed a little she kept her poise admirably.

"I suppose that is part of my interest," she admitted.

"I can think of a great many ways of saying it," said Donnegan. "I am the dry desert, you are the rain, and yet I remain dry and produce no grass."

"A very pretty comparison," said the girl with a smile.

"A very green one," and Donnegan smiled. "I am the wind and you are the wild geese, and yet I keep on blowing after you are gone and do not carry away a feather of you."

"Pretty again."

"And silly. But, really, you are very kind to me, and I shall try not to take too much advantage of it."

"Will you answer a question?"

"I had rather ask one; but go on."

"What made you so dry a desert, Mr. Donnegan?"

"There is a very leading question again."

"I don't mean it that way. For you had the same sad, hungered look the first time I saw you—when you came into Milligan's in that beggarly disguise."

"I shall confess one thing. It was not a disguise. It was the fact of me; I am a beggarly person."

"Nonsense! I'm not witless, Mr. Donnegan. You talk well. You have an education."

"In fact I have an educated taste; I disapprove of myself, you see, and long ago learned not to take myself too seriously."

"Which leads to——"

"The reason why I have wandered so much."

"Like a hunter on a trail. Hunting for what?"

"A chance to sit in a saddle—or a chair—and talk as we are talking."

"Which seems to he idly."

"Oh, you mistake me. Under the surface I am as serious as fire."

"Or ice."

At the random hit he glanced sharply at her, but she was looking a little past him, thinking.

"I have tried to get at the reason behind all your reasons," she said. "You came on me in a haphazard fashion, and yet you are not a haphazard sort."

"Do you see nothing serious about me?"

"I see that you are unhappy," said the girl gently. "And I am sorry."

Once again Donnegan was jarred, and he came within an ace of opening his mind to her, of pouring out the truth about Lou Macon. Love is a talking madness in all men and he came within an ace of confessing his troubles.

"Let's go on," she said, loosening her rein.

"Why not cut back in a semicircle toward The Corner?"

"Toward The Corner? No, no!"

There was a brightening of his eye as he noted her shudder of distaste or fear, and she strove to cover her traces.

"I'm sick of the place," she said eagerly. "Let's get as far from it as we may."

"But yonder is a very good trail leading past it."

"Of course we'll ride that way if you wish, but I'd rather go straight ahead."

If she had insisted stubbornly he would have thought nothing, but the moment she became politic he was on his guard.

"You dislike something in The Corner," he said, thinking carelessly and aloud. "You are afraid of something back there. But what could *you* be afraid of? Then you may be afraid of something for me. Ah, I have it! They have decided to 'get' me for taking Jack Landis away; Joe Rix and The Pedlar are waiting for me to come back!"

He looked steadily and she attempted to laugh.

"Joe Rix and the Pedlar? I would not stack ten like them against you!"

"Then it is some one else."

"I haven't said so. Of course there's no one."

She shook her rein again, but Donnegan sat still in his saddle and looked fixedly at her.

"That's why you brought me out here," he announced. "Oh, Nelly Lebrun, what's behind your mind? Who is it? By Heaven, it's this Lord Nick!"

"Mr. Donnegan, you're letting your imagination run wild."

"It's gone straight to the point. But I'm not angry. I think I may get back in time."

He turned his horse, and the girl swung hers beside him and caught his arm.

"Don't go!" she pleaded. "You're right; it's Nick, and it's suicide to face him!"

The face of Donnegan set cruelly.

"The main obstacle," he said. "Come and watch me handle it!"

But she dropped her head and buried her face in her hands, and, sitting there for a long time, she heard his careless whistling blow back to her as he galloped toward The Corner.

# CHAPTER XXXI

## HE REVEALS HIMSELF

IF Nelly Lebrun had consigned him mentally to the worms, that thought made not the slightest impression upon Donnegan. A chance for action was opening before him, and above all a chance of action in the eye of Lou Macon; and he welcomed with open arms the thought that he would have an opportunity to strike for her, and keep Landis with her. He went arrowy straight and arrowy fast to the cabin on the hill, and he found ample evidence that it had become a center of attention in The Corner. There was a scattering of people in the distance, apparently loitering with no particular purpose, but undoubtedly because they awaited an explosion of some sort. He went by a group at which the chestnut shied, and as Donnegan straightened out the horse again he caught a look of both interest and pity on the faces of the men.

Did they give him up so soon as it was known that Lord Nick had entered the lists against him? Had all his display in The Corner gone for nothing as against the repute of this terrible mystery man? His vanity made him set his teeth again.

Dismounting before the cabin of the colonel, he found that worthy in his invalid chair, enjoying a sun bath in front of his house. But there was no sign of Lord Nick—no sign of Lou. A grim fear came to Donnegan that he might have to attack Nick in his own stronghold, for Jack Landis might already have been taken away to the Lebrun house.

So he went straight to the colonel, and when he came close he saw that the fat man was apparently in the grip of a chill. He had gathered a vast blanket about his shoulders and kept drawing it tighter; beneath his eyes, which looked down to the ground, there were violet shadows.

"I've lost," said Donnegan through his teeth. "Lord Nick has been here?"

The invalid lifted his eyes, and Donnegan saw a terrible thing—that the nerve of the fat man had been crushed. The folds of his face quivered as he answered huskily: "He has been here!"

"And Landis is gone?"

"No."

"Not gone? Then——"

"Nick has gone to get a horse litter. He came up just to clear the way."

"When he comes back he'll find me!"

The glance of the colonel cleared long enough to survey Donnegan slowly from head to foot, and his amusement sent the familiar hot flush over the face of the little man. He straightened to his full height, which, in his high heels, was not insignificant. But the colonel was apparently so desperate that he was willing to throw caution away.

"Compared with Lord Nick, Donnegan," he said, "you don't look half a man—even with those heels."

And he smiled calmly at Donnegan in the manner of one who, having escaped the lightning bolt itself, does not fear mere thunder.

"There is no fool like a fat fool," said Donnegan with childish viciousness. "What did Lord Nick, as you call him, do you? He's brought out the yellow, my friend."

The colonel accepted the insult without the quiver of an eyelid. Throughout he seemed to be looking expectantly beyond Donnegan.

"My young friend," he said, "you have been very useful to me. But I must confess that you are no longer a tool equal to the task. I dismiss you. I thank you cordially for your efforts. They are worthless. You see that crowd gathering yonder? They have come to see Lord Nick prepare you for a hole in the ground. And make no mistake: if you are here when he returns that hole will have to be dug—unless they throw you out for the claws of the buzzards. In the meantime, our efforts have been wasted completely. I hadn't enough time. I had thrown the fear of sudden death into Landis, and in another hour he would have signed away his soul to me for fear of poison."

The colonel paused to chuckle at some enjoyable memory.

"Then Nick came. You see, I know all about Nick."

"And Nick knows all about you?"

For a moment the agate, catlike eyes of the colonel clouded and cleared again in their unfathomable manner.

"At moments, Donnegan," he said, "you have rare perceptions. That is exactly it—Nick knows just about everything concerning me. And so—roll your pack and climb on your horse and get away. I think you may have another five minutes before he comes."

Donnegan turned on his heel. He went to the door of the hut and threw it open. Lou sat beside Landis holding his hand, and the murmur of her voice was still pleasant as an echo through the room when she looked up and saw Donnegan. At that she rose and her face hardened as she looked at him. Landis, also, lifted his head, and his face was convulsed with hatred. So Donnegan closed the door and went softly away to his own shack.

She hated him even as Landis hated him, it seemed. He should have known that he would not be thanked for bringing back her lover to her with a bullet through his shoulder. Sitting in his cabin, he took his head between his hands and thought of life and death, and made up his mind. He was afraid. If Lord Nick had been the devil himself Donnegan could not have been more afraid. But if the big stranger had been ten devils instead of one Donnegan would not have found it in his soul to run away.

Nothing remained for him in The Corner, it seemed, except his position as a man of power—a dangerous fighter. It was a less than worthless position, and yet, once having taken it up, he could not abandon it. More than one gunfighter has been in the same place, forced to act as a public menace long after he has ceased to feel any desire to fight. Of selfish motives there remained not a scruple to him, but there was still the happiness of Lou Macon. If the boy were taken back to Lebrun's it would be fatal to her. For even if Nelly wished, she could not teach her eyes new habits, and she would ceaselessly play on the heart of the wounded man.

It was the cessation of all talk from the gathering crowd outside that made Donnegan lift his head at length, and know that Lord Nick had come. But before he had time to prepare himself, the door was cast open and into it, filling it from side to side, stepped Lord Nick.

There was no need of an introduction. Donnegan knew him by the aptness with which the name fitted that glorious figure of a man and by the calm, confident eye which now was looking him slowly over, from head to foot. Lord Nick closed the door carefully behind him.

"The colonel told me," he said in his deep, smooth voice, "that you were waiting for me here."

And Donnegan recognized the snakelike malice of the fat man in drawing him into the fight. But he dismissed that quickly from his mind. He was staring, fascinated, into the face of the other. He was a reader of men, was Donnegan; he was a reader of mind, too. In his life of battle he had learned to judge the prowess of others at a glance, just as a musician can tell the quality of a violin by the first note he hears played upon it. So Donnegan judged the quality of fighting men, and, looking into the face of Lord Nick, he knew that he had met his equal at last.

It was a great and a bitter moment to him. The sense of physical smallness he had banished a thousand times by the recollection of his speed of hand and his surety with weapons. He had looked at men muscularly great and despised them in the knowledge that a gun or a knife would make him their master. But in Lord Nick he recognized his own nerveless speed of hand, his own hair-trigger balance, his own deadly seriousness and contempt of life. The experience in battle was there, too. And he began to feel that the size of the other crushed him to the floor and made him hopeless.

It was unnatural, it was wrong, that this giant in the body should be a giant in adroitness also.

Already Donnegan had died one death before he rose from his chair and stood to the full of his height ready to die again and summoning his nervous force to meet the enemy. He had seen that the big man had followed his own example and had measured him at a glance.

Indeed the history of some lives of action held less than the concentrated silence of these two men during that second's space.

And now Donnegan felt the cold eye of the other eating into his own, striving to beat him down, break his nerve. For an instant panic got hold on Donnegan. He, himself, had broken the nerve of other men by the weight of his unaided eye. Had he not reduced poor Jack Landis to a trembling wreck by five minutes of silence? And had he not seen other brave men become trembling cowards unable to face the light, and all because of that terrible power which lies in the eye of some? He fought away the panic, though perspiration was pouring out upon his forehead and beneath his armpits.

"The colonel is very kind," said Donnegan.

And that moment he sent up a prayer of thankfulness that his voice was smooth as silk, and that he was able to smile into the face of Lord Nick. The brow of the other clouded and then smoothed itself deftly. Perhaps he, too, recognized the clang of steel upon steel and knew the metal of his enemy.

"And therefore," said Lord Nick, "since most of The Corner expects business from us, it seems much as if one of us must kill the other before we part."

"As a matter of fact," said Donnegan, "I have been keeping that in mind." He added, with that deadly smile of his that never reached his eyes: "I never disappoint the public when it's possible to satisfy them."

"No," and Lord Nick nodded, "you seem to have most of the habits of an actor—including an inclination to make up for your part."

Donnegan bit his lip until it bled, and then smiled.

"I have been playing to fools," he said. "Now I shall enjoy a discriminating critic."

"Yes," remarked Lord Nick, "actors generally desire an intelligent audience for the death scene."

"I applaud your penetration and I shall speak well of you when this disagreeable duty is finished."

"Come," and Lord Nick smiled genially, "you are a game little cock!"

The telltale flush crimsoned Donnegan's face. And if the fight had begun at that moment no power under heaven could have saved Lord Nick from the frenzy of the little man.

"My size keeps me from stooping," said Donnegan, "I shall look up to you, sir, until the moment you fall."

"Well, hit again! You are also a wit, I see! Donnegan, I am almost sorry for the necessity of this meeting. And if it weren't for the audience——"

"Say no more," said Donnegan, bowing. "I read your heart and appreciate all you intend."

He had touched his stock as he bowed, and now he turned to the mirror and carefully adjusted it, for it was a little awry from the ride; but in reality he used that moment to examine his own face, and the set of his jaw and the clearness of his eye reassured him. Turning again, he surprised a glint of admiration in the glance of Lord Nick.

"We are at one, sir, it appears," he said. "And there is no other way out of this disagreeable necessity?"

"Unfortunately not. I have a certain position in these parts. People are apt to expect a good deal of me. And for my part I see no way out except a gunplay—no way out between the devil and the moon!"

Astonishment swept suddenly across the face of the big man, for Donnegan, turning white as death, shrank toward the wall as though he had that moment received cold steel in his body.

"Say that again!" said Donnegan hoarsely.

"I said there was no way out," repeated Lord Nick, and though he kept his right hand in readiness, he passed his left through his red hair and stared at Donnegan with a tinge of contempt; he had seen men buckle like this at the last moment when their backs were to the wall.

"Between——" repeated Donnegan.

"The devil and the moon. Do you see a way yourself?"

He was astonished again to see Donnegan wince as if from a blow. His lips were trembling and they writhed stiffly over his words.

"Who taught you that expression?" said Donnegan.

"A gentleman," said Lord Nick.

"Ah?"

"My father, sir!"

"Oh, Heaven," moaned Donnegan, catching his hands to his breast. "Oh, Heaven, forgive us!"

"What the devil is in you?" asked Lord Nick.

The little man stood erect again and his eyes were now on fire.

"You are Henry Nicholas Reardon," he said.
Lord Nick set his teeth.

"Now," he said, "it is certain that you must die!"
But Donnegan cast out his arms and broke into a wild laughter.

"Oh, you fool, you fool!" he cried. "Don't you know me? I am the cripple!"

# CHAPTER XXXII

### HE OPENS HIS HEART

THE big man crossed the floor with one vast stride, and, seizing Donnegan by both shoulders, dragged him under the full light of the window; and still the crazy laughter shook Donnegan and made him helpless.

"They tied me to a board—like a papoose," said Donnegan, "and they straightened my back—but they left me this way—weazened up." He was stammering; hysterial, and the words tumbled from his lips in a jumble. "That was a month after you ran away from home. I was going to find you. Got bigger. Took the road. Kept hunting. Then I met a yegg who told about Rusty Dick—described him like you—I thought—I thought you were dead!"

And the tears rolled down his face; he sobbed like a woman.

A strange thing happened then. Lord Nick lifted the little man in his arms as if he were a child and literally carried him in that fashion to the bunk. He put him down tenderly, still with one mighty arm around his back.

"You are Garry? You!"

"Garrison Donnegan Reardon. Aye, that's what I am. Henry, don't say that you don't know me!"

"But—your back—I thought——"

"I know—hopeless they said I was. But they brought in a young doctor. Now look at me. Little. I never grew big—but hard, Henry, as leather!"

And he sprang to his feet. And knowing that

Donnegan had begun life as a cripple it was easy to appreciate certain things about his expression—a cold wistfulness, and his manner of reading the minds of men. Lord Nick was like a man in a dream. He dragged Donnegan back to the bunk and forced him to sit down with the weight of his arms. And he could not keep his hands from his younger brother. As though he were blind and had to use the sense of touch to reassure him.

"I heard lies. They said everybody was dead. I thought——"

"The fever killed them all, except me. Uncle Toby took me in. He was a devil. Helped me along, but I left him when I could. And——"

"Don't tell me any more. All that matters is that I have you at last, Garry. Heaven knows it's a horrible thing to be kithless and kinless, but I have you now! Ah, lad, but the old pain has left its mark on you. Poor Garry!"

Donnegan shuddered.

"I've forgotten it. Don't bring it back."

"I keep feeling that you should be in that chair."

"I know. But I'm not. I'm hard as nails, I tell you."

He leaped to his feet again.

"And not so small as you might think, Henry!"

"Oh, big enough, Garry. Big enough to paralyze The Corner, from what I've heard."

"I've been playing a game with 'em, Henry. And now—if one of us could clear the road, what will we do together? Eh?"

The smile of Lord Nick showed his teeth.

"Haven't I been hungry all my life for a man like you, lad? Somebody to stand and guard my back while I faced the rest of the world?"

"And I'll do my share of the facing, too."

"You will, Garry. But I'm your elder."

"Man, man! Nobody's my elder except one that's spent half his life—as I have done!"

"We'll teach you to forget the pain. I'll make life roses for you, Garry."

"And the fools outside thought——"

Donnegan broke into a soundless laughter, and, running to the door, opened it a fraction of an inch and peeped out.

"They're standing about in a circle. I can see 'em gaping. Even from here. What will they think, Henry?"

Lord Nick ground his teeth.

"They'll think I've backed down from you," he said gloomily. "They'll think I've taken water for the first time."

"Why, confound 'em, the first man that opens his head——"

"I know, I know. You'd fill his mouth with lead, and so would I. But if it ever gets about—as it's sure to—that Lord Nick, as they call me, has been bluffed down without a fight, I'll have every Chinaman that cooks on the range talking back to me. I'll have to start all over again."

"Don't say that, Henry. Don't you see that I'll go out and explain that I'm your brother?"

"What good will that do? No, do we look alike?"

Donnegan stopped short.

"I'm not very big," he said rather coldly, "but then I'm not so very small, either. I've found myself big enough, speaking in general. Besides, we have the same hair and eyes."

"Why, man, people will laugh when they hear that we call ourselves brothers."

Donnegan ground his teeth and the old flush burned upon his face.

"I'll cut some throats if they do," he said, trembling with his passion.

"I can hear them say it. 'Lord Nick walked in on Donnegan prepared to eat him up. He measured him up and down, saw that he was a fighting wild cat in spite of his size, and decided to back out. And Donnegan was willing. They couldn't come out without a story of some kind—with the whole world expecting a death in that cabin—so they framed a crazy cock-and-bull story about being brothers.' I can hear them say that, Donnegan, and it makes me wild!"

"Do you call me Donnegan?" said Donnegan sadly.

"No, no. Garry, don't be so touchy. You've never got over that, I see. Still all pride and fire."

"You're not very humble yourself, Henry."

"Maybe not, maybe not. But I've been in a certain position around these parts, Don—Garry. And it's hard to see it go!"

Donnegan closed his eyes in deep reverie. And then he forced out the words one by one.

"Henry, I'll let everybody know that it was I who backed down. That we were about to fight." He was unable to speak; he tore the stock loose at his throat and went on: "We were about to fight; I lost my nerve; you couldn't shoot a helpless man. We began to talk. We found out we are brothers——"

"Damnation!" broke out Lord Nick, and he struck himself violently across the forehead with the back of his hand. "I'm a skunk, Garry, lad. Why, for a minute I was about to let you do it. No, no, no! A thousand times no!"

It was plain to be seen that he was arguing himself away from the temptation.

"What do I care what they say? We'll cram the words back down their throats and be hanged to 'em. Here I am worrying about myself like a selfish dog without letting myself be happy over finding you. But I am happy, Garry. Heaven knows it. And you don't doubt it, do you, old fellow?"

"Ah," said Donnegan, and he smiled to cover a touch of sadness. "I hope not. No, I don't doubt you, of course. I've spent my life wishing for you since you left us, you see. And then I followed you for three years on the road, hunting everywhere."

"You did that?"

"Yes. Three years. I liked the careless life. For to tell you the truth, I'm not worth much, Henry. I'm a loafer by instinct, and——"

"Not another word." There were tears in the eyes of Lord Nick, and he frowned them away. "Confound it, Garry, you unman me. I'll be weeping like a woman in a minute. But now, sit down. We still have some things to talk over. And we'll get to a quick conclusion."

"Ah, yes," said Donnegan, and at the emotion which had come in the face of Lord Nick, his own expression softened wonderfully. A light seemed to stand in his face. "We'll brush over the incidentals. And everything is incidental aside from the fact that we're together again. They can chisel iron chain apart, but we'll never be separated again, God willing!" He looked up as he spoke, and his face was for the moment as pure as the face of a child—Donnegan, the thief, the beggar, the liar by gift, and the man-killer by trade and artistry.

But Lord Nick in the meantime was looking down to the floor and mustering his thoughts.

"The main thing is entirely simple," he said. "You'll make one concession to my pride, Garry, boy?"

"Can you ask me?" said Donnegan softly, and he cast out his hands in a gesture that offered his heart and his soul. "Can you ask me? Anything I have is yours!"

"Don't say that," answered Lord Nick tenderly. "But this small thing—my pride, you know—I despise myself for caring what people think, but I'm weak. I admit it, but I can't help it."

"Talk out, man. You'll see if there's a bottom to things that I can give!"

"Well, it's this. Every one knows that I came up here to get young Jack Landis and bring him back to Lebrun's—from which you stole him, you clever young devil! Well, I'll simply take him back there, Garry; and then I'll never have to ask another favor of you."

He was astonished by a sudden silence, and looking up again, he saw that Donnegan sat with his hand at his breast. It was a singularly feminine gesture to which he resorted. It was a habit which had come to him in his youth in the invalid chair, when the ceaseless torment of his crippled back became too great for him to bear.

And clearly, indeed, those days were brought home to Lord Nick as he glanced up, for Donnegan was staring at him in the same old, familiar agony, mute and helpless.

# CHAPTER XXXIII

### HE DENIES HIS BROTHER

AT this Lord Nick very frankly frowned in turn. And when he frowned his face grew marvelously dark, like some wrathful god, for there was a noble, a Grecian purity to the profile of Henry Nicholas Reardon, and when he frowned he seemed to be scorning, from a distance, ignoble, earthly things which troubled him.

"I know it isn't exactly easy for you, Garry," he admitted. "You have your own pride; you have your own position here in The Corner. But I want you to notice that mine is different. You've spent a day for what you have in The Corner, here. I've spent ten years. You've played a prank, acted a part, and cast a jest for what you have. But for the place which I hold, brother mine, I've schemed with my wits, played fast and loose, and killed men. Do you hear? I've bought it with blood, and things you buy at such a price ought to stick, eh?"

He banished his frown; the smile played suddenly across his features.

"Why, I'm arguing with myself. But that look you gave me a minute ago had me worried for a little while."

At this Donnegan, who had allowed his head to fall, so that he seemed to be nodding in acquiescence, now raised his face and Lord Nick perceived the same white pain upon it. The same look which had been on the face of the cripple so often in the other days.

"Henry," said the younger brother, "I give you my oath that my pride has nothing to do with this. I'd let you drive me barefoot before you through the street yonder. I'd let every soul in The Corner know that I have no pride where you're concerned. I'll do whatever you wish—with one exception—and that one exception is the unlucky thing you ask. Pardner, you mustn't ask for Jack Landis! Anything else I'll work like a slave to get for you; I'll fight your battles, I'll serve you in any way you name: but don't take Landis back!"

He had talked eagerly, the words coming with a rush, and he found at the end that Lord Nick was looking at him in bewilderment.

"When a man is condemned to death," said Lord Nick slowly, "suppose somebody offers him anything in the world that he wants—palaces, riches, power— everything except his life. What would the condemned man say to a friend who made such an offer? He'd laugh at him and then call him a traitor. Eh? But I don't laugh at you, Garry. I simply explain to you why I have to have Landis back. Listen!"

He counted off his points upon the tips of his fingers, in the confident manner of a teacher who deals with a stupid child, waiting patiently for the young mind to comprehend.

"We've been bleeding Jack Landis. Do you know why? Because it was Lester who made the strike up here. He started out to file his claim. He stopped at the house of Colonel Macon. That old devil learned the location, learned everything; detained Lester with a trick, and rushed young Landis away to file the claims for himself. Then when Lester came up here he found that his claims had been jumped, and when he went to the law there was no law that could help him. He had nothing but his naked word for what he had discovered. And naturally the word of a ruffian like Lester had no weight against the word of Landis. And, you see, Landis thought that he was entirely in the right. Lester tried the other way; tried to jump the claims; and was shot down by Landis. So Lester sent for me. What was I to do? Kill Landis? The mine would go to his heirs. I tried a different way—bleeding him of his profits, after I'd explained to him that he was in the wrong. He half admitted that, but he naturally wouldn't give up the mines even after we'd almost proved to him that Lester had the first right. So Landis has been mining the gold and we've been drawing it away from him. It looks tricky, but really it's only just. And Lester and Lebrun split with me.

"But I tell you, Garry, that I'd give up everything without an afterthought. I'll give up the money and I'll make Lebrun and Lester shut up without a word. I'll make them play square and not try to knife Landis in the back. I'll do all that willingly —for you! But, Garry, I can't give up taking Landis back to Lebrun's and keeping him there until he's well. Why, man, I saw him in the hut just now. He wants to go. He's afraid of the old colonel as if he were poison—and I think he's wise in being afraid."

"The colonel won't touch him," said Donnegan.

"No?"

"No. I've told him what would happen if he does."

"Tush. Garry, Colonel Macon is the coldest-blooded murderer I've ever known. But come out in the open, lad. You see that I'm ready to listen to reason—except on one point. Tell me why you're so set on this keeping of Landis here against my will and even against the lad's own will? I'm reasonable, Garry. Do you doubt that?"

Explaining his own mildness, the voice of Lord Nick swelled again and filled the room, and he frowned on his brother. But Donnegan looked on him sadly.

"There is a girl——" he began.

"Why didn't I guess it?" exclaimed Lord Nick. "If ever you find a man unreasonable, stubborn and foolish, you'll always find a woman behind it! All this trouble because of a piece of calico?"

He leaned back, laughing thunderously in his relief.

"Come, come! I was prepared for a tragedy. Now tell me about this girl. Who and what is she?"

"The daughter of the colonel."

"You're in love with her? I'm glad to hear it, Garry. As a matter of fact I've been afraid that you were hunting in my own preserve, but if it's the colonel's daughter, you're welcome to her. So you love the girl? She's pretty, lad!"

"I love her?" said Donnegan in an indescribably tender voice. "I love her? Who am I to love her? A thief, a mankiller, a miserable play actor, a gambler, a drunkard. I love her? Bah!"

If there was one quality of the mind with which Lord Nick was less familiar than with all others, it was humbleness of spirit. He now abased his magnificent head, and resting his chin in the mighty palm of his hand, he stared with astonishment and commiseration into the face of Donnegan. He seemed to be learning new things every moment about his brother.

"Leave me out of the question," said Donnegan.

"Can't be done. If I leave you out, dear boy, there's not one of them that I care a hang about; I'd ride roughshod over the whole lot. I've done it before to better men than these!"

"Then you'll change, I know. This is the fact of the matter. She loves Landis. And if you take Landis away where will you put him?"

"Where he was stolen away. In Lebrun's."

"And what will be in Lebrun's?"

"Joe Rix to guard him and the old negress to nurse him."

"No, no! Nelly Lebrun will be there!"

"Eh? Are you glancing at her, now?"

"Henry, you yourself know that Landis is mad about that girl."

"Oh, she's flirted a bit with him. Turned the fool's head. He'll come out of it safe. She won't break his heart. I've seen her work on others!"

He chuckled at the memory.

"What do I care about Landis?" said Donnegan with unutterable scorn. "It's the girl. You'll break her heart, Henry; and if you do I'll never forgive you."

"Steady, lad. This is a good deal like a threat."

"No, no, no! Not a threat, Heaven knows!"

"By Heaven!" exclaimed Lord Nick. "I begin to be irritated to see you stick on a silly point like this. Listen to me, lad. Do you mean to say that you are making all this trouble about a slip of a girl?"

"The heart of a girl," said Donnegan calmly.

"Let Landis go; then take her in your arms and kiss her worries away. I warrant you can do it! I gather from Nell that you're not tongue-tied around women!"

"I?" echoed Donnegan, turning pale. "Don't jest at this, Henry. I'm as serious as death. She's the type of woman made to love one man, and one man only. Landis may be common as dirt; but she doesn't see it. She's fastened her heart on him. I looked in on her a little while ago. She turned white when she saw me. I brought Landis to her, but she hates me because I had to shoot him down."

"Garry," said the big man with a twinkle in his eye, "you're in love!"

It shook Donnegan to the core, but he replied instantly: "If I were in love, don't you suppose that I would have shot to kill when I met Landis?"

At this his brother blinked, frowned, and shook his head. The point was apparently plain to him and wiped out his previous convictions. Also, it eased his mind.

"Then you don't love the girl?"

"I?"

"Either way, my hands are cleared of the worry. If you want her, let me take Landis. If you don't want her, what difference does it make to you except silly sentiment?"

Donnegan made no answer.

"If she comes to Lebrun's house, I'll see that Nell doesn't bother him too much."

"Can you control her? If she wants to see this fool can you keep her away, and if she goes to him can you control her smiling?"

"Certainly," said Lord Nick, but he flushed heavily.

Donnegan smiled.

"She's a devil of a girl," admitted Henry Reardon. "But this is beside the point: which is, that you're sticking on a matter that means everything to

me, and which is only a secondhand interest to you
—a point of sentiment. You pity the girl. What's
pity? Bah! I pity a dog in the street, but would I
cross you, Garry, lad, to save the dog? Sentiment,
I say, silly sentiment."

Donnegan rose.

"It was a silly sentiment," he said hoarsely, "that
put me on the road following you, Henry. It was
a silly sentiment that turned me into a wastrel, a
wanderer, a man without a home and without
friends."

"It's wrong to throw that in my face," muttered
Lord Nick.

"It is. And I'm sorry for it. But I want you
to see that matters of sentiment may be matters of
life and death with me."

"Aye, if it were for you it would be different.
I might see my way clear—but for a girl you have
only a distant interest in——"

"It is a matter of whether or not her heart shall
be broken."

"Come, come. Let's talk man talk. Besides,
girls' hearts don't break in this country. You're
old-fashioned."

"I tell you the question of her happiness is worth
more than a dozen lives like yours and mine."

There had been a gathering impatience in Lord
Nick. Now he, also, leaped to his feet; a giant.

"Tell me in one word: You stick on this point?"

"In one word—yes!"

"Then you deny me, Garry. You set me aside for
a silly purpose of your own—a matter that really
doesn't mean much to you. It shows me where I
stand in your eyes—and nothing between the devil
and the moon shall make me side-step!"

They remained silent, staring at each other. Lord Nick stood with a flush of anger growing; Donnegan became whiter than ever, and he stiffened himself to his full height, which, in all who knew him well, was the danger signal.

"You take Landis?" he said softly.

"I do."

"Not," said Donnegan, "while I live!"

"You mean——" cried Lord Nick.

"I mean it!"

They had been swept back to the point at which that strangest of scenes began, but this time there was an added element—horror.

"You'd fight?"

"To the death, Henry!"

"Garry, if one of us should kill the other, he'd be cursed forever!"

"I know it."

"And she's worth even this?"

"A thousand times more! What are we? Dust in the wind; dust in the wind. But a woman like that is divine, Henry!"

Lord Nick swayed a little, setting himself in balance like an animal preparing for the leap.

"If it comes to the pinch, it is you who will die," he said. "You've no chance against me, Garry. And I swear to you that I won't weaken. You prove that you don't care for me. You put another above me. It's my pride, my life, that you'd sacrifice to the whim of a girl!" His passion choked him.

"Are you ready?" said Donnegan.

"Yes!"

"Move first!"

"I have never formed the habit."

"Nor I? You fool, take what little advantage you can, because it won't help you in the end."

"You shall see. I have a second sight, Henry, and it shows me you dead on the floor there, looking bigger than ever, and I see the gun smoking in my hand and my heart as dead as ashes! Oh, Henry, if there were only some other way!"

They were both pale now.

"Aye," murmured Lord Nick, "if we could find a judge. My hand turns to lead when I think of fighting you, Garry."

Perspiration stood on the face of Donnegan.

"Name a judge; I'll abide by the decision."

"Some man——"

"No, no. What man could understand me? A woman, Henry!"

"Nell Lebrun."

"The girl who loves you? You want me to plead before her?"

"Put her on her honor and she'll be as straight as a string with both of us."

For a moment Donnegan considered, and at length: "She loves you, Henry. You have that advantage. You have only to let her know that this is a vital matter to you and she'll speak as you wish her to speak."

"Nonsense. You don't know her. You've seen yourself that no man can control her absolutely."

"Make a concession."

"A thousand, Garry, dear boy, if they'll get us clear from this horrible mess."

"Only this. Leave The Corner for a few hours. Give me until—to-night. Let me see Nelly during that time. You've had years to work on her. I want only this time to put my own case before her."

"Thank Heaven that we're coming to see light and a way out!"

"Aye, Henry."

The big man wiped his forehead and sighed in his relief.

"A minute ago I was ready—but we'll forget all this. What will you do? How will you persuade Nelly? I almost think that you intend to make love to her, Garry!"

The little man turned paler still.

"It is exactly what I intend," he said quietly.

The brow of Lord Nick darkened solemnly, and then he forced a laugh.

"She'll be afraid to turn me down, Garry. But try your own way." He bit his lips. "Why, if you influence her that way—do it. What's a fickle jade to me? Nothing!"

"However I do it, you'll stick by her judgment, Henry?"

The perspiration had started on Lord Nick's forehead again. Doubt swayed him, but pride forced him on.

"I'll come again to-night," he said gloomily. "I'll meet you in—Milligan's?"

"In Milligan's, then."

Lord Nick, without a word of farewell, stamped across the hut and out.

As for Donnegan, he stepped backward, his legs buckled beneath him, and when big George entered, with a scared face, he found the little man half sitting on the bunk, half lying against the wall with the face and the staring eyes of a dead man.

## CHAPTER XXXIV

### HE ENTERS THE BLACK PIT

IT was a long time before Donnegan left the hut, and when he came out the crowd which had gathered to watch the fight, or at least to mark the reports of the guns when those two terrible warriors met, was scattered. There remained before Donnegan only the colonel in his invalid's chair. Even from the distance one could see that his expression was changed, and when the little red-headed man came near the colonel looked up to him with something akin to humility.

"Donnegan," he said, stopping the other as Donnegan headed for the door of the hut, "Donnegan, don't go in there just now."

Donnegan turned and came slowly toward him.

"The reason," said the colonel, "is that you probably won't receive a very cheery reception. Unfortunate—very unfortunate. Lou has turned wrong-headed for the first time in her life and she won't listen to reason."

He chuckled softly.

"I never dreamed there was so much of my metal in her. Blood will tell, my boy; blood will tell. 'And when you finally get her you'll find that she's worth waiting for."

"Let me tell you a secret," said Donnegan dryly. "I am no longer waiting for her!"

"Ah?" smiled the colonel. "Of course not. This bringing of Landis to her—it was all pure self-sacrifice. It was not an attempt to soften her heart. It was not a cunning maneuver. Tush! Of course not!"

"I am about to make a profound remark," said Donnegan carelessly.

"By all means."

"You read the minds of other people through a colored glass, colonel. You see yourself everywhere."

"In other words I put my own motives into the actions and behind the actions of people? Perhaps. I am full of weaknesses. Very full. In the meantime let me tell you one important thing—if you have not made the heart of Lou tender toward you, you have at least frightened her."

The jaw of Donnegan set.

"Excellent!" he said huskily.

"Perhaps better than you think; and to keep you abreast with the times, you must know another thing. Lou has a silly idea that you are a lost soul, Donnegan, but she attributes your fall entirely to my weakness. Nothing can convince her that you did not intend to kill Landis; nothing can convince her that you did not act on my inspiration. I have tried arguing. Bah! she overwhelmed me with her scorn. You are a villain, says Lou, and I have made you one. And for the first time in my memory of her, her eyes fill with tears."

"Tears?"

"Upon my honor, and when a girl begins to weep about a man I don't need to say he is close to her heart."

"You are full of maxims, Colonel Macon."

"As a nut is full of meat. Old experience, you know. In the meantime Lou is perfectly certain that I intend to make away with Landis. Ha, ha, ha!" The laughter of the colonel was a cheery thunder, and soft as with distance. "Landis is equally convinced. He begs Lou not to fall asleep lest I should steal in on him. She hardly dares leave him to cook his food. I actually think she would have been glad to see that fiend, Lord Nick, take Landis away!"

Donnegan smiled wanly. But could he tell her, poor girl, the story of Nelly Lebrun? Landis, in fear of his life, was no doubt at this moment pouring out protestations of deathless affection.

"And they both consider you an archdemon for keeping Lord Nick away!"

Again Donnegan winced, and coughed behind his hand to cover it.

"However," went on the colonel, "when it comes to matters with the hearts of women, I trust to time. Time alone will show her that Landis is a puppy."

"In the meantime, colonel, she keeps you from coming near Landis?"

"Not at all! You fail to understand me and my methods, dear boy. I have only to roll my chair into the room and sit and smile at Jack in order to send him into an hysteria of terror. It is amusing to watch. And I can be there while Lou is in the room and through a few careful innuendoes convey to Landis my undying determination to either remove him from my path and automatically become his heir, or else secure from him a legal transfer of his rights to the mines."

"I have learned," said Donnegan, "that Landis has not the slightest claim to them himself. And that you set him on the trail of the claims by trickery."

The colonel did not wince.

"Of course not," said the fat trickster. "Not the slightest right. My claim is a claim of superior wits, you see. And in the end all your labor shall be rewarded, for my share will go to Lou and through her it shall come to you. No?"

"Quite logical."

The colonel disregarded the other's smile.

"But I have a painful confession to make."

"Well?"

"I misjudged you, Donnegan. A moment since, when I was nearly distraught with disappointment, I said some most unpleasant things to you."

"I have forgotten them."

But the colonel raised his strong forefinger and shook his head, smiling.

"No, no, Donnegan. If you deny it, I shall know that you are harboring the most undying grudge against me. As a matter of fact, I have just had an interview with Lord Nick, and the cursed fellow put my nerves on edge."

The colonel made a wry face.

"And when you came, I saw no manner in which you could possibly thwart him."

His eyes grew wistful.

"Between friends—as a son to his future father," he said softly, "can't you tell me what the charm was that you used on Nick to send him away? I watched him come out of the shack. He was in a fury. I could see that by the way his head thrust out between his big shoulders. And when he went down the hill he was striding like a giant, but every now and then he would stop short, and his head would go up as if he were tempted to turn around and go back, but didn't quite have the nerve. Donnegan, tell me the trick of it?"

"Willingly. I appealed to his gambling instinct."

"Which leaves me as much in the dark as ever."

But Donnegan smiled in his own peculiar and mirthless manner and he went on to the hut. Not that he expected a cheery greeting from Lou Macon, but he was drawn by the same perverse instinct which tempts a man to throw himself from the great height. At the door he paused a moment. He could distinguish no words, but he caught the murmur of Lou's voice as she talked to Jack Landis, and it had that infinitely gentle quality which only a woman's voice can have, and only when she nurses the sick. It was a pleasant torture to Donnegan to hear it. At length he summoned his resolution and tapped at the door.

The voice of Lou Macon stopped. He heard a hurried and whispered consultation. What did they expect? Then swift footfalls on the floor, and she opened the door. There was a smile of expectancy on her lips; her eyes were bright; but when she saw Donnegan her lips pinched in. She stared at him as if he were a ghost.

"I knew; I knew!" she said piteously, falling back a step but still keeping her hand upon the knob of the door as if to block the way to Donnegan. "Oh, Jack, he has killed Lord Nick and now he is here——"

To do what? To kill Landis in turn? Her horrified eyes implied as much. He saw Landis in the distance raise himself upon one elbow and his face was gray, not with pain but with dread.

"It can't be!" groaned Landis.

"Lord Nick is alive," said Donnegan. "And I have not come here to torment you; I have only come to ask that you let me speak with you alone for a moment, Lou!"

He watched her face intently. All the cabin was in deep shadow, but the golden hair of the girl glowed as if with an inherent light of its own, and the same light touched her face. Jack Landis was stricken with panic; he stammered in a dreadful eagerness of fear.

"Don't leave me, Lou. You know what it means. He wants to get you out of the way so that the colonel can be alone with me. Don't go, Lou! Don't go!"

As though she saw how hopeless it was to try to bar Donnegan by closing the door against him, she fell back to the bed. She kept her eye on the little man, as if to watch against a surprise attack, and, fumbling behind her, her hand found the hand of Landis and closed over it with the reassurance of a mother.

"Don't be afraid, Jack. I won't leave you. Not unless they carry me away by force."

"I give you my solemn word," said Donnegan in torment, "that the colonel shall not come near Landis while you're away with me."

"Your word!" murmured the girl with a sort of horrified wonder. "*Your* word!"

And Donnegan bowed his head.

But all at once she cast out her free hand toward him, while the other still cherished the weakness of Jack Landis.

"Oh, give them up!" she cried. "Give up my father and all his wicked plans. There *is* something good in you. Give him up; come with us; stand for us; and we shall be grateful all our lives!"

The little man had removed his hat, so that the sunshine burned brightly on his red hair. Indeed, there was always a flamelike quality about him. In inaction he seemed femininely frail and pale; but when his spirit was roused his eyes blazed as his hair burned in the sunlight.

"You shall learn in the end," he said to the girl, "that everything I do, I do for you."

She cried out as if he had struck her.

"It's not worthy of you," she said bitterly. "You are keeping Jack here—in peril—for my sake?"

"For your sake," said Donnegan.

She looked at him with a queer pain in her eyes.

"To keep you from needless lying," she said, "let me tell you that Jack has told me everything. I am not angry because you come and pretend that you do all these horrible things for my sake. I know my father has tempted you with a promise of a great deal of money. But in the end you will get nothing. No, he will twist everything away from you and leave you nothing! But as for me—I know everything; Jack told me."

"He has told you what? What?"

"About the woman you love."

"The woman I love?" echoed Donnegan, stupefied.

It seemed that Lou Macon could only name her with an effort that left her trembling.

"The Lebrun woman," she said. "Jack has told me."

"Did you tell her that?" he asked Landis.

"The whole town knows it," stammered the wounded man.

The cunning hypocrisy spurred Donnegan. He put his foot on the threshold of the shack, and at this the girl cried out and shrank from him; but Landis was too paralyzed to stir or speak. For a moment Donnegan was wildly tempted to pour his torrent of contempt and accusation upon Landis. To what end? To prove to the girl that the big fellow had coolly tricked her? That it was to be near Nelly Lebrun as much as to be away from the colonel that he wished so ardently to leave the shack? After all, Lou Macon was made happy by an illusion; let her keep it.

He looked at her sadly again. She stood defiant over Landis; ready to protect the helpless bulk of the man.

So Donnegan closed the door softly and turned away with ashes in his heart.

# CHAPTER XXXV

### HE IS TALKED OF

WHEN Nelly Lebrun raised her head from her
hands, Donnegan was a far figure; yet even
in the distance she could catch the lilt and easy
sway of his body; he rode as he walked, lightly, his
feet in the stirrups half taking his weight in a
semi-English fashion. For a moment she was on
the verge of spurring after him, but she kept the
rein taut and merely stared until he dipped away
among the hills. For one thing she was quite assured that she could not overtake that hard rider;
and, again, she felt that it was useless to interfere.
To step between Lord Nick and one of his purposes
would have been like stepping before an avalanche
and commanding it to halt with a raised hand.

She watched miserably until even the dust cloud
dissolved and the bare, brown hills alone remained
before her. Then she turned away, and hour after
hour let her black jog on.

To Nelly Lebrun this day was one of those still
times which come over the life of a person, and in
which they see themselves in relation to the rest of
the world clearly. It would not be true to say that
Nelly loved Donnegan. Certainly not as yet, for
the familiar figure of Lord Nick filled her imagination. But the little man was different. Lord Nick
commanded respect, admiration, obedience; but there
was about Donnegan something which touched her
in an intimate and disturbing manner. She had

felt the will-o'-the-wisp flame which burned in him in his great moments. It was possible for her to smile at Donnegan; it was possible to even pity him for his fragility, his touchy pride about his size; to criticize his fondness for taking the center of the stage even in a cheap little mining camp like this and strutting about, the center of all attention. Yet there were qualities in him which escaped her, a possibility of metallic hardness, a pitiless fire of purpose.

To Lord Nick, he was as the bull terrier to the mastiff.

But above all she could not dislodge the memory of his strange talk with her at Lebrun's. Not that she did not season the odd avowals of Donnegan with a grain of salt, but even when she had discounted all that he said, she retained a quivering interest. Somewhere beneath his words she sensed reality. Somewhere beneath his actions she felt a selfless willingness to throw himself away.

As she rode she was comparing him steadily with Lord Nick. And as she made the comparisons she felt more and more assured that she could pick and choose between the two. They loved her, both of them. With Nick it was an old story; with Donnegan it might be equally true in spite of its newness. And Nelly Lebrun felt rich. Not that she would have been willing to give up Lord Nick. By no means. But neither was she willing to throw away Donnegan. Diamonds in one hand and pearls in the other. Which handful must she discard?

She remained riding an unconscionable length of time, and when she drew rein again before her father's house, the black was flecked with foam from his clamped bit, and there was a thick lather under the stirrup leathers. She threw the reins to the servant who answered her call and went slowly into the house.

Donnegan, by this time, was dead. She began to feel that it would be hard to look Lord Nick in the face again. His other killings had often seemed to her glorious. She had rejoiced in the invincibility of her lover.

Now he suddenly took on the aspect of a murderer.

She found the house hushed. Perhaps every one was at the gaming house; for now it was mid-afternoon. But when she opened the door to the apartment which they used as a living room she found Joe Rix and The Pedlar and Lester sitting side by side, silent. There was no whisky in sight; there were no cards to be seen. Marvel of marvels, these three men were spending their time in solemn thought. A sudden thought rushed over her, and her cry told where her heart really lay, at least at this time.

"Lord Nick—has he been——"

The Pedlar lifted his gaunt head and stared at her without expression. It was Joe Rix who answered.

"Nick's upstairs."

"Safe?"

"Not a scratch."

She sank into a chair with a sigh, but was instantly on edge again with the second thought.

"Donnegan?" she whispered.

"Safe and sound," said Lester coldly.

She could not gather the truth of the statement.

"Then Nick got Landis back before Donnegan returned?"

"No."

Like any other girl, Nelly Lebrun hated a puzzle above all things in the world, at least a puzzle which affected her new friends.

"Lester, what's happened?" she demanded.

At this Lester, who had been brooding upon the floor, raised his eyes and then switched one leg over the other. He was a typical cowman, was Lester, from his crimson handkerchief knotted around his throat to his shop-made boots which fitted slenderly about his instep with the care of a gloved hand.

"I dunno what happened," said Lester. "Which looks like what counts is the things that didn't happen. Landis is still with that devil, Macon. Donnegan is loose without a scratch, and Lord Nick is in his room with a face as black as a cloudy night."

And briefly he described how Lord Nick had gone up the hill, seen the colonel, come back, taken a horse litter, and gone up the hill again, while the populace of The Corner waited for a crash. For Donnegan had arrived in the meantime. And how Nick had gone into the cabin, remained a singularly long time, and then come out, with a face half white and half red and an eye that dared any one to ask questions. He had strode straight home to Lebrun's and gone to his room; and there he remained, never making a sound.

"But I'll give you my way of readin' the sign on that trail," said Lester. "Nick goes up the hill to clean up on Donnegan. He sees him; they size each other up in a flash; they figure that if they's a gun it means a double killin'—and they simply haul off and say a perlite fare-thee-well."

The girl paid no attention to these remarks. She was sunk in a brown study.

"There's something behind it all," she said, more to herself than to the men. "Nick is proud as the devil himself. And I can't imagine why he'd let Donnegan go. Oh, it might have been done if they'd met alone in the desert. But with the whole town looking on and waiting for Nick to clean up on Donnegan—no, it isn't possible. There *must* have been a show-down of some kind."

There was a grim little silence after this.

"Maybe there was," said The Pedlar dryly. "Maybe there was a show-down—and the wind-up of it is that Nick comes home meek as a six-year-old broke down in front."

She stared at him, first astonished, and then almost frightened.

"You mean that Nick may have taken water?"

The three, as one man, shrugged their shoulders, and met her glance with cold eyes.

"You fools!" cried the girl, springing to her feet. "He'd rather die!"

Joe Rix leaned forward, and to emphasize his point he stabbed one dirty forefinger into the fat palm of his other hand.

"You just start thinkin' back," he said solemnly, "and you'll remember that Donnegan has done some pretty slick things."

Lester added with a touch of contempt: "Like shootin' down Landis one day and then sittin' down and havin' a nice long chat with you the next. I dunno how he does it."

"That hunch of yours," said the girl fiercely, "ought to be roped and branded—lie! Lester, don't look at me like that. And if you think Nick has lost his grip on things you're dead wrong. Step light, Lester—and the rest of you. Or Nick may hear you walk—and think."

She flung out of the room and raced up the stairs to Lord Nick's room. There was an interval without response after her first knock. But when she rapped again he called out to know who was there. At her answer she heard his heavy stride cross the room, and the door opened slowly. His face, as she looked up to it, was so changed that she hardly knew him. His hair was unkempt, on end, where he had sat with his fingers thrust into it, buried in thought. And the marks of his palms were red upon his forehead.

"Nick," she whispered, frightened, "what is it?"

He looked down half fiercely, half sadly at her. And though his lips parted they closed again before he spoke. Fear jumped coldly in Nelly Lebrun.

"Did Donnegan——" she pleaded, white-faced. "Did he——"

"Did he bluff me out?" finished Nick. "No, he didn't. That's what everybody'll say. I know it, don't I? And that's why I'm staying here by myself, because the first fool that looks at me with a question in his face, why—I'll break him in two."

She pressed close to him, more frightened than before. That Lord Nick should have been driven to defend himself with words was almost too much for credence.

"You know I don't believe it, Nick? You know that I'm not doubting you?"

But he brushed her hands roughly away.

"You want to know what it's all about? Then go over to—well, to Milligan's. Donnegan will be there. He'll explain things to you, I guess. He wants to see you. And maybe I'll come over later and join you."

Seeing Lord Nick before her, so shaken, so gray of face, so dull of eye, she pictured Donnegan as a devil in human form, cunning, resistless.

"Nick, dear——" she pleaded.

He closed the door in her face, and she heard his heavy step go back across the room. In some mysterious manner she felt the Promethean fire had been stolen from Lord Nick, and Donnegan's was the hand that had robbed him of it.

# CHAPTER XXXVI

## HE TELLS NEW LIES

IT was fear that Nelly Lebrun felt first of all.
It was fear because the impossible had happened
and the immovable object had been at last moved.
Going back to her own room, the record of Lord
Nick flashed across her mind; one long series of
thrilling deeds. He had been a great and widely
known figure on the mountain desert while she herself was no more than a girl. When she first met
him she had been prepared for the sight of a fire-
breathing monster; and she had never quite recovered from the first thrill of finding him not devil
but man.

Quite oddly, now that there seemed another man
as powerful as Lord Nick or even more terrible, she
felt for the big man more tenderly than ever; for
like all women, there was a corner of her heart into
which she wished to receive a thing she could cherish
and protect. Lord Nick, the invincible, had seemed
without any real need of other human beings. His
love for her had seemed unreal because his need of
her seemed a superficial thing. Now that he was in
sorrow and defeat she suddenly visualized a Lord
Nick to whom she could truly be a helpmate. Tears
came to her eyes at the thought.

Yet, very contradictorily and very humanly, the
moment she was in her room she began preparing
her toilet for that evening at Lebrun's. Let no one
think that she was already preparing to cast Lord

Nick away and turn to the new star in the sky of the mountain desert. By no means. No doubt her own heart was not quite clear to Nelly. Indeed, she put on her most lovely gown with a desire for revenge. If Lord Nick had been humbled by this singular Donnegan, would it not be a perfect revenge to bring Donnegan himself to her feet? Would it not be a joy to see him turn pale under her smile, and then, when he was well-nigh on his knees, spurn the love which he offered her?

She set her teeth and her eyes gleamed with the thought. But nevertheless she went on lavishing care in the preparation for that night.

As she visioned the scene, the many curious eyes that watched her with Donnegan; the keen envy in the faces of the women; the cold watchfulness of the men, were what she pictured.

In a way she almost regretted that she was admired by such fighting men, Landis, Lord Nick, and now Donnegan, who frightened away the rank and file of other would-be admirers. But it was a pang which she could readily control and subdue.

To tell the truth the rest of the day dragged through a weary length. At the dinner table her father leaned to her and talked in his usual murmuring voice which could reach her own ear and no other by any chance.

"Nelly, there's going to be the devil to pay around The Corner. You know why. Now, be a good girl and wise girl and play your cards. Donnegan is losing his head; he's losing it over you. So play your cards."

"Turn down Nick and take up Donnegan?" she asked coldly.

"I've said enough already," said her father, and

would not speak again. But it was easy to see that he already felt Lord Nick's start to be past its full glory.

Afterward, Lebrun himself took his daughter over to Milligan's and left her under the care of the dance-hall proprietor.

"I'm waiting for some one," said Nelly, and Milligan sat willingly at her table and made talk. He was like the rest of The Corner—full of the subject of the strange encounter between Lord Nick and Donnegan. What had Donnegan done to the big man? Nelly merely smiled and said they would all know in time; one thing was certain—Lord Nick had not taken water. But at this Milligan smiled behind his hand.

Ten minutes later there was that stir which announced the arrival of some public figures; and Donnegan with big George behind him came into the room. This evening he went straight to the table to Nelly Lebrun. Milligan, a little uneasy, rose. But Donnegan was gravely polite and regretted that he had interrupted.

"I have only come to ask you for five minutes of your time," he said to the girl.

She was about to put him off merely to make sure of her hold over him, but something she saw in his face fascinated her. She could not play her game. Milligan had slipped away before she knew it, and Donnegan was in his place at the table. He was as much changed as Lord Nick, she thought. Not that his clothes were less carefully arranged than ever, but in the compression of his lips and something behind his eyes she felt the difference. She would have given a great deal indeed to have learned what went on behind the door of Donnegan's shack when Lord Nick was there.

"Last time you asked for one minute and stayed half an hour," she said. "This time it's five minutes."

No matter what was on his mind he was able to answer fully as lightly.

"When I talk about myself, I'm always long-winded."

"To-night it's some one else?"

"Yes."

She was, being a woman, intensely disappointed, but her smile was as bright as ever.

"Of course I'm listening."

"You remember what I told you of Landis and the girl on the hill?"

"She seems to stick in your thoughts, Mr. Donnegan."

"Yes, she's a lovely child."

And by his frankness he very cunningly disarmed her. Even if he had hesitated an instant she would have been on the track of the truth, but he had foreseen the question and his reply came back instantly.

He added: "Also, what I say has to do with Lord Nick."

"Ah," said the girl a little coldly.

Donnegan went on. He had chosen frankness to be his rôle and he played it to the full.

"It is a rather wonderful story," he went on. "You know that Lord Nick went up the hill for Landis? And The Corner was standing around waiting for him to bring the youngster down?"

"Of course."

"There was only one obstacle—which you had so kindly removed—myself."

"For your own sake, Mr. Donnegan."

"Ah, don't you suppose that I know?" And his voice touched her. "He came to kill me. And no doubt he could have done so."

Such frankness shocked her into a new attention.

Perhaps Donnegan overdid his part a little at this point, for in her heart of hearts she knew that the little man would a thousand times rather die than give way to any living man.

"But I threw my case bodily before him—the girl —her love for Landis—and the fear which revolved around your own unruly eyes, you know, if he were sent back to your father's house. I placed it all before him. At first he was for fighting at once. But the story appealed to him. He pitied the girl. And in the end he decided to let the matter be judged by a third person. He suggested a man. But I know that a man would see in my attitude nothing but foolishness. No man could have appreciated the position of that girl on the hill. I myself named another referee—yourself."

She gasped.

"And so I have come to place the question before you, because I know that you will decide honestly."

"Then I shall be honest," said the girl.

She was thinking: Why not have Landis back? It would keep the three men revolving around her. Landis on his feet and well would have been nothing; either of these men would have killed him. But Landis sick she might balance in turn against them both. Nelly had the instincts of a fencer; she loved balance.

But Donnegan was heaping up his effects. For

by the shadow in her eyes he well knew what was passing through her mind, and he dared not let her speak too quickly.

"There is more hanging upon it. In the first place, if Landis is left with the girl it gives the colonel a chance to work on him, and like as not the colonel will get the young fool to sign away the mines to him—frighten him, you see, though I've made sure that the colonel will not actually harm him."

"How have you made sure? They say the colonel is a devil."

"I have spoken with him. The colonel is not altogether without sensibility to fear."

She caught the glint in the little man's eye and she believed.

"So much for that. Landis is safe, but his money may not be. Another thing still hangs upon your decision. Lord Nick wanted to know why I trusted to you? Because I felt you were honest. Why did I feel that? There was nothing to do. Besides, how could I conceal myself from such a man? I spoke frankly and told him that I trusted you because I love you."

She closed her hand hard on the edge of the table to steady herself.

"And he made no move at you?"

"He restrained himself."

"Lord Nick?" gasped the incredulous girl.

"He is a gentleman," said Donnegan with a singular pride which she could not understand.

He went on: "And unfortunately I fear that if you decide in favor of my side of the argument, I fear that Lord Nick will feel that you—that you——"

He was apparently unable to complete his sentence.

"He will feel that you no longer care for him," said Donnegan at length.

The girl pondered him with cloudy eyes.

"What is behind all this frankness?" she asked coldly.

"I shall tell you. Hopelessness is behind it. Last night I poured my heart at your feet. And I had hope. To-day I have seen Lord Nick and I no longer hope."

"Ah?"

"He is worthy of a lovely woman's affection; and I——" He called her attention to himself with a deprecatory gesture.

"Do you ask me to hurt him like this?" said the girl. "His pride is the pride of the fiend. Love me? He would hate me!"

"It might be true. Still I know you would risk it, because——" he paused.

"Well?" asked the girl, whispering in her excitement.

"Because you are a lady."

He bowed to her.

"Because you are fair; because you are honest, Nelly Lebrun. Personally I think that you can win Lord Nick back with one minute of smiling. But you might not. You might alienate him forever. It will be clumsy to explain to him that you were influenced not by me, but by justice. He will make it a personal matter, whereas you and I know that it is only the right that you are seeing."

She propped her chin on the tips of her fingers, and her arm was a thing of grace. For the last moments that clouded expression had not cleared.

"If I only could read your mind," she murmured
now. "There is something behind it all."

"I shall tell you what it is. It is the restraint
that has fallen upon me. It is because I wish to
lean closer to you across the table and speak to
you of things which are at the other end of the
world from Landis and the other girl. It is because I have to keep my hands gripped hard to
control myself. Because, though I have given up
hope, I would follow a forlorn chance, a lost cause,
and tell you again and again that I love you, Nelly
Lebrun!"

He had half lowered his eyes as he spoke; he had
called up a vision, and the face of Lou Macon
hovered dimly between him and Nelly Lebrun. If
all that he spoke was a lie, let him be forgiven for
it; it was to the golden-haired girl whom he ad-
dressed, and it was she who gave the tremor and
the fiber to his voice. And after all was he not
pleading for her happiness as he believed?

He covered his eyes with his hand; but when he
looked up again she could see the shadow of the
pain which was slowly passing. She had never
seen such emotion in any man's face, and if it was
for another, how could she guess it? Her blood was
singing in her veins, and the old, old question was
flying back and forth through her brain like a shut-
tle through a loom: Which shall it be?

She called up the picture of Lord Nick, half
broken, but still terrible, she well knew. She pitied
him, but when did pity wholly rule the heart of a
woman? And as for Nelly Lebrun, she had the
ambition of a young Cæsar; she could not fill a
second place. He, who loved her must stand first,
and she saw Donnegan as the invincible man. She

had not believed half of his explanation. No, he was shielding Lord Nick; behind that shield the truth was that the big man had quailed before the small.

Of course she saw that Donnegan, pretending to be constrained by his agreement with Lord Nick, was in reality cunningly pleading his own cause. But his passion excused him. When has a woman condemned a man for loving her beyond the rules of fair play?

"Whatever you may decide," Donnegan was saying, "I shall be prepared to stand by it without a murmur. Send Landis back to your father's house and I submit; I leave The Corner and say farewell. But now, think quickly. For Lord Nick is coming to receive your answer."

# CHAPTER XXXVII

## HE CONQUERS

IF the meeting between Lord Nick and Donnegan earlier that day had wrought up the nerves of The Corner to the point of hysteria; if the singular end of that meeting had piled mystery upon excitement; if the appearance of Donnegan, sitting calmly at the table of the girl who was known to be engaged to Nick, had further stimulated public curiosity, the appearance of Lord Nick was now a crowning burden under which The Corner staggered.

Yet not a man or a woman stirred from his chair, for every one knew that if the long-delayed battle between these two gun fighters was at length to take place, neither bullet was apt to fly astray.

But what happened completed the wreck of The Corner's nerves, for Lord Nick walked quietly across the floor and sat down with Nelly Lebrun and his somber rival.

Oddly enough, he looked at Donnegan, not at the girl, and this token of the beaten man decided her.

"Well?" said Lord Nick.

"I have decided," said the girl. "Landis should stay where he is."

Neither of the two men stirred hand or eye. But Lord Nick turned gray. At length he rose and asked Donnegan, quietly, to step aside with him. Seeing them together, the difference between their sizes was more apparent: Donnegan seemd hardly larger than a child beside the splendid bulk of Lord Nick. But she could not overhear their talk.

"You've won," said Lord Nick, "both Landis and Nelly. And——"

"Wait," broke in Donnegan eagerly. "Henry, I've persuaded Nelly to see my side of the case, but that doesn't mean that she has turned from you to——"

"Stop!" put in Lord Nick, between his teeth. "I've not come to argue with you or ask advice or opinions. I've come to state facts. You've crawled in between me and Nelly like a snake in the grass. Very well. You're my brother. That keeps me from handling you. You've broken my reputation just as I said you would do. The bouncer at the door looked me in the eye and smiled when I came in."

He had to pause a little, breathing heavily, and avoiding Donnegan's eyes. Finally he was able to continue.

"I'm going to roll my blankets and leave The Corner and everything I have in it. You'll get my share of most things, it seems." He smiled after a ghastly, mirthless fashion. "I give you a free road. I surrender everything to you, Donnegan. But there are two things I want to warn you about. It may be that my men will not agree with me. It may be that they'll want to put up a fight for the mine. They can't get at it without getting at Macon. They can't get at him without removing you. And they'll probably try it. I warn you now.

"Another thing: from this moment there's no blood tie between us. I've found a brother and lost him in the same day. And if I ever cross you again, Donnegan, I'll shoot you on sight. Remember, I'm not threatening. I simply warn you in advance. If I were you, I'd get out of the country. Avoid me, Donnegan, as you'd avoid the devil."

And he turned on his heel. He felt the eyes of the people in the room follow him by jerks, dwelling on every one of his steps. Near the door, stepping aside to avoid a group of people coming in, he half turned and he could not avoid the sight of Donnegan and Nelly Lebrun at the other end of the room. He was leaning across the table, talking with a smile on his lips—at that distance he could not mark the pallor of the little man's face—and Nelly Lebrun was laughing. Laughing already, and oblivious of the rest of the world.

Lord Nick turned, a blur coming before his eyes and made blindly for the door. A body collided with him; without a word he drew back his massive right fist and knocked the man down. The stunned body struck against the wall and collapsed along the floor. Lord Nick felt a great madness swell in his heart. Yet he set his teeth, controlled himself, and went on toward the house of Lebrun. He had come within an eyelash of running amuck, and the quivering hunger for action was still swelling and ebbing in him when he reached the gambler's house.

Lebrun was not in the gaming house, no doubt, at this time of night—but the rest of Nick's chosen men were there. They stood up as he entered the room—Harry Masters, newly arrived—The Pedlar —Joe Rix—three names famous in the mountain desert for deeds which were not altogether a pleasant aroma in the nostrils of the law-abiding, but whose sins had been deftly covered from legal proof by the cunning of Nick, and whose bravery itself had half redeemed them. They rose now as three wolves rise at the coming of the leader. But this time there was a question behind their eyes, and he read it in gloomy silence.

"Well?" asked Harry Masters.

In the old days not one of them would have dared to voice the question, but now things were changing, and well Lord Nick could read the change and its causes.

"Are you talking to me?" asked Nick, and he looked straight between the eyes of Masters.

The glance of the other did not falter, and it maddened Nick.

"I'm talking to you," said Masters coolly enough. "What happened between you and Donnegan?"

"What should happen?" asked Lord Nick.

"Maybe all this is a joke," said Masters bitterly. He was a square-built man, with a square face and a wrinkled, fleshy forehead. In intelligence, Nick ranked him first among the men. And if a new leader were to be chosen there was no doubt as to where the choice of the men would fall. No doubt that was why Masters put himself forward now, ready to brave the wrath of the chief. "Maybe we're fooled," went on Masters. "Maybe they ain't any call for you to fall out with Donnegan?"

"Maybe there's a call to find out this," answered Lord Nick. "Why did you leave the mines? What are you doing up here?"

The other swallowed so hard that he blinked.

"I left the mines," he declared through his set teeth, "because I was run off 'em."

"Ah," said Lord Nick, for the devil was rising in him, "I always had an idea that you might be yellow, Masters."

The right hand of Masters swayed toward his gun, hesitated, and then poised idly.

"You heard me talk?" persisted Lord Nick brutally. "I call you yellow. Why don't you draw on me? I called you yellow, you swine, and I call the rest of you yellow. You think you have me down? Why, curse you, if there were thirty of your cut, I'd say the same to you!"

There was a quick shift, the three men faced Lord Nick, but each from a different angle. And opposing them, he stood superbly indifferent, his arms folded, his feet braced. His arms were folded, but each hand, for all they knew, might be grasping the butt of a gun hidden away in his clothes. Once they flashed a glance from face to face; but there was no action. They were remembering only too well some of the wild deeds of this giant.

"You think I'm through," went on Lord Nick. "Maybe I am—through with you. You hear me talk?"

One by one, his eyes dared them, and one by one they took up the challenge, struggled, and lowered their glances. He was still their master and in that mute moment the three admitted it, The Pedlar last of all.

Masters saw fit to fall back on the last remark.

"I've swallowed a lot from you, Nick," he said gravely. "Maybe there'll be an end to what we take one of these days. But now I'll tell you how yellow I was. A couple of gents come to me and tell me I'm through at the mine. I told them they were crazy. They said old Colonel Macon had sent them down to take charge. I laughed at 'em. They went away and came back. Who with? With the sheriff. And he flashed a paper on me. It was all drawn up clean as a whistle. Trimmed up with a lot of 'whereases' and 'as hereinbefore mentioned' and such like things. But the sheriff just gimme a look and then he tells me what it's about. Jack Landis has signed over all the mines to the colonel and the colonel has taken possession."

As he stopped, a growl came from the others.

"Lester is the man that has the complaint," said Lord Nick. "Where do the rest of you figure in it? Lester had the mines; he lost 'em because he couldn't drop Landis with his gun. He'd never have had a smell of the gold if I hadn't come in. Who made Landis see light? I did! Who worked it so that every nickel that came out of the mines went through the fingers of Landis and came back to us? I did! But I'm through with you. You can hunt for yourselves now. I've kept you together to guard one another's backs. I've kept the law off your trail. You, Masters, you'd have swung for killing the McKay brothers. Who saved you? Who was it bribed the jury that tried you for the shooting up of Derbyville, Pedlar? Who took the marshal off your trail after you'd knifed 'Lefty' Waller, Joe Rix? I've saved you all a dozen times. Now you whine at me. I'm through with you forever!"

Stopping, he glared about him. His knuckles stung from the impact of the blow he had delivered in Milligan's place. He hungered to have one of these three stir a hand and get into action.

And they knew it. All at once they crumbled and became clay in his hands.

"Chief," said Joe Rix, the smoothest spoken of the lot, and one who was supposed to stand specially well with Lord Nick on account of his ability to bake beans, Spanish. "Chief, you've said a whole pile. You're worth more'n the rest of us all rolled together. Sure. We know that. There ain't any argument. But here's just one little point that I want to make.

"We was doing fine. The gold was running fine and free. Along comes this Donnegan. He busts up our good time. He forks in on your girl——"

A convulsion of the chief's face made Rix waver in his speech and then he went on: "He shoots Landis, and when he misses killing him—by some accident, he comes down here and grabs him out of Lebrun's own house. Smooth, eh? Then he makes Landis sign that deed to the mines. Oh, very nice work, I say. Too nice.

"Now, speakin' man to man, they ain't any doubt that you'd like to get rid of Donnegan. Why don't you? Because everybody has a jinx, and he's yours. I ain't easy scared, maybe, but I knew an albino with white eyes once, and just to look at him made me some sick. Well, chief, they ain't nobody can say that you ever took water or ever will. But maybe the fact that this Donnegan has hair just as plumb red as yours may sort of get you off your feed. I'm just suggesting. Now, what I say is, let the rest of us take a crack at Donnegan, and you sit back and come in on the results when we've cleaned up. D'you give us a free road?"

How much went through the brain of Lord Nick? But in the end he gave his brother up to death. For he remembered how Nelly Lebrun had sat in Milligan's laughing.

"Do what you want," he said suddenly. "But I want to know none of your plans—and the man that tells me Donnegan is dead gets paid—in lead!"

# CHAPTER XXXVIII

## HE IS TEMPTED WITH GOLD

THE smile of Joe Rix was the smile of a diplomat. It could be maintained upon his face as unwaveringly as if it were wrought out of marble while Joe heard insult and lie. As a matter of fact Joe had smiled in the face of death more than once, and this is a school through which even diplomats rarely pass. Yet it was with an effort that he maintained the characteristic good-natured expression when the door to Donnegan's shack opened and he saw big George and, beyond the negro, Donnegan himself.

"Booze," said Joe Rix to himself instantly.

For Donnegan was a wreck. The unshaven beard —it was the middle of morning—was a reddish mist over his face. His eyes were sunken in shadow. His hair was uncombed. He sat with his shoulders hunched up like one who suffers from cold. Altogether his appearance was that of one whose energy has been utterly sapped.

"The top of the morning, Mr. Donnegan," said Joe Rix, and put his foot on the threshold.

But since big George did not move it was impossible to enter.

"Who's there?" asked Donnegan.

It was a strange question to ask, for by raising his eyes he could have seen. But Donnegan was staring down at the floor. Even his voice was a weak murmur.

"What a party! What a party he's had!" thought Joe Rix, and, after all, there was cause for a celebration. Had not the little man in almost one stroke won the heart of the prettiest girl in The Corner, and also did he not probably have a working share in the richest of the diggings?

"I'm Joe Rix," he said.

"Joe Rix?" murmured Donnegan softly. "Then you're one of Lord Nick's men?"

"I *was*," said Joe Rix, "sort of attached to him, maybe."

Perhaps this pointed remark won the interest of Donnegan. He raised his eyes, and Joe Rix beheld the most unhappy face he had ever seen. "A bad hang-over," he decided, "and that makes it bad for me!"

"Come in," said Donnegan in the same monotonous, lifeless voice.

Big George reluctantly, it seemed, withdrew to one side, and Rix was instantly in the room and drawing out a chair so that he could face Donnegan.

"I was," he proceeded, "sort of tied up with Lord Nick. But"—and here he winked broadly—"it ain't much of a secret that Nick ain't altogether a lord any more. Nope. Seems he turned out sort of common, they say."

"What fool," murmured Donnegan, "has told you that? What ass has told you that Lord Nick is a common sort?"

It shocked Joe Rix, but being a diplomat he avoided friction by changing his tactics.

"Between you and me," he said calmly enough, "I took what I heard with a grain of salt. There's something about Nick that ain't common, no matter what they say. Besides, they's some men that nobody but a fool would stand up to. It ain't hardly a shame for a man to back down from 'em."

He pointed this remark with a nod to Donnegan.

"I'll give you a bit of free information," said the little man, and his weary eyes lighted a little. "There's no man on the face of the earth who could make Lord Nick back down."

Once more Joe Rix was shocked to the verge of gaping, but again he exercised a power of marvelous self-control.

"About that," he remarked as pointedly as before, "I got my doubts. Because there's some things that any gent with sense will always clear away from. Maybe not one man—but say a bunch all standin' together."

Donnegan leaned back in his chair and waited. Both of his hands remained drooping from the edge of the table, and the tired eyes drifted slowly across the face of Joe Rix.

It was obviously not the after effects of liquor. The astonishing possibility occurred to Joe Rix that this seemed to be a man with a broken spirit and a great sorrow. He blinked that absurdity away.

"Coming to cases," he went on, "there's yourself, Mr. Donnegan. Now, you're the sort of a man that don't sidestep nobody. Too proud to do it. But even you, I guess, would step careful if there was a whole bunch agin' you."

"No doubt," remarked Donnegan.

"I don't mean any ordinary bunch," explained Joe Rix, "but a lot of hard fellows. Gents that handle their guns like they was born with a holster on the hip."

"Fellows like Nick's crowd," suggested Donnegan quietly.

At this thrust the eyes of Joe narrowed a little.

"Yes," he admitted, "I see you get my drift."

"I think so."

"Two hard fighters would give the best man that ever pulled a gun a lot of trouble. Eh?"

"No doubt."

"And three men—they ain't any question, Mr. Donnegan—would get him ready for a hole in the ground."

"I suppose so."

"And four men would make it no fight—jest a plain butchery."

"Yes?"

"Now, I don't mean that Nick's crowd has any hard feeling about you, Mr. Donnegan."

"I'm glad to hear that."

"I knew you'd be. That's why I've come, all friendly, to talk things over. Suppose you look at it this way——"

"Joe Rix," broke in Donnegan, sighing, "I'm very tired. Won't you cut this short? Tell me in ten words just how you stand."

Joe Rix blinked once more, caught his breath, and fired his volley.

"Short talk is straight talk, mostly," he declared. "This is what Lester and the rest of us want—the mines!"

"Ah?"

"Macon stole 'em. We got 'em back through Landis. Now we've got to get 'em back through the colonel himself. But we can't get at the colonel while you're around."

"In short, you're going to start out to get me? I expected it, but it's kind of you to warn me."

"Wait, wait, wait! Don't rush along to conclusions. We ain't so much in a hurry. We don't want you out of the way. We just want you on our side."

"Shoot me up and then bring me back to life, eh?"

"Mr. Donnegan," said the other, spreading out his hands solemnly on the table, "you ain't doin' us justice. We don't hanker none for trouble with you. Anyway it comes, a fight with you means somebody dead besides you. We'd get you. Four to one is too much for any man. But one or two of us might go down. Who would it be? Maybe The Pedlar, maybe Harry Masters, maybe Lester, maybe me! Oh, we know all that. No gun play if we can keep away from it."

"You've left out the name of Lord Nick," said Donnegan.

Joe Rix winked.

"Seems like you tended to him once and for all when you got him alone in this cabin. Must have thrown a mighty big scare into him. He won't lift a hand agin' you now."

"No?" murmured Donnegan hoarsely.

"Not him! But that leaves four of us, and four is plenty, eh?"

"Perhaps."

"But I'm not here to insist on that point. No, we put a value on keepin' up good feeling between us and you, Mr. Donnegan. We ain't fools. We know a man when we see him—and the fastest gunman that ever slid a gun out of leather ain't the sort of a man that me and the rest of the boys pass over lightly. Not us! We know you, Mr. Donnegan; we respect you; we want you with us; we're going to have you with us."

"You flatter me and I thank you. But I'm glad to see that you are at last coming to the point."

"I am, and the point is five thousand dollars that's tied behind the hoss that stands outside your door."

He pushed his fat hand a little way across the table, as though the gold even then were resting in it, a yellow tide of fortune.

"For which," said Donnegan, "I'm to step aside and let you at the colonel?"

"Right."

Donnegan smiled.

"Wait," said Joe Rix. "I was makin' a first offer to see how you stood, but you're right. Five thousand ain't enough and we ain't cheap skates. Not us. Mr. Donnegan, they's ten thousand cold iron men behind that saddle out there and every cent of it belongs to you when you come over on our side."

But Donnegan merely dropped his chin upon his hand and smiled mirthlessly at Joe Rix. A wild thought came to the other man. Both of Donnegan's hands were far from his weapons. Why not a quick draw, a snap shot, and then the glory of having killed this man slayer in single battle for Joe Rix?

The thought rushed red across his brain and then faded slowly. Something kept him back. Perhaps it was the singular calm of Donnegan; no matter how quiet he sat he suggested the sleeping cat which can leap out of dead sleep into fighting action at a touch. By the time a second thought had come to Joe Rix the idea of an attack was like an idea of suicide.

"Is that final?" he asked, though Donnegan had not said a word.

"It is."

Joe Rix stood up.

"You put it to us kind of hard. But we want you, Mr. Donnegan. And here's the whole thing in a nutshell. Come over to us. We'll stand behind you. Lord Nick is slipping. We'll put you in his place. You won't even have to face him; we'll get rid of him."

"You'll kill him and give his place to me?" asked Donnegan.

"We will. And when you're with us, you cut in on the whole amount of coin that the mines turn out—and it'll be something tidy. And right now, to show where we stand and how high we put you, I'll let you in on the rock-bottom truth. Mr. Donnegan, out there tied behind my saddle there's thirty thousand dollars in pure gold. You can take it in here and weigh it out!"

He stepped back to watch this blow take effect. To his unutterable astonishment the little man had not moved. His chin still rested upon the back of his hand, and the smile which was on the lips and not in the eyes of Donnegan remained there, fixed.

"Donnegan," muttered Joe Rix, "if we can't get you, we'll get rid of you. You understand?"

But the other continued to smile.

It gave Joe Rix a shuddering feeling that some one was stealing behind him to block his way to the door. He cast one swift glance over his shoulder and then, seeing that the way was clear, he slunk back, always keeping his face to the red-headed man. But when he came to the doorway his nerve collapsed. He whirled, covered the rest of the distance with a leap, and emerged from the cabin in a fashion ludicrously like one who has been kicked through a door.

His nerve returned as soon as the sunlight fell warmly upon him again; and he looked around hastily to see if any one had observed his flight.

There was no one on the whole hillside except Colonel Macon in the invalid chair, and the colonel was smiling broadly, beneficently. He had his perfect hands folded across his breast and seemed to cast a prayer of peace and good will upon Joe Rix.

# CHAPTER XXXIX

### HE HAS AN ALLY

NELLY LEBRUN smelled danger. She sensed it as plainly as the deer when the puma comes between her and the wind. The many tokens that something was wrong came to her by small hints which had to be put together before they assumed any importance.

First of all, her father, who should have burst out at her in a tirade for having left Lord Nick for Donnegan said nothing at all, but kept a dark smile on his face when she was near him. He even insinuated that Nick's time was done and that another was due to supercede him.

In the second place, she had passed into a room where Masters, Joe Rix, and The Pedlar sat cheek by jowl in close conference with a hum of deep voice. But at her appearance all talk was broken off.

It was not strange that they should not invite her into their confidence if they had some dark work ahead of them; but it was exceedingly suspicious that Joe Rix attempted to pass off their whispers by immediately breaking off the soft talk and springing into the midst of a full-fledged jest; also, it was strangest of all that when the jest ended even The Pedlar, who rarely smiled, now laughed uproariously and smote Joe soundingly upon the back.

Even a child could have strung these incidents into a chain of evidence which pointed toward danger. Obviously the danger was not directly hers, but then it must be directed at some one near to her. Her father? No, he was more apt to be the mainspring of their action. Lord Nick? There was nothing to gain by attacking him. Who was left? Donnegan!

As the realization came upon her it took her breath away for a moment. Donnegan was the man. At breakfast every one had been talking about him. Lebrun had remarked that he had a face for the cards—emotionless. Joe Rix had commented upon his speed of hand, and The Pedlar had complimented the little man on his dress.

But at lunch not a word was spoken about Donnegan even after she had dexterously introduced the subject twice. Why the sudden silence? Between morning and noon Donnegan must have grievously offended them.

Fear for his sake stimulated her; but above and beyond this, indeed, there was a mighty feminine curiosity. She smelled the secret; it reeked through the house, and she was devoured by eagerness to know. She hand-picked Lord Nick's gang in the hope of finding a weakness among them; some weakness upon which she could play in one of them and draw out what they were all concealing. The Pedlar was as unapproachable as a crag on a mountaintop. Masters was wise as an outlaw broncho. Lester was probably not even in the confidence of the others because since the affair with Landis his nerve had been shattered to bits and the others secretly despised him for being beaten by the youngster at the draw. There remained, therefore, only Joe Rix.

But Joe Rix was a fox of the first quality. He

lied with the smoothness of silk. He could show
a dozen colors is as many moments. Come to the
windward of Joe Rix? It was a delicate business!
But since there was nothing else to do, she fixed her
mind upon it, working out this puzzle. Joe Rix
wished to destroy Donnegan for reasons that were
evidently connected with the mines. And she must
step into his confidence to discover his plans. How
should it be done? And there was a vital need
for speed, for they might be within a step of
executing whatever mischief it was that they were
planning.

She went down from her room; they were there
still, only Joe Rix was not with them. She went
to the apartment where he and the other three of
Nick's gang slept and rapped at the door. He
maintained his smile when he saw her, but there
was an uncertain quiver of his eyebrows that told
her much. Plainly he was ill at ease. Suspicious?
Ay, there were always clouds of suspicion drifting
over the red, round face of Joe Rix. She put a
tremor of excitement and trouble in her voice.

"Come into my room, Joe, where we won't be
interrupted."

He followed her without a word, and since she
led the way she was able to relax her expression
for a necessary moment. When she closed the door
behind him and faced Joe again she was once more
ready to step into her part. She did not ask him
to sit down. She remained for a moment with her
hand on the knob and searched the face of Joe Rix
eagerly.

"Do you think he can hear?" she whispered,
gesturing over her shoulder.

"Who?"

"Who but Lord Nick!" she exclaimed softly.

The bewilderment of Joe clouded his face a second and then he was able to smooth it away. What on earth was the reason of her concern about Lord Nick he was obviously wondering.

"I'll tell you why," she said, answering the unspoken question at once. "He's as jealous as the devil, Joe!"

The fat little man sighed as he looked at her.

"He can't hear. Not through that log wall. But we'll talk soft, if you want."

"Yes, yes. Keep your voice down. He's already jealous of you, Joe."

"Of me?"

"He knows I like you, that I trust you; and just now he's on edge about every one I look at."

The surprising news which the first part of this sentence contained caused Joe to gape, and the girl looked away in concern, enabling him to control his expression. For she knew well enough that men hate to appear foolishly surprised. And particularly a fox like Joe Rix.

"But what's the trouble, Nelly?" He added with a touch of venom: "I thought everything was going smoothly with you. And I thought you weren't worrying much about what Lord Nick had in his mind."

She stared at him as though astonished.

"Do you think just the same as the rest of them?" she asked sadly. "Do you mean to say that you're fooled just the same as Harry Masters and The Pedlar and the rest of those fools—including Nick himself?"

Joe Rix was by no means willing to declare himself a fool beforehand. He now mustered a look of much reserved wisdom.

"I have my own doubts, Nell, but I'm not talking about them."

He was so utterly at sea that she had to bite her lip hard to keep from breaking into ringing laughter.

"Oh, I knew that you'd seen through it, Joe," she cried softly. "You see what an awful mess I've gotten into?"

He passed a hurried hand across his forehead and then looked at her searchingly. But he could not penetrate her pretense of concern.

"No matter what I think," said Joe Rix, "you come out with it frankly. I'll listen."

"As a friend, Joe?"

She managed to throw a plea into her voice that made Joe sigh.

"Sure. You've already said that I'm your friend, and you're right."

"I'm in terrible, terrible trouble! You know how it happened. I was a fool. I tried to play with Lord Nick. And now he thinks I was in earnest."

As though the strength of his legs had given way, Joe Rix slipped down into a chair.

"Go on," he said huskily. "You were playing with Lord Nick?"

"Can't you put yourself in my place, Joe? It's always been taken for granted that I'm to marry Nick. And the moment he comes around everybody else avoids me as if I were poison. I was sick of it. And when he showed up this time it was the same old story. A man would as soon sign his own death warrant as ask me for a dance. You know how it is?"

He nodded, still at sea, but with a light beginning to dawn in his little eyes.

"I'm only a girl, Joe. I have all the weakness
of other girls. I don't want to be locked up in a
cage just because I—love one man!"

The avowal made Joe blink. It was the second
time that day that he had been placed in an astonishing scene. But some of his old cunning remained
to him.

"Nell," he said suddenly, rising from his chair
and going to her. "What are you trying to do to
me? Pull the wool over my eyes?"

It was too much for Nelly Lebrun. She knew
that she could not face him without betraying her
guilt and therefore she did not attempt it. She
whirled and flung herself on her bed, face down,
and began to sob violently, suppressing the sounds.
And so she waited.

Presently a hand touched her shoulder lightly.

"Go away," cried Nelly in a choked voice. "I
hate you, Joe Rix. You're like all the rest!"

His knee struck the floor with a soft thud.

"Come on, Nell. Don't be hard on me. I thought
you were stringing me a little. But if you're
playing straight, tell me what you want?"

At that she bounced upright on the bed, and
before he could rise she caught him by both shoulders.

"I want Donnegan," she said fiercely.

"What?"

"I want him dead!"

Joe Rix gasped.

"Here's the cause of all my trouble. Just because
I flirted with him once or twice, Nick thought I
was in earnest and now he's sulking. And Donnegan

puts on airs and acts as if I belonged to him. I hate him, Joe. And if he's gone Nick will come back to me. He'll come back to me, Joe; and I want him so!"

She found that Joe Rix was staring straight into her eyes, striving to probe her soul to its depths, and by a great effort she was enabled to meet that gaze. Finally the fat little man rose slowly to his feet. Her hands trailed from his shoulders as he stood up and fell helplessly upon her lap.

"Well, I'll be hanged, Nell!" exclaimed Joe Rix. "What do you mean?"

"You're not acting a part? No, I can see you mean it. But what a cold-blooded little——" He checked himself. His face was suddenly jubilant. "Then we've got him, Nell. We've got him if you're with us. We had him anyway, but we'll make sure of him if you're with us. Look at this! You saw me put a paper in my pocket when I opened the door of my room? Here it is?"

He displayed before the astonished eyes of Nelly Lebrun a paper covered with an exact duplicate of her own swift, dainty script. And she read:

Nick is terribly angry and is making trouble. I have to get away. It isn't safe for me to stay here. Will you help me? Will you meet me at the shack by Donnell's ford to-morrow morning at ten o'clock?

"But I didn't write it," cried Nelly Lebrun, bewildered.

"Nelly," Joe Rix chuckled, flushing with pleasure, "you didn't. It was me. I kind of had an idea that you wanted to get rid of this Donnegan, and I was going to do it for you and then surprise you with the good news."

"Joe, you forged it?"

"Don't bother sayin' pretty things about me and my pen," said Rix modestly. "This is nothin'! But if you want to help me, Nelly——"

His voice faded partly out of her consciousness as she fought against a tigerish desire to spring at the throat of the little fat man. But gradually it dawned on her that he was asking her to write out that note herself. Why? Because it was possible that Donnegan might have seen her handwriting and in that case, though the imitation had been good enough to deceive Nelly herself, it probably would not for a moment fool the keen eyes of Donnegan. But if she herself wrote out the note, Donnegan was already as good as dead.

"That is," concluded Joe Rix, "if he really loves you, Nell."

"The fool!" cried Nelly. "He worships the ground I walk on, Joe. And I hate him for it."

Even Joe Rix shivered, for he saw the hate in her eyes and could not dream that he himself was the cause and the object of it. There was a red haze of horror and confusion in front of her eyes, and yet she was able to smile while she copied the note for Joe Rix.

"But how are you going to work it?" she asked. "How are you going to kill him, Joe?"

"Don't bother your pretty head," said the fat man, smiling. "Just wait till we bring you the good news."

"But are you sure?" she asked eagerly. "See what he's done already. He's taken Landis away from us; he's baffled Nick himself, in some manner; and he's gathered the mines away from all of us.

He's a devil, Joe, and if you want to get him you'd better take ten men for the job."

"You hate him, Nell, don't you?" queried Joe Rix, and his voice was both hard and curious. "But how has he harmed you?"

"Hasn't he taken Nick away from me? Isn't that enough?"

The fat man shivered again.

"All right. I'll tell you how it works. Now, listen!"

And he began to check off the details of his plan.

# CHAPTER XL

### HE IS BOTH WARNED AND BETRAYED

THE day passed and the night, but how very slowly for Nelly Lebrun; she went up to her room early for she could no longer bear the meaning glances which Joe Rix cast at her from time to time. But once in her room it was still harder to bear the suspense as she waited for the noise to die away in the house. Midnight, and half an hour more went by, and then, at last, the murmurs and the laughter stopped; she alone was wakeful in Lebrun's. And when that time came she caught a scarf around her hair and her shoulders, made of a filmy material which would veil her face but through which she could see, and ventured out of her room and down the hall.

There was no particular need for such caution, however, it seemed. Nothing stirred. And presently she was outside the house and hurrying behind the houses and up the hill. Still she met nothing. If The Corner lived to-night, its life was confined to Milligan's and the gambling house.

She found Donnegan's shack and the one next to it, which the terrible colonel occupied, entirely dark, but only a moment after she tapped at the door it was opened. Donnegan, fully dressed, stood in the entrance, outlined blackly by the light which came faintly from the hooded lantern hanging on the wall. Was he sitting up all the night, unable to sleep because he waited breathlessly for that false tryst on the morrow? A great tenderness came over the heart of Nelly Lebrun.

"It is I?" she whispered.

There was a soft exclamation, then she was drawn into the room.

"Is there any one here?"

"Only big George. But he's in the kitchen and he won't hear. He never hears anything except what's meant for his ear. Take this chair!"

He was putting a blanket over the rough wood to make it more comfortable, and she submitted dumbly to his ministrations. It seemed terrible and strange to her that one so gentle should be the object of so much hate—such deadly hate as the members of Nick's gang felt for him. And now that he was sitting before her she could see that he had indeed been wakeful for a long time. His face was grimly wasted; the lips were compressed as one who has endured long pain; and his eyes gleamed at her out of a profound shadow. He remained in the gloom; the light from the lantern fell brightly upon his hands alone—meager, fleshless hands which seemed to represent hardly more strength than that of a child. Truly this man was all a creature of spirit and nerve. Therein lay his strength, as also his weakness, and again the cherishing instinct grew strong and swept over her.

"There is no one near," he said, "except the colonel and his daughter. They are up the hillside, somewhere. Did you see them?"

"No. What in the world are they out for at this time of night?"

"Because the colonel only wakes up when the sun goes down. And now he's out there humming to himself and never speaking a word to the girl.

But they won't be far away. They'll stay close to see that no one comes near the cabin to get at Landis."

He added: "They must have seen you come into my cabin!"

And his lips set even harder than before. Was it fear because of her?

"They may have seen me enter, but they won't know who it was. You have the note from me?"

"Yes."

"It's a lie! It's a ruse. I was forced to write it to save you! For they're planning to murder you. Oh, my dear!"

"Hush! Hush! Murder?"

"I've been nearly hysterical all day and all the night. But, thank Heaven, I'm here to warn you in time! You mustn't go. You mustn't go!"

"Who is it?"

He had drawn his chair closer; he had taken her hands, and she noted that his own were icy cold, but steady as rock. Their pressure soothed her infinitely.

"Joe Rix, The Pedlar, Harry Masters. They'll be at the shack at ten o'clock, but not I!"

"Murder, but a very clumsy scheme. Three men leave town and commit a murder and then expect to go undetected? Not even in the mountain desert!"

"But you don't understand, you don't understand! They're wise as foxes. They'll take no risk. They don't even leave town together or travel by the same routes. Harry Masters starts first. He rides out at eight o'clock in the morning and takes the north trail. He rides down the gulch and winds out of it and strikes for the shack at the ford. At half past eight The Pedlar starts. He goes past

Sandy's place and then over the trail through the marsh. You know it?"

"Yes."

"Last of all, Joe Rix starts at nine o'clock. Half an hour between them."

"How does he go to the shack?"

"By the south trail. He takes the ridge of the hills. But they'll all be at the shack long before you and they'll shoot you down from a distance as you come up to it. Plain murder, but even for cowardly murder they daren't face you except three to one."

He was thoughtful.

"Suppose they were to be met on the way?"

"You're mad to think of it!"

"But if they fail this time they'll try again. They must be taught a lesson."

"Three men? Oh, my dear, my dear! Promise!"

"Very well. I shall do nothing rash. And I shall never forget that you've come to tell me this and been in peril, Nell, for if they found you had come to me——"

"The Pedlar would cut my throat. I know him!"

"Ah! But now you must go. I'll take you down the hill, dear."

"No, no! It's much easier to get back alone. My face will be covered. But there's no way you could be disguised. You have a way of walking—good night—and God bless you!"

She was in his arms, straining him to her; and then she slipped out the door.

And sure enough, there was the colonel in his chair not fifty feet away with a girl pushing him. The moonlight was too dim for Nelly Lebrun to make out the face of Lou Macon, but even the light which escaped through the filter of clouds was

enough to set her golden hair glowing. The color
was not apparent, but its luster was soft silver in
the night. There was a murmur of the colonel's
voice as Nelly came out of the cabin.

And then, from the girl, a low cry.

It brought the blood to the cheeks of Nelly as she
hurried down the hill, for she recognized the pain
that was in it; and it occurred to her that if the
girl was in love with Jack Landis she was strangely
interested in Donnegan also.

The thought came so sharply home to her that
she paused abruptly on the way down the hill. After
all, this Macon girl would be a very strange sort if
she were not impressed by the little red-headed
man, with his gentle voice and his fiery ways, and
his easy way of making himself a brilliant spectacle
whenever he appeared in public. And Nelly remembered, also, with the keen suspicion of a woman
in love how weakly Donnegan had responded to her
embrace this night. How absent-mindedly his arms
had held her, and how numbly they had fallen away
when she turned at the door.

But she shook her head and made the suspicion
shudder its way out of her. Lou Macon, she decided, was just the sort of girl who would think
Jack Landis an ideal. Besides, she had never had
an opportunity to see Donnegan in his full glory
at Milligan's. And as for Donnegan? He was
wearied out; his nerves relaxed; and for the deeds
with which he had startled The Corner and won
her own heart he was now paying the penalty in the
shape of ruined nerves. Pity again swelled in her
heart, and a consuming hatred for the three mur-
derers who lived in her father's house.

And when she reached her room again her heart

was filled with a singing happiness and a glorious knowledge that she had saved the man she loved.

And Donnegan himself?

He had seen Lou and her father; he had heard that low cry of pain; and now he sat bowed again over his table, his face in his hands and a raging devil in his heart.

# CHAPTER XLI

### TOKENS OF HIS HANDIWORK

THERE was one complication which Nelly Lebrun might have foreseen after her pretended change of heart and her simulated confession to Joe Rix that she still loved the lionlike Lord Nick. But strangely enough she did not think of this phase; and even when her father the next morning approached her in the hall and tapping her arm whispered: "Good girl! Nick has just heard and he's hunting for you now!" Even then the full meaning did not come home to her. It was not until she saw the great form of Lord Nick stalking swiftly down the hall that she knew. He came with a glory in his face which the last day had graven with unfamiliar lines; and when he saw her he threw up his hand so that it almost brushed the ceiling, and cried out.

What could she do? Try to push him away; to explain?

There was nothing to be done. She had to submit when he swept her into his arms.

"Rix has told me. Rix has told me. Ah, Nell, you little fox!"

"Told you what, Nick?"

Was he, too, a party to the murderous plan?

But he allowed himself to be pushed away.

"I've gone through something in the last few days. Why did you do it, girl?"

She saw suddenly that she must continue to play her part.

"Some day I'll tell you why it was that I gave you up so easily, Nell. You thought I was afraid of Donnegan?" He ground his teeth and turned pale at the thought. "But that wasn't it. Some day I can tell you. But after this, the first man who comes between us—Donnegan or any other— I'll turn him into powder—under my heel!"

He ground it into the floor as he spoke. She decided that she would see how much he knew.

"It will never be Donnegan, at least," she said. "He's done for to-day. And I'm almost sorry for him in spite of all that he's done."

He became suddenly grave.

"What are you saying, Nell?"

"Why, Joe told you, didn't he? They've drawn Donnegan out of town, and now they're lying in wait for him. Yes, they must have him, by this time. It's ten o'clock!"

A strangely tense exclamation broke from Lord Nick. "They've gone for Donnegan?"

"Yes. Are you angry?"

The big man staggered; one would have said that he had been stunned with a blow.

"Garry!" he whispered.

"What are you saying?"

"Nell," he muttered hoarsely, "did you know about it?"

"But I did it for you, Nick. I knew you hated——"

"No, no! Don't say it!" He added bitterly, after a moment. "This is for my sins."

And then, to her: "But you knew about it and didn't warn him? You hated him all the time you were laughing with him and smiling at him? Oh, Nell! What a merciless witch of a woman you are! For the rest of them—I'll wait till they come back!"

"What are you going to do, Nick?"

"I told them I'd pay the man who killed Donnegan—with lead. Did the fools think I didn't mean it?"

Truly, no matter what shadow had passed over the big man, he was the lion again, and Nell shrank from him.

"We'll wait for them," he said. "We'll wait for them here."

And they sat down together in the room. She attempted to speak once in a shaken voice, but he silenced her with a gesture, and after that she sat and watched in quiet the singular play of varying expressions across his face. Grief, rage, tenderness, murderous hate—they followed like a puppet play.

What was Donnegan to him? And then there was a tremor of fear. Would the three suspect when they reached the shack by the ford and no Donnegan came to them? The moments stole on. Then the soft beat of a galloping horse in the sand. The horse stopped. Presently they saw Joe Rix and Harry Masters pass in front of the window. And they looked as though a cyclone had caught them up, juggled them a dizzy distance in the air, and then flung them down carelessly upon bruising rocks. Their hats were gone; and the clothes of burly Harry Masters were literally torn from his back. Joe Rix was evidently far more terribly hurt, for he leaned on the arm of Masters and they came on together, staggering.

"They've done the business!" exclaimed Lord Nick. "And now, curse them, I'll do theirs!"

But the girl could not speak. A black haze

crossed before her eyes. Had Donnegan gone out madly to fight the three men in spite of her warning?

The door opened. They stood in the doorway, and if they had seemed a horrible sight passing the window, they were a deadly picture at close range. And opposite them stood Lord Nick; in spite of their wounds there was murder in his face and his revolver was out.

"You've met him? You've met Donnegan?" he asked angrily.

Masters literally carried Joe Rix to a chair and placed him in it. He had been shot through both shoulders, and though tight bandages had stanched the wound he was still in agony. Then Masters raised his head.

"We've met him," he said.

"What happened?"

But Masters, in spite of the naked gun in the hand of Lord Nick, was looking straight at Nelly Lebrun.

"We fought him."

"Then say your prayers, Masters."

"Say prayers for The Pedlar, you fool," said Masters bitterly. "He's dead, and Donnegan's still living!"

There was a faint cry from Nelly Lebrun. She sank into her chair again.

"We've been double-crossed," said Masters, still looking at the girl. "I was going down the gulch the way we planned. I come to the narrow place where the cliffs almost touch, and right off the wall above me drops a wild cat. I thought it was a cat at first. And then I found it was Donnegan.

"The way he hit me from above knocked me off

the horse. Then we hit the ground. I started for my gun; he got it out of my hand; I pulled my knife. He got that away, too. His fingers work with steel springs and act like a cat's claws. Then we fought barehanded. He didn't say a word. But kept snarling in his throat. Always like a cat. And his face was devilish. Made me sick inside. Pretty soon he dived under my arms. Got me up in the air. I came down on my head.

"Of course I went out cold. When I came to there was still a mist in front of my eyes and this lump on the back of my head. He'd figured that my head was cracked and that I was dead. That's the only reason he left me. Later I climbed on my hoss and fed him the spur.

"But I was too late. I took the straight cut for the ford, and when I got there I found that Donnegan had been there before me. Joe Rix was lyin' on the floor. When he got to the shack Donnegan was waitin' for him. They went for their guns and Donnegan beat him to it. The hound didn't shoot to kill. He plugged him through both shoulders, and left him lyin' helpless. But I got a couple of bandages on him and saved him.

"Then we cut back for home and crossed the marsh. And there we found The Pedlar.

"Too late to help him. Maybe Donnegan knew that The Pedlar was something of a flash with a gun himself, and he didn't take any chances. He'd met him face to face the same way he met Joe Rix and killed him. Shot him clean between the eyes. Think of shooting for the head with a snapshot! That's what he done and Joe didn't have time to think twice after that slug hit him. His gun wasn't even fired, he was beat so bad on the draw.

"So Joe and me come back home. And we come full of questions!"

"Let me tell you something," muttered Lord Nick, putting up the weapon which he had kept exposed during all of the recital. "You've got what was coming to you. If Donnegan hadn't cleaned up on you, you'd have had to talk turkey with me. Understand?"

"Wait a minute," protested Harry Masters.

And Joe Rix, almost too far gone for speech, set his teeth over a groan and cast a look of hatred at the girl.

"Wait a minute, chief. There's one thing we all got to get straight. Somebody had tipped off Donnegan about our whole plan. Was it The Pedlar or Rix or me? I guess good sense'll tell a man that it wasn't none of us, eh? Then who was it? The only other person that knew about the plan—Nell—Nell, the crooked witch—and it's her that murdered The Pedlar—curse her!"

He thrust out his bulky arm as he spoke.

"Her that lied her way into our confidence with a lot of talk about you, Nick. Then what did she do? She goes runnin' to the gent that she said she hated. Don't you see her play? She makes fools of us—she makes a fool out of you!"

She dared not meet the glance of Lord Nick. Even now she might have acted out her part and filled in with lies, but she was totally unnerved.

"Get Rix to bed," was all he said, and he did not even glance at Nelly Lebrun.

Masters glowered at him, and then silently obeyed, lifting Joe as a helpless bulk, for the fat man was nearly fainting with pain. Not until they had gone and he had closed the door after them and upon

the murmurs of the servants in the hall did Lord
Nick turn to Nelly.

"Is it true?" he asked shortly.

Between relief and terror her mind was whirling.
"Is what true?"

"You haven't even sense enough to lie, Nell, eh?
It's all true, then? And last night, after you'd
wormed it out of Joe, you went to Donnegan?"

She could only stare miserably at him.

"And that was why you pushed me away when
I kissed you a little while ago?"

Once more she was dumb. But she was beginning
to be afraid. Not for herself, but for Donnegan.

"Nell, I told you I'd never let another man come
between us again. I meant it. I know you're
treacherous now; but that doesn't keep me from
wanting you. It's Donnegan again—Donnegan still?
Nell, you've killed him. As sure as if your own
finger pulled the trigger when I shoot him. He's
a dead one, and you've done it!"

If words would only come! But her throat was
stiff and cold and aching. She could not speak.

"You've done more than kill him," said Lord
Nick. "You've put a curse on me as well. And
afterward I'm going to even up with you. You hear
me? Nell, when I shoot Donnegan I'm doing a
thing worse than if he was a girl—or a baby. You
can't understand that; I don't want you to know.
But some time when you're happy again and you're
through grieving for Donnegan, I'll tell you the
truth and make your heart black for the rest of
your life."

Still words would not come. She strove to cling
to him and stop him, but he cast her away with a
single gesture and strode out the door.

# CHAPTER XLII

## HE MAKES A PRAYER

THERE was no crowd to block the hill at this second meeting of Donnegan and Lord Nick. There was a blank stretch of brown hillside with the wind whispering stealthily through the dead grass when Lord Nick thrust open the door of Donnegan's shack and entered.

The little man had just finished shaving and was getting back into his coat while George carried out the basin of water. And Donnegan, as he buttoned the coat, was nodding slightly to the rhythm of a song which came from the cabin of the colonel near by. It was a clear, high music, and though the voice was light it carried the sound far. Donnegan looked up to Lord Nick; but still he kept the beat of the music.

He seemed even more fragile this morning than ever before. Yet Lord Nick was fresh from the sight of the torn bodies of the two fighting men whom this fellow had struck and left for dead, or dying, as he thought.

"Dismiss your servant," said Lord Nick.

"George, you may go out."

"And keep him out."

"Don't come back until I call for you."

Big George disappeared into the kitchen and the outside door was closed. Yet even with all the doors

closed the singing of Lou Macon kept running
through the cabin in a sweet and continuous thread.

> What made the ball so fine?
> Robin Adair!
> What made the assembly shine?
> Robin Adair!

And no matter what Lord Nick could say, it
seemed that with half his mind Donnegan was listening to the song of the girl.

"First," said the big man, "I've broken my word."

Donnegan waved his hand and dismissed the
charge. He pointed to a chair, but Lord Nick paid
no heed.

"I've broken my word," he went on. "I promised that I'd give you a clear road to win over
Nelly Lebrun. I gave you the road and you've
won her, but now I'm taking her back!"

"Ah, Henry," said Donnegan, and a flash of
eagerness came in his eyes. "You're a thousand
times welcome to her."

Lord Nick quivered.

"Do you mean it?"

"Henry, don't you see that I was only playing
for a purpose all the time? And if you've opened
the eyes of Nelly to the fact that you truly love her
and I've been only acting out of a heartless sham—
why, I'm glad of it—I rejoice, Henry, I swear
I do!"

He came forward, smiling, and held out his hand;
Lord Nick struck it down, and Donnegan shrank
back, holding his wrist tight in the fingers of his
other hand.

"Is it possible?" murmured Henry Reardon. "Is
it possible that she loves a man who despises her?"

"Not that! If any other man said this to me, I'd call for an explanation of his meaning, Henry. No, no! I honor and respect her, I tell you. By Heaven, Nick, she has a thread of pure, generous gold in her nature!"

"Ah?"

"She has saved my life no longer ago than this morning."

"It's perfect," said Lord Nick. And he writhed under a torment. "I am discarded for the sake of a man who despises her!"

Donnegan, frowning with thought, watched his older brother. And still the thin singing entered the room, that matchless old melody of "Robin Adair;" the day shall never come when that song does not go straight from heart to heart. But because Donnegan still listened to it, Lord Nick felt that he was contemptuously received, and a fresh spur was driven into his tender pride.

"Donnegan!" he said sharply.

Donnegan raised his hand slowly.

"Do you call me by that name?"

"Aye. You've ceased to be a brother. There's no blood tie between us now, as I warned you before."

Donnegan, very white, moved back toward the wall and rested his shoulders lightly against it, as though he needed the support. He made no answer.

"I warned you not to cross me again," exclaimed Lord Nick.

"I have not."

"Donnegan, you've murdered my men!"

"Murder? I've met them fairly. Not murder, Henry."

"Leave out that name, I say!"

"If you wish," said Donnegan very faintly.

The sight of his resistlessness seemed to madden
Lord Nick. He made one of his huge strides and
came to the center of the room and dominated all
that was in it, including his brother.

"You murdered my men," repeated Lord Nick.
"You turned my girl against me with your lying
love-making and turned her into a spy. You made
her set the trap and then you saw that it was
worked. You showed her how she could wind me
around her finger again."

"Will you let me speak?"

"Aye, but be short."

"I swear to you, Henry, that I've never influenced
her to act against you; except to win her away for
just one little time, and she will return to you again.
It is only a fancy that makes her interested in me.
Look at us! How could any woman in her senses
prefer me?"

"Are you done?"

"No, no! I have more to say; I have a thousand
things!"

"I shall not hear them."

"Henry, there is a black devil in your face. Be-
ware of it."

"Who put it there?"

"It was not I."

"What power then?"

"Something over which I have no control."

"Are you trying to mystify me?"

"Listen!" And as Donnegan raised his hand, the
singing poured clear and small into the room.

"That is the power," said Donnegan.

"You're talking gibberish!" exclaimed the other
pettishly.

"I suppose I shouldn't expect you to understand."

"On the other hand, what I have to say is short and to the point. A child could comprehend it. You've stolen the girl. I tried to let her go. I can't. I have to have her. Willing or unwilling she has to belong to me, Donnegan."

"If you wish, I shall promise that I shall never see her again or speak to her."

"You fool! Won't she find you out? Do you think I could trust you? Only in one place—underground."

Donnegan had clasped his hands upon his breast and his eyes were wide.

"What is it you mean, Henry?"

"I'll trust you—dead!"

"Henry!"

"That name means nothing to me. I've forgotten it. The world has forgotten it."

"Henry, I implore you to keep cool—to give me five minutes for talk——"

"No, not one. I know your cunning tongue!"

"For the sake of the days when you loved me, my brother. For the sake of the days when you used to wheel my chair and be kind to me."

"You're wasting your time. You're torturing us both for nothing. Donnegan, my will is a rock. It won't change."

And drawing closer his right hand gripped his gun and the trembling passion of the gun fighter set him shuddering.

"You're armed, Garry. Go for your gun!"

"No, no!"

"Then I'll give you cause to fight."

And as he spoke, he drew back his massive arm and with his open hand smote Donnegan heavily across the face. The weight of that blow crushed the little man against the wall.

"Your gun!" cried Lord Nick, swaying from side to side as the passion choked him.

Donnegan fell upon his knees and raised his arms.

"God have mercy on me, and on yourself!"

At that the blackness cleared slowly on the face of the big man; he thrust his revolver into the holster.

"This time," he said, "there's no death. But sooner or later we meet, Donnegan, and then, I swear by all that lives, I'll shoot you down—without mercy—like a mad dog. You've robbed me; you've hounded me; you've killed my men; you've taken the heart of the woman I love. And now nothing can save you from the end."

He turned on his heel and left the room.

And Donnegan remained kneeling, holding a stained handkerchief to his face.

All at once his strength seemed to desert him like a tree chopped at the root, and he wilted down against the wall with closed eyes.

But the music still came out of the throat and the heart of Lou, and it entered the room and came into the ears of Donnegan. He became aware that there was a strength beyond himself which had sustained him, and then he knew it had been the singing of Lou from first to last which had kept the murder out of his own heart and restrained the hand of Lord Nick.

Perhaps of all Donnegan's life, this was the first moment of true humility.

# CHAPTER XLIII

### THE SACRIFICE

ONE thing was now clear. He must not remain in The Corner unless he was prepared for Lord Nick again; and in a third meeting guns must be drawn. From that greater sin he shrank, and prepared to leave. His orders to big George made the negro's eyes widen, but George had long since passed the point where he cared to question the decision of his master. He began to build the packs.

As for Donnegan, he could see that there was little to be won by remaining. That would save Landis to Lou Macon, to be sure, but after all, he was beginning to wonder if it were not better to let the big fellow go back to his own kind—Lebrun and the rest. For if it needed compulsion to keep him with Lou now, might it not be the same story hereafter?

Indeed, Donnegan began to feel that all his labor in The Corner had been running on a treadmill. It had all been grouped about the main purpose, which was to keep Landis with the girl. To do that now he must be prepared to face Nick again; and to face Nick meant the bringing of the guilt of fratricide upon the head of one of them. There only remained flight. He saw at last that he had been fighting blindly from the first. He had won a girl whom he did not love—though doubtless her liking was only the most fickle fancy. And she for whom he would have died he had taught to hate him. It

was a grim summing up. Donnegan walked the
room whistling softly to himself as he checked up
his accounts.

One thing at least he had done; he had taken the
joy out of his life forever.

And here, answering a rap at the door, he opened
it upon Lou Macon. She wore a dress of some very
soft material. It was a pale blue—faded, no doubt
—but the color blended exquisitely with her hair and
with the flush of her face. It came to Donnegan
that it was an unnecessary cruelty of chance that
made him see the girl lovelier than he had ever
seen her before at the very moment when he was
surrendering the last shadow of a claim upon her.

And it hurt him, also, to see the freshness of her
face, the clear eyes; and to hear her smooth, un-
troubled voice. She had lived untouched by anything
save the sunshine in The Corner.

Her glance flicked across his face and then fluttered down, and her color increased guiltily.

"I have come to ask you a favor," she said.

"Step in," said Donnegan, recovering his poise at
length.

At this, she looked past him, and her eyes widened a little. There was an imperceptible shrug of
her shoulders, as though the very thought of entering this cabin horrified her. And Donnegan had
to bear that look as well.

"I'll stay here; I haven't much to say. It's a small
thing."

"Large or small," said Donnegan eagerly. "Tell
me!"

"My father has asked me to take a letter for him
down to the town and mail it. I—I understand

that it would be dangerous for me to go alone. Will you walk with me?"

And Donnegan turned cold. Go down into The Corner? Where by five chances out of ten he must meet his brother in the street?

"I can do better still," he said, smiling. "I'll have George take the letter down for you."

"Thank you. But you see, father would not trust it to any one save me. I asked him; he was very firm about it."

"Tush! I would trust George with my life."

"Yes, yes. It is not what *I* wish—but my father rarely changes his mind."

Perspiration beaded the forehead of Donnegan. Was there no way to evade this easy request?

"You see," he faltered, "I should be glad to go——"

She raised her eyes slowly.

"But I am terribly busy this morning."

She did not answer, but half of her color left her face.

"Upon my word of honor there is no danger to a woman in the town."

"But some of the ruffians of Lord Nick——"

"If they dared to even raise their voices at you, they would hear from him in a manner that they would never forget."

"Then you don't wish to go?"

She was very pale now; and to Donnegan it was more terrible than the gun in the hand of Lord Nick. Even if she thought he was slighting her why should she take it so mortally to heart? For Donnegan, who saw all things, was blind to read the face of this girl.

"It doesn't really matter," she murmured and turned away.

A gentle motion, but it wrenched the heart of Donnegan. He was instantly before her.

"Wait here a moment. I'll be ready to go down immediately."

"No. I can't take you from your—work."

What work did she assign to him in her imagination? Endless planning of deviltry no doubt.

"I shall go with you," said Donnegan. "At first —I didn't dream it could be so important. Let me get my hat."

He left her and leaped back into the cabin.

"I am going down into The Corner for a moment," he said over his shoulder to big George, as he took his belt down from the wall.

The negro strode to the wall and took his hat from a nail.

"I shall not need you, George."

But George merely grinned, and his big teeth flashed at the master. And in the second place he took up a gun from the drawer and offered it to Donnegan.

"The gun in that holster ain't loaded," he said.

Donnegan considered him soberly.

"I know it. There'll be no need for a loaded gun."

But once more George grinned. All at once Donnegan turned pale.

"You dog," he whispered. "Did you listen at the door when Nick was here?"

"Me?" murmured George. "No, I just been thinking."

And so it was that while Donnegan went down the hill with Lou Macon, carrying an empty-chambered revolver, George followed at a distance of a few paces, and he carried a loaded weapon unknown to Donnegan.

It was the dull time of the day in The Corner. There were very few people in the single street, and though most of them turned to look at the little man and the girl who walked beside him, not one of them either smiled or whispered.

"You see?" said Donnegan. "You would have been perfectly safe—even from Lord Nick's ruffians. That was one of his men we passed back there."

"Yes. I'm safe with you," said the girl.

And when she looked up to him, the blood of Donnegan turned to fire.

Out of a shop door before them came a girl with a parcel under her arm. She wore a gay, semi-masculine outfit, bright-colored, jaunty, and she walked with a lilt toward them. It was Nelly Lebrun. And as she passed them, Donnegan lifted his hat ceremoniously high. She nodded to him with a smile, but the smile turned wan and small in an instant. There was a quick widening and then a narrowing of her eyes, and Donnegan knew that she had judged Lou Macon as only one girl can judge another who is lovelier.

He glanced at Lou to see if she had noticed, and he saw her raise her head and go on with her glance proudly straight before her; but her face was very pale, and Donnegan knew that she had guessed everything that was true and far more than the truth. Her tone at the door of the post office was ice.

"I think you are right, Mr. Donnegan. There's no danger. And if you have anything else to do, I can get back home easily enough."

"I'll wait for you," murmured Donnegan sadly,

and he stood at the door of the little building with bowed head.

And then a murmur came down the street. How small it was, and how sinister! It consisted of exclamations begun, and then broken sharply off. A swirl of people divided as a cloud of dust divides before a blast of wind, and through them came the gigantic figure of Lord Nick!

On he came, a gorgeous figure, a veritable king of men. He carried his hat in his hand and his red hair flamed, and he walked with great strides. Donnegan glanced behind him. The way was clear. If he turned, Lord Nick would not pursue him, he knew.

But to flee even from his brother was more than he could do; for the woman he loved would know of it and could never understand.

He touched the holster that held his empty gun—and waited!

An eternity between every step of Lord Nick. Others seemed to have sensed the meaning of this silent scene. People seemed to stand frozen in the midst of gestures. Or was that because Donnegan's own thoughts were traveling at such lightning speed that the rest of the world seemed standing still? What kept Lou Macon? If she were with him, not even Lord Nick in his madness would force on a gun play in the presence of a woman, no doubt.

Lord Nick was suddenly close; he had paused; his voice rang over the street and struck upon Donnegan's ear as sounds come under water.

"Donnegan!"

"Aye!" called Donnegan softly.

"It's the time!"

"Aye," said Donnegan.

Then a huge body leaped before him; it was big George. And as he sprang his gun went up with his hand in a line of light. The two reports came close together as finger taps on a table, and big George, completing his spring, lurched face downward into the sand.

Dead? Not yet. All the faith and selflessness which can make his people sometimes glorious was nerving the negro. And his master stood behind him, unarmed!

He reared himself upon his knees—an imposing bulk, even then, and fired again. But his hand was trembling, and the bullet shattered a sign above the head of Lord Nick. He, in his turn, it seemed to Donnegan that the motion was slow, twitched up the muzzle of his weapon and fired once more from his hip. And big George lurched back on the sand, with his face upturned to Donnegan. He would have spoken, but a burst of blood choked him; yet as his eyes fixed and glazed, he mustered his last strength and offered his revolver to the master.

But Donnegan let the hand fall limp to the ground. There were voices about him; steps running; but all that he clearly saw was Lord Nick with his feet braced, and his head high.

"Donnegan! Your gun!"

"Aye," said Donnegan.

"Take it then!"

But in the crisis, automatically Donnegan flipped his useless revolver out of its holster and into his hand. At the same instant the gun from Nick's hand seemed to blaze in his eyes. He was struck a crushing blow in his chest. He sank upon his knees; another blow struck his head, and Donnegan collapsed on the body of big George.

# CHAPTER XLIV.

### HE FINDS SALVATION

AN ancient drunkard in the second story of one of the stores across the street had roused himself at the sound of the shots and now he dragged himself to the window and began to scream: "Murder! Murder!" over and over, and even The Corner shuddered at the sound of his voice.

Lord Nick, his revolver still in his hand, stalked through the film of people who now swirled about him, eager to see the dead. There was no call for the law to make its appearance, and the representatives of the law were wisely dilatory in The Corner.

He stood over the two motionless figures with a stony face.

"You saw it, boys," he said. "You know what I've borne from this fellow. The nigger pulled his gun first on me. I shot in self-defense. As for— the other—it was a square fight."

"Square fight," some one answered. "You both went for your irons at the same time. Pretty work, Nick."

It was a solid phalanx of men which had collected around the moveless bodies as swiftly as mercury sinks through water. Yet none of them touched either Donnegan or the negro. And then the solid group dissolved at one side. It was the moan of a woman which had scattered it, and a yellow-haired girl slipped through them. She glanced once, in horror, at the mute faces of the men, and then there was a wail as she threw herself on the body of Donnegan. Somewhere she found the strength of a man to lift him and place him face upward on the sand, the gun trailing limply in his hand. And then she lay, half crouched over him, her face pressed to his heart—listening—listening for the stir of life.

Shootings were common in The Corner; the daily mortality ran high; but there had never been after-maths like this one. Men looked at one another, and then at Lord Nick. A bright spot of color had come in each of his cheeks, but his face was as hard as ever.

"Get her away from him," some one murmured.

And then another man cried out, stooped, wrenched the gun from the limp hand of Donnegan and opened the cylinder. He spun it; daylight was glittering through the empty cylinder.

At this the man stiffened, and with a low bow which would have done credit to a drawing-room, he presented the weapon butt first to Lord Nick.

"Here's something the sheriff will want to see," he said, "but maybe you'll be interested, too."

But Lord Nick, with the gun in his hand, stared at it dumbly, turned the empty cylinder. And the full horror crept slowly on his mind. He had not killed his brother, he had murdered him. As his eyes cleared, he caught the glitter of the eyes which sur-rounded him.

And then Lou Macon was on her knees with her hands clasped at her breast and her face glorious.

"Help!" she was crying. "Help me. He's not dead, but he's dying unless you help me!"

Then Lord Nick cast away his own revolver and the empty gun of Donnegan. They heard him shout: "Garry!" and saw him stride forward.

Instantly men pressed between, hard-jawed men who meant business. It was a cordon he would have to fight his way through; but he dissolved it with a word.

"You fools! He's my brother!"

And then he was on his knees opposite Lou Macon.

"You?" she had stammered in horror.

"His brother, girl."

And ten minutes later, when the bandages had been wound, there was a strange sight of Lord Nick striding up the street with his victim in his arms. How lightly he walked; and he was talking to the calm, pale face which rested in the hollow of his shoulder.

"He will live? He will live?" Lou Macon was pleading as she hurried at the side of Lord Nick.

"God willing, he shall live!"

It was three hours before Donnegan opened his eyes. It was three days before he recovered his senses, and looking aside toward the door he saw a brilliant shaft of sunlight falling into the room. In the midst of it sat Lou Macon. She had fallen asleep in her great weariness now that the crisis was over. Behind her, standing, his great arms folded, stood the indomitable figure of Lord Nick.

Donnegan saw and wondered greatly. Then he closed his eyes dreamily.

"Hush," said Donnegan to himself, as if afraid that what he saw was all a dream. "I'm in heaven, or if I'm not, it's still mighty good to be alive."

**THE END.**

# RIP-ROARIN' ACTION AND ADVENTURE BY THE WORLD'S MOST CELEBRATED WESTERN WRITER!

## GUN GENTLEMEN

MAX BRAND

Renowned throughout the Old West, Lucky Bill has the reputation of a natural battler. Yet he is no remorseless killer. He only outdraws any gunslinger crazy enough to pull a six-shooter first. Then Bill finds himself on the wrong side of the law, and plenty of greenhorns and gringos set their sights on collecting the price on his head. But Bill refuses to turn tail and run. He swears he'll clear his name and live a free man before he'll be hunted down and trapped like an animal.

_3937-0                                      $4.50 US/$5.50 CAN

# RIP-ROARIN' ACTION AND ADVENTURE BY THE WORLD'S MOST CELEBRATED WESTERN WRITER!

**Bull Hunter.** A man who can rip a tree trunk from the ground with his bare hands or tame the wildest stallion with his kind manner—that is Bull Hunter. Nary a sensible soul west of the Pecos dares to run afoul of the mighty frontiersman. But Pete Reeve doesn't have the reputation of a dead shot because he relies on his common sense. Then Bull Hunter and Pete Reeve cross paths, and townsfolk from Cheyenne to San Antonio brace for a battle that will end up with either a couple of gut-shot gunslingers—or a pair of living legends.
\_4047-6                                    $4.50 US/$5.50 CAN

**The Mustang Herder.** Gregg isn't a big man physically, but he is as tenacious as a terrier after a rat. Raised on the tough streets of Old New York, he can outfight any brawler, outcuss any sailor, and outdraw any gunslinger. Armed with these talents, he heads West to make his fortune, never realizing that he'll end up herding mustangs. He doesn't know a lot about horses, but he knows anyone who stands in his way is as good as buzzard bait.
\_3908-7                                    $4.50 US/$5.50 CAN

**Dorchester Publishing Co., Inc.**
**65 Commerce Road**
**Stamford, CT 06902**

Please add $1.75 for shipping and handling for the first book and $.50 for each book thereafter. NY, NYC, PA and CT residents, please add appropriate sales tax. No cash, stamps, or C.O.D.s. All orders shipped within 6 weeks via postal service book rate. Canadian orders require $2.00 extra postage and must be paid in U.S. dollars through a U.S. banking facility.

Name _____

Address _____

City _____ State _____ Zip _____

I have enclosed $_____ in payment for the checked book(s).
Payment <u>must</u> accompany all orders. ☐ Please send a free catalog.